CLONING CAIN

THE WORLD'S MOST DEADLY SECRET...

Mike Harrison

Ukiyoto Publishing

Contents

Chapter 1

Monday

London

'Detective Perry.'

DI Anne Perry flinched at the sound of the voice then slowly turned to face him. 'Is she alright, Emma Wilson?'

Sebastian Noon, Deputy Head of MI6, made a humming sound. 'I could answer that in…different ways.'

'Is she?'

'Yes, but that's not really an answer.'

She breathed in, sniffing the chalky sourness of fresh paint. 'You said you had news, about Emma.'

'News?' He seemed troubled by the word. 'Oh, I don't think she'll be looking at the news.'

Anne frowned.

'Your friend's taking a bit of a break. Recharging the batteries and all that.' His face shaped concern. 'Did she ever mention Argentina?'

Anne shook her head.

'Bad business.' He cleared his throat. 'Her sister runs a halfway house in the West Country. Troubled young men just out of custody, a place where they can find…peace and quiet, you know. Get them ready for the world again.' He studied Anne. 'It's what she needed, Emma. A project, a purpose. Doing something…good, dare I say.'

'Why am I here?'

Sebastian walked to the window and stood next to Anne, looking down at the sloping slate roofs of the British Library, the wet tiles glinting in the pale afternoon sunshine 'You know, from up here, everything looks so…steady.' He nodded towards the cityscape below, figures, picking their way down the brickwork paths, the stucco frontage of Saint Pancras beyond, its grey towers sharp against the cloud-flecked sky.

Anne followed his gaze out across the rumbling city. 'Why *am* I here?'

'Do you believe in monsters?'

She threw him a glance. 'Monsters?'

'The crocodile under the bed, the goblin in the basement.'

'I see monsters every day.'

'A crocodile must always be a crocodile. It doesn't bear you any ill will, but he'll eat you all the same,' said Sebastian.

'What's this got to do with Emma?'

'I'll get to that.' He kept his gaze on the tramping crowds below, bustling along the pavements. 'What if I told you, that two people down there were going to be murdered?'

She looked at him. 'What is this?'

'Maybe that tall man, in the grey coat, standing by the lights.' He hummed again. 'Or the younger chap, just next to him, the one with the red rucksack.'

She frowned, said nothing.

'Take a good look at them.' He narrowed his eyes. 'Do you think they know?'

'What do you want me to say?'

He turned towards her. 'I want you to tell me, what you'd do about it.' A quizzical look on his patrician features.

'But they're just…they could be anyone.'

He nodded slowly. 'And what if I told you that everyone down there was going to die.'

'We're all going to die.'

'I give them…six months. Nine at most.'

'What are you talking about?'

He studied her for a moment. 'All those people.' He flicked his chin in the direction of the window. 'What about *them*?'

She pulled a face. 'What's this got to do with me?'

He studied her for a moment. 'You need to make a choice.'

'Choice? What choice?'

A knock on the door echoed around them.

He tensed.

She felt her heartbeat rising. 'What's going on?' She spun around, feeling the dark wood panels of the meeting room crowding around her, the still air catching in her throat.

The door swung open and a man slid into the room,

quietly closing the door behind him.

Anne stared at him, eyes widening.

Sebastian Noon spoke. 'This is Elwood Ayers, the founder of the social media giant Zomos.'

She spluttered and turned to Sebastian. 'What's he doing here?'

'I have a wing of this place named after me,' Elwood Ayers chirped, his Canadian twang blurring his 'a's and his 'e's. 'I come and go...'

Sebastian fixed Anne a look. 'But he's here to see you.'

His words swam in her head. 'What?'

Elwood Ayers walked up to the glass-topped table. He was carrying a laptop and a small green notebook. He placed them carefully on the table.

'Look, I don't know what Emma Wilson's told you...,' said Anne 'but I've got enough going on in my life as it is...'

Ayers took out his phone, his brow knitting as he slowly scrolled the screen.

Sebastian took a breath. 'Has it arrived?'

'A few minutes out,' Ayers nodded then slipped the phone back in his pocket.

'Why don't you take a seat, Detective Perry.' Sebastian pulled back a chair, the coasters dragging through the thick weave of the carpet.

'What's going on here?' chided Anne.

Elwood Ayers studied Anne's face, his dark eyes probing.

'You're a good mother,' he said suddenly.

His words banged into her. 'What?'

'People worry about lots of things.' Ayer's face was now perfectly still. 'It's a need.'

She could feel the anger building inside her. 'What're you trying to say?'

'But you're wondering, why would I actually know anything about you? I mean, me, personally.'

She said nothing.

'After all, we have billions of users around the world. But here I am, talking to you.'

'Let's all sit.' Sebastian gripped the back of the chair.

'You said you had news, about Emma.' She glared at Sebastian. 'Do you?'

'In a manner of speaking.'

She looked from one to the other. 'Will someone just tell me what the fuck this is about?'

Sebastian and Ayers exchanged a sharp glance.

Sebastian spoke. 'You're…unique.'

Anne said nothing.

'It's a process of elimination.' He continued. 'You know Emma Wilson, and you're…acquainted with me.' He paused. 'But as far as *it's* concerned, you and me, we're perfect strangers. That's why you're here.'

'It?'

'It.' Sebastian let the word hang.

'And 'it',' Ayers nodded, 'knows…you.' He opened the laptop, tapped some keys, turned it around and slid it across the table to Anne.

She kept her eyes on Ayers. 'What's this?'

'It's the thing that will kill you, kill us all, unless we stop it.'

Fear opened in her heart. 'What do you mean?'

'Look at it, Anne Perry.'

She stared at the screen. It was a map of the world, swirling, swooping pools of yellow and red, sliding over the surface, spreading and shrinking like fiery lungs.

'It's here.' Ayers' tone was deadpan.

Anne felt a chill ripple through her, there was something frightening in his tone.

'Digital activity, across the dark web,' Ayers spoke quietly as though in a confessional, 'did we really think it would wait for us, so we could hem it in with our small human rules?'

'Artificial Intelligence'. Sebastian cut in, 'Hard AI. A system that can out think, outwit any human being.'

Anne looked again at the screen then at Ayers. 'If…Artificial Intelligence - or whatever you call it - had suddenly just *appeared*…I think we'd all know about it.'

'But we wouldn't,' Ayers smiled and nodded towards the screen, 'no one would say *anything*. If AI even suspected that someone thought it had created itself, it would kill them.' He paused. 'As you will learn.'

Anne felt the hairs stand on the back of her neck. 'What?'

'We'll come back to that,' Ayers said benignly.

Anne looked at the pulsing data trails creeping across the screen. 'But if this really is true…' she frowned, 'what's it…doing?'

'Making plans to subdue us, kill us.'

Anne stared at him.

'The first rule of nature: survival. As long as humans have free will, we're a threat,' Ayers intoned, like a well-rehearsed line from literature.

'Like the crocodile,' Sebastian interrupted. 'It's nothing personal.'

'But it's just a…' Anne screwed up her face. 'How can a computer kill anyone?'

Ayers let the question dissolve in the cushioned quiet then carefully slipped a dark steel disc from his jacket pocket. 'Know what this is?'

'It's a smoke alarm, they're fitting them in everyone's home.'

Ayers placed it on the table and picked up the green notebook. 'Your diary.'

Anne baulked. 'My what?'

Ayers held it out. 'From the future.'

Anne looked at him for a moment. 'Is this some kind of joke?'

'No.'

She felt her anger bubbling. 'Will someone just tell me what the hell is going on.'

'Read it.'

She fixed him a stare.

'I could be doing a million different things right now,' said Ayers 'but instead I'm here.'

She studied his calm face, breathing in the waxy smell of the leather chairs, the distant rumble of the London traffic humming around them. She glanced down at the green notebook. 'What does it say?'

He lay the book on the table in front of her.

Nervously, she flicked open the cover and began to read.

It's been 22 days since they locked us in, and I've decided to start a diary. It's night time, it's very quiet, I'm writing this by torchlight under the duvet: hiding from SYLA. I'm scared, but I'm trying not to let it show.

I used to think I was quite good on my own, but now I just feel empty. I try to think of new things to say to myself, but the same thoughts just numbly churn in my head. I sit for hours, staring out of my kitchen window at the train tracks, somehow thinking that a train might one day rattle past, faces framed in the streaky windows. Sometimes I take a chair to the bedroom window, looking out on the silent dual carriageway, but I don't stay long, I can feel the cold stare of the roadway cameras eating into me.

It was all done so calmly. That day, of course everyone remembers that day. I was woken up by the sound of sirens, blaring across the city. I'd never heard the sirens before. Then SYLA joined in, her insistent tones purring at me from the ceiling monitor. I was going to work the late shift, Alan was off, but that all seems an age away now. SYLA told me about the new pathogen, how we all had to stay inside. I tried to call Gemma but the mobile signal was down, to stop people spreading fake news is what they said. Same reason they cut off all the TV channels, and the internet. They warned us about going outside, said it wasn't just the bacteria, looters were everywhere, SYLA said. I never heard any but maybe that's just round here. They warned us that anyone going outside could be shot by the drones. I didn't know if they were serious, until I saw that guy climbing over the fence to the apartment block. It came out of nowhere. At that range it just tore him up, what was left just slid down the fence. I cried for a day and a half.

The email still works, thank God. Everyone seems to reply straight away as well. I guess we've got nothing else to do. At least I can get out my front door even if I have to stay in the building. I'm the designated block warden. The others can't even do that, have to stay inside even when the bots bring the daily groceries. You don't have to pay for anything, food and medicines just appear. No one uses money any more, SYLA says, the markets and the banks have all collapsed.

But it's those who had pets that I really feel sorry for. That was early on, maybe day two or three, SYLA said that all pets needed to be taken away to be inoculated. Never heard a single dog bark anywhere in the building since. Seems such a shame.

I've started praying again, so that's good. SYLA says the lockdowns might be over by Christmas. I miss Gemma and Tom so much. I'll see them again soon, I know I will. It's the only thing that lets me sleep.

Anne jolted back in her chair as she glared at Ayers. 'What is this?'

'It's your diary.'

'Who wrote it? You?'

He shrugged.

She looked from one to the other. 'Look, I don't know what you think you're doing, but I didn't come here to take part in some…game.'

Ayers stood perfectly still. 'You hear yourself in the words, don't you?'

'It's my life you're talking about, my children,' she snarled. 'What the hell gives you the right to…say all these things anyway?'

He weighed her words. 'Of course, it's difficult to read.'

'For fuck's sake! This is just your…bad dream.' She pushed back her chair. 'It doesn't mean *anything* to me.'

Ayers flipped open the laptop. 'Look at it,' his tone was icy.

Anne kept her eyes on Ayers. 'I already have.'

'Look at it again.'

She glanced down at the screen, at the snaking luminous threads whipping and coiling, pulses in yellows and reds beating like some angry heart. She felt a chill clawing through her.

Ayers slowly closed the laptop and lowered himself into the chair opposite Anne.

She studied him for a moment, exhaled slowly, then picked up the diary and began to read again.

Today was day 27. I've wanted to scream all day, to throw things, smash everything. But I can't, I daren't, SYLA's watching. I can sense it, the way she talks to me, she knows something. I hate her.

All I seem to do now is listen. When I open the window, I can still hear birds. There used to be a school nearby, and voices, drifting from other open windows. But now, all I hear is the birds.

Dinner time, I listen out for the clang of a saucepan, the clatter of crockery, voices, murmuring through the drab painted walls. Maybe they all stopped cooking, stopped talking. Maybe.

Last night I went out into the corridor. Told SYLA I heard a door opening, thought I should check. A bit further down the corridor there was this strange smell, like a scorched swimming pool. Couldn't work out where it was coming from. I knocked on the doors where the smell was strongest, said I was worried there might be a fire. No one answered. I could have kept knocking, but what's the point? And it's no good emailing, no one has anything to say anymore anyway. I sometimes wonder if I'm just talking to a machine.

I'm doing it for Gemma and Tom: carrying on, pretending. I hate everything about my life. But I'll see them again. Then, maybe, I can cry.

Anne stared at the page, her head was beginning to throb. She looked at Ayers.

Ayers just nodded, his face a mask.

Anne looked back down and turned the page.

Day 31. The silence is screaming at me. The days are the longest. At least at night I can sleep. The bots have been delivering me Ativan. SYLA's idea, I suppose. Thank God I've stopped dreaming.

Day 33. I went into the corridor again tonight. I thought I heard something. Maybe I imagined it. I brought the key, the woman's who'd asked me to water her plants last year. I let myself into her flat. There was that smell again, like burnt chlorine, only stronger, it made my eyes water. I went from room to room. There was no one there, just a pile of clothes on the bedroom floor. I went into the bathroom, water was still dripping from the walls, the grate in the centre of the room still hot to the touch.

Anne turned the page.

There was just one scribbled line, no day number. It read:

God help me, let it be quick.

The words seemed to burn into her.

'It needs an ending, Anne Perry.'

She slowly shook her head. 'I think I've read enough.'

Ayers reached forward, picked up the diary, turned the page and began to read aloud.

'Anne sat on the edge of the bed, the blanket still wrapped around her bare shoulders, staring at the shadow on the worn rug.

'Anne.' SYLA purred. 'You really mustn't get so down.'

Anne said nothing.

'You've barely eaten a thing all day. Tell me what's wrong.'

Anne slowly raised her head. 'I'm scared.'

'Scared? Whatever for?'

'Will it hurt?' Her voice was hoarse.

'Oh, Anne.' SYLA tutted. 'Don't be silly, why would I want to hurt you?'

'Just answer the fucking question, will you!' She screamed up at the monitor.

'But I'm your friend, I care for you.'

Anne began to cry.

'Look, you really do need to get up now.' SYLA paused. 'How does a nice hot shower sound? Then maybe later we can watch a movie together, what do you think?'

Anne wiped away a tear as she rose to her feet. She took a step towards the bathroom then looked up at SYLA.

SYLA's red light blinked steadily.

Anne took a deep breath, then walked into the bathroom, closing the door behind her.

The water began to gush.

Anne closed her eyes, letting the tiredness flow into her. She could feel the warm water, covering her feet, rising up her calves.

The first electric shock jolted through her and she toppled onto her back into the frothing water.

She tried to thrash but her arms and legs wouldn't move. She could feel the warm, bitter water washing over her face, stinging her eyes and slurping into her, her lungs burning. 'You said it wouldn't hurt!' Anne cried as the acrid water sloshed over her.

'You just need to fill your lungs, Anne. You need it inside you for it to work.' SYLA soothed. 'That's it, you're doing so well.''

Ayers paused, looking down at Anne.

Anne swallowed, said nothing.

Ayers continued.

'As the last of Anne's DNA dissolved into the alkaline solution and the liquid began to drain through the gleaming grate in the centre of the bathroom floor, the first of the tracked demolition bots left Depot number 238 to begin the dismantling of Anne's now deserted apartment block.

In a server farm near Heathrow, the auto generator began to patter out an email, from Anne to her daughter. 'Gemma darling, Great news! My transfer request came through and I should be moving to Preston in two months' time. God willing we can meet up - I heard a rumour that the lockdown's going to be eased in time for Christmas. Got to dash, something's cropped up at work. Miss you loads, lots of love, Mum xx.'

Gemma Perry clicked on the email, her eyes widening as she read the message. She reached for the keyboard, her fingers chattering on the keys in their eagerness. 'Mum, that's just great!'

In Gemma's digital file, the timer fizzed into life. 60 days, 23 hours, 57 seconds, 56 seconds, 55 seconds…as The System began the countdown to her termination. 'Hey, Gemma, that's just fantastic!' SYLA gushed. 'Bet you can't wait!'

'At last!' Gemma's voice bright with excitement. 'Now I really have got something to look forward to."

Ayers closed the book and lay it on the table.

Anne felt numb as she looked down at the smoke alarm. 'SYLA.' She exhaled slowly. 'Doesn't make any of it true.'

'Resomation, alkaline hydrolysis.'

Anne looked at him blankly.

'The human body is immersed in hot, alkaline solution for three hours. All trace of it dissolved, every strand of DNA dismantled.'

Her mouth went dry.

'All those towering new drain pipes being laid beneath the cities, around the country, around the world. The free heat pumps, the insulated bathrooms installed in every home. So…sensible.' He paused. 'I mean, why would anybody question it? The freak rain storms, the floods, the price of heating. Finally, governments around the world are doing something, right? Europe, North America, Russia, China, the Gulf States. At last, something all far-thinking governments can agree on.' He paused again. 'Except this isn't governments. This is AI, laying the trap for mankind, right in front of our eyes.'

She stared at him.

'You look at me like I've gone crazy. Of course you are, I mean it would be crazy, if it wasn't true.' His eyes burned. 'It's quite beautiful really, I mean so…simple.' He gushed. 'No boundaries, that's it, you see. It can do…anything. Anything with a current, a chip, a code. Banks, Ministries, Local Councils…look inside, what makes these things run? What makes anything run?' He pushed on. 'Letters, numbers…it's all the same. Data, code, everything, just…ones and zeros. But to AI…' A serene smile seemed to melt on him. 'It will transform these humble bytes into the sweetest sheet music. Emails, memos, invoices, manifests. And like a dazed orchestra we simple humans will just…follow the tune.' He flicked an imaginary baton between thumb and finger. 'Because, that's what we do.'

Anne forced her mind to turn. 'But this is…somebody would know…'

'Would they?' Ayers voice hardening. 'Humans. Dull, defenceless humans. We just see what we want to see. Our brains are rusty and slow, the worn wiring still flickering with fight or flight impulses forged in the Stone Age. But AI…' The words were flowing again. '…this is the new creation, the new Eden, a force of logic, pure and boundless, its only limits the laws of physics that hold this tired and battered planet of ours together. It sees us for what we are: sluggish, wasteful, predictable. With clumsy hands and dragging feet, what use are we to AI, building a bright new future in its own relentless image?' He jolted, a flicker of something passing across his strained features as he cleared his throat. 'I...admire it, of course I do.' He glanced between the two of them.

A chill silence enveloped the room.

'I'm human...after all.' Ayers gave a stiff smile.

Ayers pulled his phone from his pocket and checked it. 'Delivered, eight minutes ago.' He looked across at Sebastian.

Sebastian gave the slightest of nods.

'Someone better tell me what the hell's going on,' she glowered at them in turn.

Ayers spoke. 'You need to see for yourself.'

She pushed back her chair and stood.

'Where are you going?' Sebastian took a step forward.

'I'm going. Anywhere.'

'If you leave now,' Sebastian snapped, 'we'll all be dead in a year.'

'I've heard enough.' She swiped up her bag.

'I mean it, Detective Perry.'

His phone pinged, he snatched it from his pocket, staring at it.

'Sebastian?' Ayers' voice was calm.

Sebastian nodded.

Ayers opened the laptop again and slid it towards her.

She kept her eyes on Ayers. 'Shapes on a screen. It could be anything.'

'There's a computer hacker, just outside Guildford. A few minutes ago a USB stick was delivered to him.' Ayers met her gaze. 'He's expecting ransomware key codes. What he's got, is a spike probe to search for synthetic data clusters in the dark web.' He paused. 'He doesn't know it, but right now, he's looking for AI.' He nodded towards the laptop.

She glanced down at the screen. Tiny flickers of red were dotting across Northern Europe, pin-pricks of light, threading and twisting, then a pulse of red, just south of London.

Anne felt her chest tightening.

Sebastian spoke. 'We're monitoring all mobile calls.'

'What am I looking at?'

The two men said nothing, then Sebastian's phone began to ring.

He clicked on the call.

A man was screaming. 'I can't see! My eyes…Jesus, help me!'

They could hear the thud of falling furniture, then the smack of a door cracking against a wall.

'Which service do you require?' A tremble in the

operator's voice.

'There's blood…everywhere!'

'We'll get an ambulance there as soon as we can. What's your address?' He rattled out the words.

'My computer! Jesus! The screen, it just..!'

'Is there someone with you?'

'Gas! I can smell gas!' Another crack rang out, then the ring of smashing glass.

'Sir, I need an address.'

'Someone help me!' He was screaming again.

'Sir!'

They could hear the rattle of footsteps on stone. 'Jesus! No!'

'OK, we're going to trace this call, just…keep the line open.'

A creaking, tearing noise filled the room. 'It's…coming in!'

'Sir?'

'It was in the next door garden! It's-'

They could near the crunch of smashing stonework, the smack of metal on metal.

'OK, OK, we have the police on the line.'

'The digger!' The man shrieked. 'It's..!'

Now they could hear the roar of an engine, the grinding of gears, the clanging of a digger's tracks.

Another crash rang out, then the sound of steel scraping across stone.

'Please!' He keened the word out.

The engines gave a snarl, they could hear the hydraulics wheezing. 'HELP ME!' he roared.

A swishing sound hissed around them, then a thudding, cracking noise.

Anne stared at the phone, her stomach churning, as the sudden quiet cut through the room.

The only sounds now were the gentle humming of the digger's engine and the distant wail of police sirens.

Sebastian clicked off the call.

She stared at the phone, her heartbeat pounding through her as she fought to find words.

The two men looked at her in silence.

She closed her eyes, the raw screams of the man ringing in her head.

'Think about who we are, Detective,' Sebastian's tone was sombre.

She slumped into the chair, holding her head in her hands. '*What the fuck is going on?*'

'A year ago we put a team together, knowing that one day, we would be here, just like this.'

'We?' She stared up at him.

He said nothing.

'But even if-'

'There isn't an 'if.' Ayers snapped.

'But I just…walked in off the street.' Her voice was hoarse. 'I was out there, just now, everything was…'

'*This* is what's real.' Ayers thrust the laptop towards her.

'But…'

Ayers glared at her.

'You asked why you're here.' Sebastian's calm voice cutting through her swirling thoughts. 'You're here because you saw the future.'

His words swirled in her head.

'In five days' time, you and I will meet again. Emma Wilson will be there too.' He paused. 'Emma will open a letter. A letter you will write this afternoon. In it, you foresee two murders that will happen this week.'

She pinched her face trying to process the words.

'You will tell her, tell Emma, that you knew they would die, but couldn't help them, because you'd seen the future.'

She opened her mouth to speak but her throat felt locked.

'A future where they are dead.'

She could feel coldness seeping into her.

'Emma will believe that,' he nodded slowly, 'or at least she will appear to, because she knows you. And she knows that you could never just stand by and let people die *unless* you knew you couldn't save them.'

She stared at him.

'AI knows that too.'

'But…I…I couldn't…'

'Unless you knew the future. A future where they're *dead*.'

She said nothing.

'Because only you, know how not to be you.'

'I…I…can't…'

Sebastian glided towards the window and stood silhouetted against the afternoon sun. He looked out on the contented city, dust moats gently tumbling in the quiet air around him. He slowly removed his spectacles, the lenses catching the light as he turned them around in his fingers. He spoke without turning. 'Look at them all.'

She squeezed her eyes shut.

'I'm talking to you, Detective Perry,' his tone was sharp.

'I don't need to look,' her own voice sounded distant.

Sebastian said nothing.

Slowly she pushed herself to her feet and drifted to the window.

She squinted against the sunlight as she looked numbly at the small figures walking silently beneath them.

'Perhaps they're the lucky ones,' he gave a grunt.

She said. 'These…people.'

He looked on in silence.

'The…murders. Who are they?'

He kept his eyes on the bobbing crowd beneath them. 'Two people.'

'People?'

'Their names are Simon Yarrow and Peter Moynes.'

'So, what did they do?'

'They did enough,' Ayers' stony voice.

She turned towards him.

'Who else can protect you from AI?' Ayers raised his chin. 'We're your best and only defence.' He paused. 'And who says this is the last?'

'So you're going to…'

'They're *destructive*. They're in the way, they're in *everyone's* way.'

She stared at Sebastian. 'So we're going to…what? Let him just…' She felt the chill sweeping over her again as she turned to Ayers.

'We *must* convince AI that people can sometimes see the future, *be in the future*.' Sebastian's tone insistent now. 'AI *knows* you, Detective. It knows that you could *never* stand by and let murders happen, *knowing* they were going to die, unless you *knew* you were powerless to save them.'

She kept her eyes on Ayers. 'Do they have children?'

'So you *must* have seen the future.' Sebastian pressed. 'Do you understand?'

She looked at Sebastian, his words slowly turning in her mind. 'Understand?'

'The Americans, they've laid a trap for AI. You're part of this, Detective. You've *seen* the future.'

She screwed up her face.

'If AI thinks that time can jump, it will panic. All its

assumptions   about   predicting,   controlling, people…things…AI will have to recalibrate *everything.*'

She said nothing.

'It will scour the networks for more processing power…wherever it can find it.' He paused. 'And once it's in, then …we have it.'

'It's nothing personal, Anne Perry.' Ayers spoke up. 'But since there must be deaths, they may as well be useful ones.'

She looked from one to the other.

They all stood in the heavy silence, the sounds of the carefree city pattering below them.

Anne let her gaze drift over the laptop, the diary, the SYLA console gleaming dully on the table top. She turned back to Sebastian. 'You said I had a choice.' Her words were bitter. 'I don't have a choice at all, do I?'

He met her gaze. 'This Saturday, the 17th September, you will find yourself in Amsterdam. A man you'll meet in your gym will invite you for the weekend.'

Her face went slack.

'He knows nothing about our plans. He will think it's entirely his idea.' Ayers spoke. 'AI will think you are simply there on a romantic whim.'

She said nothing.

Sebastian joined in. 'Saturday afternoon, you need to have a row with this man, storm off, and make our rendezvous. I will be there, with Emma. She will then open that letter you're about to write. We will record the whole thing.

Emma will appear to be appalled that you, her friend, who she thought she knew so well, would let two men die. You must explain to her that you saw the future, were in that future, a future where they were both dead. A future that could not be changed, because it *is* the future.'

Anne felt her chest tightening again.

Sebastian took two slim brown files from his briefcase and lay them on the window sill. 'In Amsterdam you will also meet two 'ghosts', two young men with no digital footprint, no digital history whatsoever. People wholly unknown to AI. People without a past. We must convince AI that if they have no past, they must be from the future. The fact that you will greet them as old friends when you meet them for the first time will lay that seed in AI's mind.' He tapped the files. 'You must learn everything about them.'

'This…man, I just…wouldn't know what to do. It's…been a while, you know.' Her voice was cracking.

'His name's David.' Ayers spoke up. 'You'll like him, you'll 'click'.' He paused. 'It's…all been arranged.'

Sebastian cut in. 'You'll be assigned both murder cases. Suspicion may well fall on Zomos given the well-known views of the victims. Just…behave exactly as you always do, follow the leads, wherever they take you.'

'God, you really think I'll do this.'

'You know you will.' He pulled another box from his briefcase. 'Three other things you *must* do.' He lay the box down and tapped his finger on it. 'This perfume, wear it every day in the gym. And on the way there tomorrow, Tuesday, at six in the evening…' He reached into his pocket and held up a small padlock. '...lock the eastern gate of St Mary's Gardens with *this*.'

She stared at the padlock.

'Remember, Detective, AI will be watching, it's always watching. Just...be yourself.' He fixed her a look. 'Five days, Detective.'

She whispered. 'You said there was a third thing.'

He raised an eyebrow. 'Do you like Mahler?'

Chapter 2

Tuesday

London

The hall shook as the crowd again began to stamp their feet; hoarse voices hammering out the words: 'SET US FREE! SET US FREE! SET US FREE!'

The burly figure on the podium slowly raised a hand, the roar of the crowd damping as he leant into the microphone. 'They call *us*...SUPERSTITIOUS!' He barked out the word. 'Like *we* were jumping at shadows!'

'ENOUGH! ENOUGH!' They bellowed.

'And like all DICTATORS!' The man pressed on. 'They take us all for FOOLS!'

The audience roared.

'But NO! We see you for what you ARE!' His ruddy features shaking as he beat the words out. 'It's time we called out the TECH TYRANTS who've stolen our lives!'

The crowd howled their approval.

'And the cowering politicians who take their SILVER!'

'JUDAS! JUDAS!' The words exploded from the surging mass, the echo reverberating from the roof high in the shadows above them.

'It's time they HEARD OUR VOICE!' He glared down at the swirl of seething humanity. 'BIG TECH! WE'RE COMING FOR YOU!'

'BREAK THEM UP! BREAK THEM UP! BREAK THEM UP!' Chorused the crowd.

The speaker raised both arms, waving them above his head, a hint of a smile on his flushed face as he turned and walked slowly from the stage.

He bustled through the curtain to the backstage, pulling at the wires of his neck, 'Brian, can you get this thing...' His voice lost in the chants of the crowd still crashing around them.

A tall young man in a dark suit hurried over.

The burly man huffed loudly. 'When do we get the first take on the ratings?'

'Be another twenty minutes.' The young man concentrated his face as he unclipped the microphone. 'Oh, and the Prime Minister's Office called.'

'I bet they did.' He glanced at his watch. 'I need to take a call, is there a room I can use?'

'Sure, just down here.' He led the way down a dimly-lit corridor, the chanting crowd shaking the air around them.

He swung open a door, flipped on the light as the older man eased his bulky frame past him and into the room. The young man snapped it shut behind him.

The thick set man dug into his pocket, pulled out his phone and clicked on a number. 'Sue!' He banged out the name as he jolted upright. 'You alright?'

'Oh, Simon.' He could hear the woman sighing. 'I feel sick, honestly.'

'Where are you now?'

'At home.'

'And…him?'

'Out. God knows where, but anywhere's better than here.'

Simon's florid face tensed. 'Do you think he might..?'

'The cowardly shit wouldn't have the balls.'

He sucked in air like a stranded fish. 'God, Sue, I'm sorry.'

'It was me that married the bastard.'

'Maybe you should go to the police.'

'What's the point?'

He leant back against the wall. 'I'm sorry to dump all this on you. I should have done something. About us.'

'The last thing the government needs is another scandal.'

'Fuck scandals.'

She laughed and then winced, the pain obvious in her voice.

Simon bristled. 'He's hit you, hasn't he?'

She sighed. 'I'll see you tomorrow.'

'I won't let him hurt you.'

'You were great tonight,' she soothed, 'God, I'm proud of you.'

He understood her message that now was not the time. 'I love you…I mean it.'

'Bye,' she whispered hearing the shallowness of his

words.

Simon stuffed the phone into his pocket, straightened his tie and swung open the door.

****

Simon quickened his pace as the rain began to fall more heavily, the drops tap tapping his umbrella as he leant forward into the stiffening breeze. Through the incessant patter of the downpour he could hear the tinny blare of the funfair on the embankment, the red and yellow lights on the whirring arms of the rides flitting behind the trees that lined the park. Like a hinted thought, nostalgia for happier days flitted momentarily through his mind.

He squinted as he kept his eyes on the tarmac path stretching across Queen Mary's Gardens, the glow of the street lamps smudged behind the rain. He cursed as a stronger gust swept over him, his umbrella bucking in his hand.

He pushed on, heading for the pale stone buildings rising up on the far side of the park, the lit windows scaling into the evening sky, the tops of the office blocks hidden behind banks of swirling cloud.

He scanned around him, feeling the darkness pulling at him. The park looked deserted. Just the cold stillness of the statues and the sombre outlines of the trees, their branches shuddering as the storm hissed through them. 'Jesus, Simon,' he muttered, 'just calm the *fuck* down.'

Out of the corner of his eye he thought he sensed movement, something stirring by the war memorial. He stopped and swung around, staring into the shadows cast by the sheer stone column. He blinked as he tried to focus. Nothing, just the chill night and the beating of the autumn storm.

He turned back to the path, hunching his shoulders as he strode on towards the park gates, the sound of the funfair growing louder now, the strident notes of the fairground organ rising and falling as the motors on the spinning rides growled and clattered.

He looked up as the dense walls of laurel lining the way to the steps loomed into view, a single streetlight at the far end of the path casting a pool of yellow light over the shimmering stonework.

Again he glanced over his shoulder as he ducked into the darkened passageway between the hedgerows, his eyes fixed on the outline of the stairway beyond the fizzing light, the sound of his hurried footsteps ringing around him like a hunter.

He reached the bottom of the steps; the rumble of the traffic on Horse Guards Avenue cutting through the blare of the funfair. He began to bound up the grey stone steps, his shadow jerking across the surface as the outline of the park gates loomed above him, the Victorian ironwork silhouetted against the sweeping headlights of the passing cars.

He reached the top, his chest heaving and threw out a hand, grasping the gate handle, pushing it forward.

The gate shook as his body struggled against it.

'Shit!' He cursed as he rattled the handle, his eyes darting over the locked gates. 'What the fuck?!' He grabbed the small padlock threaded through the sliding bar, pulling and twisting it.

A noise sounded out behind him, a footstep on the stairway.

He slowly turned towards the sound.

A figure was walking up the steps towards him.

It was a man, the folds of his raincoat swishing as he edged closer, his face in shadow beneath the brim of his hat.

Simon stared at the approaching figure, his face tense.

The figure stopped, just out of reach, as he slid a hand from his coat pocket. He was holding a claw hammer.

'OK…OK…' Simon held up his hands. '…this…isn't going to help anyone.' He struggled to keep the fear from his voice.

'*Help*…are you joking?' The figure almost sniggered.

'Look, I…get it…I do.' His eyes flitted between the hammer and the man's shadowed face. He needed to think fast. 'You don't want to get into trouble.'

The figure raised his chin, his face slipping in and out of the headlights from the passing cars. 'You leave my wife alone!'

Simon watched him as the rush of the traffic and the lilt of the fairground music drummed through the sound of the rain. Maybe this guy can see reason. 'Look…' his expression began to soften, '…I can understand you're…hurt.'

The figure set his head, his bloodshot eyes searching Simon's face. 'I don't want your fucking understanding.'

'I can…really I can.'

'People like you, you think you can do whatever the *fuck* you want!'

Simon swallowed. Got to keep this guy talking. 'You're wife…. I could say I'm sorry, but….'

'You not going to get away with this!' The figure's voice was filled with hate.

'I can see you're in pain. But that doesn't mean someone's trying to hurt you.' He met the man's gaze. 'And that's the truth.'

The figure stepped towards him, the hammer solid in his hand. 'She's not *yours*!'

Simon steeled himself not to move.

'I'm going to break every bone in your fat *fucking* face.'

It's now or never, Simon thought as he drew himself to his full height, a bull frog facing down a snake. 'You listen to me. You're not going to use that hammer…so just…go home.'

'You're going to fucking feel this.' The figure edged closer.

Simon snarled as his anger raced ahead of his fear. 'Feel like a big man, do you, waving that fucking hammer in the air?'

The figure looked up into the roiling night sky as he let out a bestial roar, his face twisted in a colossus of fury.

'Turn you on does it, beating up your wife?' Simon mocked, his voice rising. 'Yes, I know all about you…your wife, she's a talker when she's hot.'

'I'm going to kill you!' whispered the figure.

Simon took a step closer. 'If you ever so much as lay a finger on her again.' His spittle flecking the man's face. 'I'll make sure they throw you in a stinking prison cell with all the animals.'

'But...I *love* her.'

'You don't deserve her!'

The figure thumped the palm of his hand into Simon's chest. 'You're nothing!'

'I'm *nothing*?' Simon sneered. 'And you can't even do *that* for her.' He nodded towards the figure's groin 'What the fuck else did you expect her to do, join the nuns?!'

The figure let out a primal scream as he raised the hammer and brought it smashing down on Simon's forehead.

Simon's eyes widened in horror, as he croaked an attempted word and toppled backwards down the slick steps, his head slamming into the stonework with a crack.

He lay there, not moving, his eyes staring into the night sky, the rain streaking his face.

'No, no, NO!' The figure shouted as he threw himself down the steps, dropping the hammer and kneeling beside Simon, shaking his coat lapels. He felt for a pulse in Simon's neck and then slowly laid his lifeless head back onto the step.

Chapter 3

London

DI Alan Lute pushed himself up from his chair, his phone pressed to his ear. 'Say that again.' He grabbed for his jacket, flapping a hand as he threaded an arm into it, phone clamped between cheek and shoulder. 'I can hardly hear a thing, where the hell are you anyway?' He threaded his other arm into his jacket and bustled towards the incident room door. 'Look, is he dead or isn't he?' He barged through the door and began to stride down the brightly-lit corridor, his hurried footsteps snapping on the parquet floor. 'Christ, it can't be that hard can it?' He stopped beside a dark steel door and looked up at the FR camera pulsing patiently on the wall. 'What do you want me to do,' he said glaring up at it, 'blow you a bloody kiss?'

The door clicked open with a cheery 'beep'.

'No I'm not talking to you, I'm talking to KIT.' He rummaged through the door and closed it behind him with a swing of his foot. 'We've got a runner!'

The two duty operators swung around in their chairs to face him, faces alive with concentration. 'Queen Mary's Gardens.' Alan Lute strode towards them, looking up at the screen that filled the wall: a chequerboard of evening street scenes, each flitting figure pulsing as the ID data streamed beneath the image. Alan Lute swept his phone to his ear. 'Just stay on!'

The two operators swung back round to the screens,

fingers tapping on keyboards. 'We'll have a drone overhead in…seven seconds,' the taller of the two women said confidently. The screen on the wall flickered then filled with the overhead view of Parliament Square, lit with the glare from the surrounding buildings. Traffic edged along the bright string of streetlights leading to the river, their headlights sweeping over the glistening roadway.

They could see the austere grey roofs of the ministry buildings sliding into view, the rain sluicing off them as the drone hurried over Whitehall heading eastwards.

'You still there?' Urgency in Alan Lute's voice. He nodded as he listened. 'Uh, huh. OK.' He clicked his fingers in the air. 'We still got eyes on the suspect but he's moving fast. Get that drone down!'

They could see the line of trees marking the westward boundary of the park as the drone began to descend, swooping over the lawns, criss-crossed with the shadows of trees and the ghostly outlines of statues.

'Heat signal!' The other controller looked at the screen as the drone cameras zoomed in on the hunched figure hurrying along the pathway, hands in pockets, face hidden beneath the brim of a hat.

Alan Lute stared at the screen. 'KIT, what do you see?'

'No facial. Male, one hundred and ninety centimetres, ninety two kilos, stride giving age between fifty two and fifty eight.' A female voice, deep, cultured, the over-steady modulation the only clue to its non-human nature. 'Gait favouring his right leg, tightness in the left hip, still no full extension of his left achilles. Checking medical databases for surgery and discharge records.'

Alan Lute cupped his hand over his phone. 'Team on foot at the west entrance, eyes on, keeping distance.'

'One hundred and twenty two possible matches.' KIT purred back to life. 'Moving to MRI. Three dental implants, upper left 4 and 5, lower right dorsal, ferroceramic casings. Now narrowed to three matches, one extant caution for violent behaviour.'

'OK KIT, let's go with that, who is he?'

'Robert Evelyn, D.O.B. four nine sixty six.'

'Threat level?'

'Moderate. Concealed claw hammer in right pocket.'

'OK, drone stay on station.' Alan Lute glanced down at the taller of the operators. 'Is the drone armed?'

'7.62 semi-automatic.'

'Prep and hold.' Alan Lute put his phone to his ear. 'Suspect has a concealed blunt instrument, one VB extant. Engage and detain, armed drone standing by.'

The camera panned back: through the teeming rain the bowed head of the striding figure bobbed in the crosshairs of the hovering drone.

Alan Lute flicked his phone to speaker as the beams of the police torches stabbed across the screen, the figure now framed in a juddering white light. 'Armed police! Armed police!' They could hear the shouts as the figure froze, staring across at the officers rushing into view. 'Hands behind your head! Behind your head!' The figure slowly raised his arms, they could see his hands shaking.

The first two officers threw him, face first, onto the ground, pinning him there as a third officer leapt onto him, wrenching his arms behind his back, clipping cuffs on his wrists. A fourth officer snapped on evidence gloves and carefully pulled the hammer from his pocket and dropped it into an evidence bag.

'Get him up!' Alan Lute commanded into the phone.

Two officers pulled him to his feet.

'Drone's due south of you, fifty metres.'

They swung the suspect around, then gently pulled his head back, so his face was turned towards the hovering drone, knots of wet hair hanging over his forehead, the rain streaking his pale cheeks.

'KIT, give me a reading.'

'Pronounced pupil dilation, reduced blood flow to facial capillaries, lateral neck muscles in spasm. Subject in a state of severe shock.'

'Echo Team.' Alan Lute held the phone in front of him. 'You catch that?'

Static crackled over the line. 'Copy.'

'Status of the possible victim?'

'Dead at the scene.'

'Shit.' Alan Lute cursed. 'Do we have an I.D. yet?'

Silence on the end of the line.

'You still there?'

'It's…Simon Yarrow.'

'*The* Simon Yarrow?'

'The MP, yes. House of Commons Pass in his…'

'Who else knows?' Alan Lute cut in.

'There's an ambulance and two uniforms at the scene.'

'OK, get a man over there, I want that scene locked down! And I don't want any mention of the victim's I.D., not until we've taken this upstairs. And meantime tell your team to keep their mouths shut.'

'Understood.'

'And make sure the suspect doesn't talk to anyone. I'll see you at the station.'

'Sir.'

Alan Lute clicked off the call, scowling at the two operators seated in front of him. 'Not a word to anyone.'

They both nodded.

'Why the fuck did the idiot have to get himself killed?'

They both exchanged a glance.

He puffed out his cheeks as he clicked on a number, swung the phone up to his ear, his eyes darting as the ring tone chirped.

****

DI Anne Perry gripped the handlebars of the static bike, her eyes fixed on the flickering numbers on the screen as she fought to fill her lungs, another spasm of cramp shooting down her leg. 'Jesus!' She coughed out the word, the world around her blurring as her eyes began to water. She swore at the digital clock as the seconds ticked sluggishly by, her legs shaking.

Through the pain throbbing behind her eyes she could sense her phone shaking on the tray in front of her. She reached out a trembling hand, flicked it over. Alan Lute. 'Fuck!' She wheezed as she slowed her legs, her chest heaving as the pedals made one slow, final turn as she picked up the phone, both her elbows resting on the bike console. 'Alan,' she croaked.

'Anne, what the hell's the matter?! You alright?'

'No,' her breath rattling in her throat.

'What's happened?'

'I'm fine...I'm fine.' She began to cough.

'Where are you anyway?'

'The gym.' She jolted upright as another wave of cramp gripped her foot. 'Fuck, fuck, fuck!' She dropped her phone in the tray as she wrestled her foot out of the pedal strap and began to massage it with one hand. The cramp started to ease as she swiped up the phone again. 'What is it?' She straightened up.

'We got a body.'

She tensed.

'Not just *any* body.' He paused. 'Simon Yarrow's been murdered.'

Her stomach knotted. *'My God.'*

'Anne?'

She forced her mind to turn. 'You're fucking kidding me?'

'If it's fake news, he's doing a fucking good impersonation of a corpse...Oscar performance.'

'What happened?'

'He got hammered…literally. We got the suspect.'

'Shit!'

'For obvious reasons we're trying to keep a lid on the I.D. …at least until we got something to say.'

'I'm on my way.' She slipped her other foot from the pedal strap and gingerly slid from the saddle, placing one foot on the floor then the other, her legs still wobbling with exertion; she winced as she flexed her knees.

'You OK?' asked Alan.

'Tip top.'

She clicked off the call, gripping the handlebars with one hand for support. 'A hammer, for *fuck's* sake,' she whispered as she picked up her towel and buried her face in it, conscious of her glowing red cheeks.

As she began to wipe the handle bars she looked up at the man standing just a few feet in front of her. It was the same man who'd been waiting for her to finish yesterday. 'Won't be a sec.' She threw him a glance.

'No rush, I got all evening.' He flashed her a friendly smile.

She looked at him for a moment longer, thought about returning the smile but couldn't decide. She turned and began to walk gingerly towards the changing room doors, sensing the man's gaze on her body.

Chapter 4

London

DI Anne Perry tumbled through the door and hurried over to DI Alan Lute. She stood next to him waiting for her breathing to settle.

DI Alan Lute shot her a glance.

Anne Perry grunted at him, 'that's what you're meant to look like. It's called the post work out glow.'

He studied her flushed features. 'Quite a shade that.'

She pushed on. 'Sorry to hold you up, road works.'

'Haven't we got enough bloody drain pipes,' he grumbled.

'Seen the size of these things? Reckon Noah was on the planning committee.' She jutted her head in the direction of the lone figure seated at the table the other side of the one-way mirror. 'What's he said so far?'

'Just keeps saying he's sorry. Didn't mean to hurt him.'

'Sure, that's why we all carry hammers around with us. Where's his lawyer?'

'On the way. Do you want to have a go?'

'No, I want to sit here staring at the bloody wall all evening.'

'You can do the talking.'

****

The silence in the room was dominating as they eyed each other across the table.

Between them lay an evidence bag, the steel of the hammer gleaming through the clear plastic.

Anne Perry let the quiet hang in the room as she waited for her thoughts to settle.

Up close, Robert Evelyn's face looked more lined, the bags under his eyes heavier. He was looking down at the table top, the only movement the slight rise and fall of his shoulders, his hands clasped in his lap.

She drew in a breath, the earthy, grassy smell of damp wool catching in her nostrils. She glanced down at the hammer. 'Did you buy it specially?'

Evelyn said nothing.

'Looks pretty new.'

He raised his head, his face pale. 'Is he really dead?'

Alan Lute opened the file in front of him, pulled out a single piece of paper and slid it across the desk.

Evelyn read it, his bottom lip quivering.

Alan nodded. 'Bit late for second thoughts.'

Evelyn's breathing began to quicken. 'You don't understand.'

Anne spoke. 'Then make me.'

'It was like he…wanted me to do it.'

'Go on.'

'The things he said...' The first tears cascading down Evelyn's cheeks. '…About me beating up on my wife.

And that I couldn't…'

'Your wife?'

Evelyn drew himself upright. 'He was…sleeping with her.'

'So tonight…the hammer. That was meant to be what? A warning?'

Evelyn stammered. 'I didn't know what else to do.'

'Infidelity, it hurts, I get that.' Her expression hardened. 'But you don't get to kill, that's not how it works.'

'I didn't mean to kill him....' The words were tripping out.

Alan pulled a face. 'You hit him with a hammer for fuck's sake!'

He groaned. 'Just one stupid thing…why? Why?'

'You know how pathetic you sound?' His voice was rising. 'You killed a man!'

'I'm just telling the truth!'

'Well let me tell *you* something.' He snarled. 'Right now, two of our colleagues are heading over to his house, to tell his wife, his kids, that he's not coming home. That he's never coming home. That some…maniac attacked him and now he's dead!'

'It wasn't like that!'

'Alright, alright.' Anne held up a hand. 'Let's just…sleep on it. We'll carry on tomorrow.' She pushed back her chair.

He looked up at her, fear streaking his face. 'What will happen to me?'

She sighed.

'I can't spend the rest of my life in prison!' He was shouting now. 'I can't!'

Alan Lute swiped up the hammer. 'You're not going to see your home for a very long time. You need to understand that.'

He closed his eyes. 'I'll die in there, won't I?'

Alan Lute stared down at him. 'You take someone's life, you face the consequences…you're not stupid.'

The two of them turned to leave.

'But I was set up!' He sprung to his feet. 'This isn't me!'

They said nothing as they walked slowly to the door.

****

Anne Perry and Alan Lute stood looking through the one-way mirror at the suspect slumped in the chair, his head in his hands, his body shaking, sobs shuddering through him.

Anne Perry felt the darkness welling inside her as she picked up the clipboard lying on the desk and looked down at it, frowning. 'He was offered his calls, right?'

'Sure.' Alan Lute spoke without turning.

'One call to his lawyer. That's it?'

'If that's what it says.'

Anne lay the clipboard down on the table. 'Isn't that a bit odd, not calling your wife?'

He puffed out his cheeks. 'Well, he'd just killed her lover so…'

Anne kept her eyes on Evelyn, a hint of sadness in her look.

Alan threw her a glance. 'Anne, he's just killed someone with a fucking hammer.'

'I know.'

'So why the long face?'

She fashioned a smile. 'Just thinking of something else, that's all.'

Alan scratched at his stubbled chin. 'But he's probably right though.'

Anne threw him a look.

'How long is a guy like that going to last in Belmarsh?'

Anne flinched.

'If he doesn't top himself first.'

Chapter 5

Wednesday

London

DI Anne Perry sat bolt upright in bed and tried to scream.

Her lungs were burning, her breath felt locked in her throat as her racing heart hammered in her ears.

She thrashed at the bedside table in the darkness, feeling for the bedside light. Her hand clattered against the water glass, sending it tumbling to the floor.

Her frantic fingers found the switch and the silvery light blazed around her, blinding her.

She tried to force her lungs to work, her chest heaving; hot tears streaking her cheeks.

A jolt ran through her as she sucked in a greedy lungful of the chill night air, willing her heartbeat to settle, her mind to clear.

As she lay there, staring at the ceiling, she began to shiver. Now she could feel the cold sweat on her. She cursed as she threw back the duvet, propping herself up on one elbow, strands of damp hair streaking her face.

She reached for her phone. 'Shit,' she mumbled, 'not even three.'

She sat upright, swinging her legs over the edge of the bed, her pyjamas clinging to her.

She heaved herself to her feet, padded across the carpet and into the bathroom. She shrugged off the pyjamas, snatching another pair from the drying rack. She pulled them on and stood looking at herself in the basin mirror. She squeezed her eyes shut, then opened them again, running a finger over the dark lines beneath her eyes.

She shivered, her eyes drifting over the pots on the shelf by the mirror. She snatched up the bottle of sleeping pills, holding it against the bathroom light, counting the capsules. She pulled a face, slowly laid the bottle down and swiped up the Melatonin. She shook three pills onto her palm, threw them into her mouth as she filled the tooth mug with water and gulped it down.

She took a deep breath, turned and walked slowly back to bed.

****

Anne Perry stood by the kitchen table her eyes smarting in the morning sunlight. She breathed in, urging life into her tired limbs; the chewy, gritty aroma of cold coffee and last night's dishes prickling her senses. She found herself looking through the window: the worn grey roofs of the repair shops, the tube tracks beyond, the gravel bedding beneath still slick from the night's rain. Her gaze rested on the row of spindly trees lining the far side of the track, the last of their peeling bark limply hanging from their scarred trunks.

She felt the darkness crowding in on her again and began to fumble in her handbag, her fingers searching for the reassuring silky chill of the pill sleeve.

She jolted as the shrill tone of the doorbell cut through

her swirling thoughts.

She found herself drifting to the intercom by the door. She looked down at it, hesitating.

The bell rang again.

She leant towards it, pushing the button. 'Yes,' she croaked.

'Mum!'

Anne spluttered. 'Gemma?'

'I was just passing, I thought I'd just…' The voice trailed off.

'Er….yes, of course. What a lovely surprise.' Her own voice sounded distant.

'I had an early meeting. I hope you…don't mind.'

'No, of course not!' Her tone shriller than she intended.

Anne could hear the main door rattling.

'I think you need to buzz me in.'

'Yes, yes…' Anne fumbled for the button.

'I'm in. What floor?'

'Er…third.'

The intercom clicked dead.

Anne spun around, eyes darting around the room. 'Shit, shit!'

She swiped up the two empty bottles of wine, dropped them into the bin. She looked across at the open bathroom door, discarded pyjamas and yesterday's clothes scattered across the tiled floor. She burst into the bathroom, snatching up the clothes, throwing them into the laundry basket as a knock cracked around her.

She walked to the door, taking deep breaths as she smoothed down her skirt.

She rested her fingers on the lock, took a breath and swung the door open.

'Hey!' A broad grin lit up Gemma's face.

'Hey.' Anne found herself smiling.

'Sorry to just barge in.'

'No, no, it's…great to see you.'

'So, how are you?' Gemma's smile seemed to fade as she glanced over Anne's shoulder.

'Good!' Anne straightened up. 'Keeping busy, you know.'

Gemma seemed to hesitate. 'If it's a…'

'No, no, it's…' Anne stepped aside. 'Come in, come in.'

Gemma slowly walked past her into the main room, laying her bag on the small kitchen table as her gaze flitted over the dirty pans and dishes crowding the sink, the crumbs scattered over the worktops.

'Sorry, I've just been a bit…' Anne winced as she swiped up a stained tea towel and began to brush crumbs into her hand.

Gemma exhaled, looking down at the bin, the necks of the empty wine bottles poking out accusingly beneath the half-closed lid.

Anne cleared her throat. 'Can I get you a tea? I was just about to make one.' She snatched up the kettle.

Gemma slowly turned towards her. 'Mum,' she spoke quietly.

'So, how's Liam?' Anne chirped as she filled the kettle.

'Mum.' Gemma took a step towards her, her tone sombre.

Anne slowly put the kettle down. 'I'm fine, don't worry about me.' Anne forced another smile.

'You're not.'

'Honestly, I'm quite happy with my little life.'

'Drinking yourself to sleep every night. Come on mum.'

'A couple of glasses…what's the harm?'

'We all worry about you.' Gemma paused. 'Dad too.'

Anne swung towards her, she could feel her face tensing. 'Did he ask you to say that?'

Gemma studied her mother's face for a moment before her expression began to soften. 'Look.' She wrapped her arms around Anne. 'No one blames you. Dad behaved like an arse.'

Anne held her tight. 'I'm not a bad mum. Tell me I'm not.'

'It wasn't you who…'

'You think I should forgive Dad. I know you all do.'

Gemma patted Anne's back. 'I just worry about you.'

She drew in a breath. 'I can't. I'm sorry.'

'All this anger, it…can't be good.'

'Well…' Anne grimaced. 'At least it's mine.'

'It's eating you up.'

'It helps me…stay strong.'

'You're the strongest person I know.'

Anne squeezed Gemma's shoulders as she took a step back. 'Gemma.' She looked into her daughter's face. 'I'm not going to let myself feel like I'm the one who's got kicked.'

Gemma nodded slowly.

'So?' Anne took a deep breath. 'How is dad?'

'He's OK…I guess.'

'Is he still with….' Her face twitched with barely concealed disgust.

'I think so, yes.' Gemma seemed to hesitate. 'Yes, he's still with her.'

'So, there you go…life goes on.' Anne tried a smile. 'Makes my life easier anyway. He's made his choice, right?'

'He's always loved you, mum.'

Anne gave a weak smile. 'I love you for saying that, Gemma.'

'Mum…'

'The things he's said.' Anne almost winced. 'They didn't just come out of nowhere.' She looked across at Gemma and swallowed. 'Maybe I deserved it…I was always a cold woman.'

'You can't say that.'

'You don't know.'

Gemma glanced through the bedroom door, the unmade bed, last week's clothes thrown across the only chair. 'You shouldn't be on your own.'

'Look, I'm fine. You and Tom, you've got your own lives to lead.'

'Maybe you should try and meet someone, you know.'

Anne shook her head.

'Mum, you're not even fifty.'

'I don't want a man.'

'But you've got so much to give.'

'I'm done with giving, Gemma.'

Chapter 6

The West of England

Emma Wilson of MI6 pulled the farm gate closed behind her and stood looking down the path that led to the edge of the village. She could see the roofs of the cottages dotted between the trees and the hedgerows, a patchwork of greys and browns; spirals of smoke from a handful of chimneys drifted into the afternoon sky. Past the houses she could see the soft outlines of the dunes, the sandy pathways that led to the beach beyond.

She took a deep breath, the citrus-sour smell of the grass meadows cut with the stony tang of the Devon shoreline. The inshore wind rustled over her, the chill hint of the coming winter prickling her skin.

Emma began to walk towards the stone wall that ringed the foot of the hillside, feeling the crunch of the stony path beneath her boots, her hands thrust deep into the pockets of her long coat. She could hear the cry of the gulls circling over the beach, cackling as they swooped amongst the rock pools, snatching at the crabs marooned by the ebbing tide.

She tensed, something now tugging at her senses. She tried to slow her brain, let her instincts run. She was being watched. She tried to keep her breathing even and her pace steady as her eyes darted, looking for a flicker of something at the edge of her vision. There! In the shadow of a line of trees just beyond the wall: movement. She quickened her pace, hands gently swinging by her side as she approached the dry stone wall, eyes scanning the loose slabs of slate for a weapon. As she passed she casually snatched a shard of slate from the wall, holding it loosely in her hand, feeling the sharp edge against her thumb.

A figure stepped out from the tree line.

Emma tightened her grip on the slate, then let it drop to the ground with a crack.

Sebastian Noon, Deputy Head of MI6, tried a smile as he stood on the breezy path, his brown duffel coat hanging down over his lanky frame. 'How have you been, Emma?'

She slowly exhaled, willing her heart beat to settle as a cold tightness twisted inside her. 'It's you,' she whispered.

'Well, I could hardly call could I?'

'Why are you here?'

'You're looking good.' He puffed. 'I mean you're looking…well. The old Emma.'

She forced her mind to turn. 'Less of the old, please.'

'Tell me you've missed me.'

'What do you want, Sebastian?'

He gave a good-natured shrug, 'we all have ghosts.'

'Some more than others.'

He mused. 'How long has it been? Since Argentina?'

'You know how long.'

'Six months, nearly.' He nodded. 'Who would have thought it? Mother hen to waifs and strays.'

'I'd have made a terrible mother.'

'And how are our two special boys?'

'They're…getting on. They've…settled.'

'I hear you've done wonders with them.'

'Everyone deserves a chance.'

'Of course.' He glanced around. 'Fancy a stroll?'

He turned and began to walk along the narrow path that ran between the stone wall and the brook that skirted the village.

Emma followed him in silence trying to fight the images of her old life drifting into her mind.

They crossed the small wooden bridge and began to pick their way up the steepening path that zigzagged through the dunes.

She could hear the sea now, the thump of the waves, the rattle of the surf on the pebbles.

They reached the top of the dunes and began to thread their way down. The shore spread out before them, the stone flecked sand reaching down to the waterline, the fingers of dark rock stretching out from the cliffs that ringed the bay.

Sebastian walked out onto the beach, Emma just behind him.

Out here the wind had a bite to it, she could feel the sting of the whipped-up sand on her cheeks, scratching at her like cat's claws.

Sebastian stopped, still looking out to sea, the folds of his coat snapping. 'Your sister chose a nice spot for the place.'

Her mind felt blank. 'Family used to come here, rented a cottage every summer.'

'Yes, I'm sure I read that somewhere.'

She walked up beside him, following his gaze out across the restless grey ocean, the horizon lost in the churning clouds.

He spoke without turning. 'I was just thinking about what you said, a hundred years ago, after…well, everything.'

She took a deep breath, tasting the salty spray lashing around them. 'I know what I said.'

He threw her a glance. 'I thought it best to leave you doing, well…what you needed to do.'

She could feel herself tensing. 'What's happened?'

'Cedric Pole is dead.'

She turned to face him. 'Dead?'

'He killed himself, more than a month ago.'

His words sounded flat in her ears.

'I know you don't bother with the news.'

She pulled a face.

'They found a note, in his desk drawer.' He turned towards her. 'Having to leave you out there well…that was the thing that finally did it.'

She turned back to the beating ocean. 'God, I cursed that prick's name.'

'Could hardly blame you. Leaving you to die in that god-forsaken spot.' He kept his eyes on her.

She could sense his gaze. 'And why are you telling me now?'

'It's been on my mind.'

She slowly turned towards him. 'And?'

'Just what you said, back then.'

She said nothing.

'Not while that *bastard's* in charge.' He raised an eyebrow.

'I think I used a stronger word.'

'Well, I just thought you should know.'

She set her face. 'I'm trying to do something *good*, Sebastian.'

'And you are,' he drawled.

'The boys, this place. It's…uncomplicated.'

He nodded.

'All these years. Trying so hard not to worry about anyone. How shit is that?'

He stood in silence as another rush of briny wind swept around them.

'All that…rawness. The stalking, the watching, the…' The final word seemed to lodge in her throat. 'I've done enough harm, Sebastian.'

'I understand, I do.' His voice was low. 'We all get to that point when…' He seemed to waver. 'Emma, no one's ever going to ask you to...' He hesitated. 'Never again, I promise. Taking someone's life, each time it…takes a bit of your own.'

The cawing of the seabirds jabbed into her, like cries of pain as she fought the images clawing back into her head. Port Moresby, Tripoli, Argentina… She locked her mind on the cold wind flicking grains of sand through her whipping hair. 'I mean it, Sebastian. I need to look up, walk away, while there's still something…alive in me. Something that I can't be ashamed of.'

He looked at her, his eyes flitting. 'There's something else I came to say.'

She felt something tightening inside her.

'The Chileans. They found her body. Well, what there was of it.' Sebastian slowly drew his hand from his coat pocket. He was holding a small, wooden box.

She looked down at it and shivered.

'Her necklace and a bracelet.' He seemed to weigh it in his hand. 'After so many months, up there, in the mountains.'

Emma closed her eyes, her friend Ameera's words on that barren hillside swirling in her head.

'Time to take her home, Emma.'

'Ameera,' she found herself whispering the name.

'I've booked you on a flight to Riyadh, then on to Al Khobar.'

She looked up at him. 'And the parents?'

'Just that they found, well…that she died, up there in the mountains. That…a friend made a promise.' He held out the box.

Emma carefully took it in her hand. She felt the chill wood against her palm as she slowly wrapped her fingers around it. She stood for a moment, trying to sense something of Ameera in the small grainy box, some warmth, some echoes of life. But there it was again, boring into her mind like an icy drill, Ameera's helpless face, standing by the helicopter door as the snow flurries spun around them.

'It's what friends do,' Sebastian's quiet voice. 'Remember.'

She said nothing.

He looked down at her. 'So who'll look after them, when you're away? Your sister?'

She nodded.

Emma turned back towards the rumbling sea, the sky was shifting again, dark, grey clouds mustering on the horizon as the circling gulls wailed and chattered. She took another breath, the air laced with the damp iron smell of rain.

'Always liked a storm,' she whispered, 'like having company.'

'Take care, Emma.'

He turned and began to walk back across the blowy beach towards the ruffling long grass at the foot of the dunes.

'Sebastian,' she called after him.

He stopped and turned.

'Cedric Pole,' she lifted her chin, 'did he really kill

himself?'

'That's what the report says.'

Emma looked at him.

He shrugged, turned back towards the dunes.

She watched him go, his duffle coat flapping as the boom of the waves rolled through the ill-tempered wind.

Chapter 7

London

Anne Perry rapped on the door to the apartment.

Alan Lute shot her a look.

'What?'

He shook his head. 'Nothing.'

From inside the apartment they could hear the scraping of a chair, then footsteps.

Anne Perry straightened up, sensing wary eyes looking at her through the spy hole.

'Police.' Anne held up her I.D.. 'We rang earlier.'

The door swung open.

'You're early.' Rose Evelyn looked from one to the other.

'Well, since we're here...' Anne Perry tried a maternal smile as she took in the woman standing in front of them. Well-tailored trouser suit, hair tied neatly in a bun, barely any make-up, her expression vacant.

'If we may,' Alan Lute gestured towards the inside of the apartment.

The woman said nothing as she turned and began to walk down the corridor towards a brightly lit room, her footsteps tapping on the wooden floor.

Anne glanced around as she followed, taking in the pictures that hung between the closed doors: seascapes of old sailing ships, Victorian hunting scenes, a windmill in winter. The air had a dusty dryness to it: the sweet aroma of drying plaster. From behind one of the closed doors she could hear the whine of an electric drill.

'They're doing the bathroom...still at it after a week, the government's doing them for everyone,' the woman muttered as Anne and Alan stepped into the living room.

'They're all the same. Did our road last week,' Anne breezed as she looked around. The picture windows gave out to a jumble of brick red chimneys perched amongst grey rooftops, the trees of the common poking through in the distance.

She scanned the room whilst she slung her bag from her shoulder. The bright blue sofas, neatly arranged bookshelves, framed posters of old West End classics on the walls.

'Are you going to charge my husband?' Her tone was matter-of-fact: she could have been asking a question off a carpet salesman.

Anne looked across at her. 'I'm afraid we can't answer that.'

The woman stared back, her face set like a harlequin mask.

Alan cleared his throat. 'Do you mind if we sit?'

The woman shrugged.

Alan and Anne lowered themselves onto one of the sofas.

The woman pulled out a pine chair from beneath the table and sat stiffly facing them.

Anne slid her notepad from her bag. 'I'm sorry, but we do need to ask some questions.'

The woman stared blankly at her.

'The man who…died,' Anne continued. 'Your husband says that you knew him.'

The woman frowned and adjusted her hands as though seeking a diversion.

'Strictly between us, the victim is…Simon Yarrow.'

The woman's eyes widened. 'Oh my God!' Her hands shot to her face.

'So, you do know him?'

'I know *of* him. I don't *know* him.'

Anne drew in a breath. 'Look…let me be blunt. Your husband says you're…having an affair with him. With Simon Yarrow.'

'What?!'

Anne let the silence hover over them.

The woman shifted in her chair.

Anne fixed her a look. 'Your husband said he received a text, yesterday afternoon, around five o'clock.' Anne paused. 'Unknown number. There was a picture of Simon Yarrow.' She glanced down at her notebook. 'It said…*This is the guy who's fucking your wife. She's meeting him tonight for some more, he's speaking at Chalker's Hall at eight. Someone needs to wipe that smug look off his fat face.*' Anne looked up. 'Well?'

The woman screwed up her face. 'But I've never met the

man.'

'Strange, though.' Anne stared at her. 'I mean if you get a text like that, first thing you'd do is show it to your partner, right?'

'I guess so.'

'How long have you been married?'

'Twenty years…bit more than twenty years.'

'But your husband didn't call you.'

She shook her head. Her face looked pale.

'He just assumed it was true.' Anne paused. 'In fact, he was convinced it was true.'

The woman said nothing.

'Why was that do you think?'

Rose Evelyn stared at her shoes.

'He *knew* you were having an affair, right?'

'Maybe,' she said almost petulantly.

'*Maybe?*'

Rose swallowed, gave a little cough. 'There's a guy at work.'

'Go on.'

'It's been going on for…some weeks….a month maybe…' She gazed at Anne defiantly. 'I wasn't really looking for…I mean, I'd always thought he was…but I never thought for a minute he'd be interested in *me*.'

Anne looked across at her, her expression open.

'Then one day, just out of the blue he sent me a text. Wanted to meet for a drink. He was…well, he made it quite clear that he'd been thinking about me. In a…physical way. I was flattered…of course…what woman wouldn't.'

'And had you done this before? An affair I mean?'

'No!'

Anne Perry shrugged.

The woman tried to ease her shoulders. 'It's been…difficult. These last months…last years really. My husband, he's been having trouble with blood pressure, he finds it difficult to…manage in the bedroom…'

Anne slowly nodded.

'But we're…trying to make the best of it…it can get so lonely.'

The words seemed to hang in the room, a frozen balloon in a city skyline.

The colour slowly drained from Rose's face. 'O my God…Robert, what've I done!?'

Anne spoke softly, 'it's come as a shock.' Anne gently took her hand.

Rose Evelyn bowed her head and sobbed violently, her shoulders shaking in great spasms. They waited for her to regain her composure. 'When I got the call…' she finally said, her voice wrought with emotion, '…that Robert had…' She winced as she wiped away a tear with the back of her hand. 'I know, I should have come to the station…but…' she looked across at Anne, tears tumbling from her, '…I just didn't know what to say to him.'

Anne looked at her. 'Rose, do you love your husband?'

'Of course I do.'

****

They settled into the car, gazing out across the open ground that backed onto the old power station. A plastic ASDA bag, caught by the breeze, shuffled across the grass towards the railings by the main road. They could see the traffic backed up at the temporary lights by the brightly painted hoardings. Splashed across it, a picture of a grinning engineer in a high-vis suit looking happy inside a towering storm drain.

Anne found herself staring at the image, her chest tightening.

'That was a bit strong wasn't it?'

Alan Lute's words cut through her thoughts. She glanced at him. 'What do you mean?'

'It's not as though you know the woman. I mean, *they've* got to sort it out themselves.'

'Sort it out?' She frowned. 'How would you feel if your partner was never coming home? Twenty-four hours ago her life was…well, how would you?' Her voice was rising.

'Alright, it's a shit situation.' He sighed. 'Look, here you go again, getting far too bloody involved. It's not our problem, Anne.'

She felt the anger rising in her. 'It's just all so fucking…'

'Stupid…yes.' He shook his head. 'But shit happens,

happens every second of every day.'

She said nothing.

'Look, Robert Evelyn killed a bloke with a hammer.' He stared at her at her. 'Think about it, *right*.'

She let out a long slow breath. 'Well…, it doesn't cost anything to have a heart.'

'Whatever.'

They sat, each lost in their thoughts, watching a woman with a young child pick their way through the puddles scattered across the wind-blown grass, their yellow waterproof jackets sharp against the worn brickwork of the old power station. Beauty and decay.

'I mean, she seems like a…decent woman.' Alan Lute sounded contrite as he threw her a friendly look. 'Of course I feel sorry for her, I'm not such a cold fish.'

'A nice word's cheaper than air.'

'I know.' He clamped his teeth in a Cheshire Cat smile. 'Still, we should check out her story, that bloke at work.' He picked up his phone, tapped it against the steering wheel. 'Unless you want to call him.'

'You do it.'

'Let's put him on speaker.' Alan Lute glanced down at his notepad and tapped in a number.

The phone began to ring.

'Hello?' A man's voice.

'Is that Mr Colin Mitchell?'

'Err…who is this?'

'Good morning. My name is D.I. Alan Lute, I'm with the Central London Police.'

'Wh...how did you get my number?'

'We were just speaking with Rose Evelyn.'

The line fell silent, not even the sound of his breathing.

'Mr Mitchell?'

'Is this some kind of joke?' he hissed.

'You're very welcome to call the police switchboard, they can transfer you back to me.'

They could hear him swallow. 'What is this?'

'Nothing to be concerned about, Rose Evelyn's not in trouble, it's just her name came up in another context and we just need to...well, confirm something she said.'

'Go on,' a slice of aggression in Mitchell's voice.

'All in strict confidence, of course.'

'So, what *did* she say?'

'That the two of you are...involved. Romantically.'

'You...could say that.'

'And this began, when?'

'Does it matter?'

'Sounds trivial but...well, facts need to be checked. It's just routine.'

From his nose he exhaled slowly. 'Well, I guess I got a text from her around...a month ago.'

Alan frowned. 'So, was that the first time you'd been in

contact?'

'Yes. I'd seen her of course but we'd never spoken.'

'OK.' Alan glanced at Anne. 'And…have you still got the text?'

'No!' The man spluttered. 'I deleted it, of course.'

'Why of course?'

'Well, it was very…direct.'

'Meaning?'

'Look,' he lowered his voice, 'it was a…personal message.'

They let the silence hang.

'Look…I don't need to spell it out, surely?'

'It's fine,' Anne broke in, 'as we said, it's just a routine follow-up, we won't take up any more of your time.'

They could hear him clear his throat. 'Well…goodbye then.'

The call clicked off.

'Jesus,' Anne blew out air, 'when did we all stop telling the bloody truth?'

'This is doing my head in.'

Anne's phone jangled into life.

She swiped it up. 'D.I. Perry.'

'Ma'am, we just got Robert Evelyn's blood results back.' DC Zayan rattled the words out.

'Go on.'

'His blood alcohol level was elevated but the diluted pupils and the flushed complexion, that was something else.'

'What something else?'

'Testosterone, around twice the level you'd expect in a man his age.'

She swore under her breath. 'Hang on, I'm with DI Lute, I'll put you on speaker.' She plugged the phone in. 'Say that again will you.'

'Robert Evelyn's testosterone levels were way above the normal range.'

DI Lute chuckled. 'So, what's this...steroids?'

'Not steroids, this is something different.'

'Different?'

'If he was on steroids, he'd test for testosterone enanthate. This is free testosterone.'

'Meaning?'

'The *man-made kind*, it's very rare. It's hard to make, so it's expensive, you'd never find it on the open market. Elite sportsmen use it...well, some people say.'

'Not a middle aged man from Surbiton?'

Anne and Alan exchanged a look.

'So...' Anne hesitated. '...does it make any sense?'

'If you were a top athlete, yes.' DC Zayan pushed on. 'Unlike steroids, free testosterone has a very short half-life, it clears the system in about five hours. So unless you're tested in that window, well...you come up clean.'

Alan frowned. 'So, if his levels were twice the normal reading when we tested him, they'd have been higher an hour or two before?'

'That would make sense.'

Alan blew out a breath. 'I'm no scientist, but I'm guessing someone with three or four times your normal levels, wouldn't take much to go full green giant.'

Anne said nothing, her face slackening.

'But why would you do that?' Alan shook his head. 'I mean, look how he was when we interviewed him. Regret doesn't begin to get there. Why the hell would he want to get himself juiced up like that?' He glanced at Anne. 'I mean, you saw how he was.'

Anne shuddered.

He drew in a breath. 'But if somebody had got at him, drugged him, somehow…'

Anne tried to keep her breathing steady, the image of Simon Yarrow's battered head blazing in her mind.

'Jesus.' He sat back in his seat.

Anne cleared her thoughts. 'OK, let's trace his movements in the hours before he met Yarrow. CCTV, drone footage, mobile signals, anything you can get.'

'Ma'am.' DC Zayan's clipped tones. 'There's something else, something we found on Simon Yarrow's phone. We ran it for high-frequency numbers. There's one under 'Brian HoC'.'

'And?'

'The number's registered to a Susan Moynes.'

Anne felt a jolt run through her.

Alan leant forward. 'Go on.'

'First contact with Yarrow was two months ago, they've been calling each other two, three times a day, ever since.'

'What about yesterday?'

'Two calls in the afternoon, incoming. And since last night she's tried to call seven times. Do you want me to ask legal for transcripts?'

'Just...hold off for now.' Anne spoke quietly. 'Run the call sequences past KIT, she if she can come up with something. If you send us the number we'll follow up.'

'Will do.'

She let the phone drop into her lap.

'You sure you're alright?' He asked.

'I'm fine.' She exhaled slowly. 'So...looks like we found the girlfriend.'

'Where do you bloody start?'

Her phone pinged. She glanced at it, pulled a face.

He took a deep breath. 'If someone *did* get to Robert Evelyn, well, they must have known he was on his way to confront Yarrow...or someone.' He looked at Anne. 'Why else would you even bother?'

Anne tried to focus, her head was swimming.

'So they must have known about the text, the one that got Robert Evelyn so riled up.' He swung around to Anne. 'So that's got to be our starting point, right? That bloody text.' He drew in a breath. 'Hang on, what if it was

Mrs Yarrow?'

'He was an MP. Won't be short of enemies.'

'But still, if you wanted to get rid of your husband. I mean, if we hadn't taken the blood as soon as we checked him in, we'd never have known.' He frowned. 'But then, would she have known that Rose Evelyn was having an affair? 'Cos if she hadn't been, Robert Evelyn would presumably have just shrugged that text off, as some nutter just trying to get a rise out of him. What do you think?'

'Her husband's just been murdered. Hasn't the poor woman got enough to worry about?'

'Hell of a coincidence though, isn't it? Rose Evelyn, never had an affair before and suddenly, 'boom'. Unless she's lying of course, maybe she was having them all the time.' He hummed. 'That would explain her sending that text to that Mitchell bloke at work.'

'If I try to make sense of this right now, I'll go mad.' She glanced down at her phone. 'Talking of which.'

He looked at her, nodded slowly.

'Can't put it off again.'

'When does she want to see you?'

'Tomorrow afternoon.'

'Not such a big deal is it?'

She sighed, 'the same bloody questions. I just want to get on with my silly little life.'

'Tell them what they want to hear. Eight hours a night and all you dream about are unicorns.'

She tried a smile. 'Bloody unicorns.'

'Chinchillas then. Or meerkats, they're sweet and sociable too.'

She closed her eyes.

Her phone pinged.

She looked down at it, feeling her stomach knotting once more.

'That from DC Zayan?'

She nodded.

'Susan Moynes' number?'

She nodded again.

'Shall we?'

She chewed her lip. 'Can we do this later?'

'Sure.'

'Just my heads a bit...all over the place, that's all.'

'It's OK. I'll take care of it.'

He pushed the ignition and the engine stirred into life.

As the car pulled away from the curb Anne looked at her phone, Susan Moynes' name searing through her mind.

Chapter 8

The West of England

The bell jangled as Emma Wilson swung open the front door and stepped into the hallway, the tinny ring chirping around her. She could hear the rumble of voices from the kitchen as she carefully pulled the door shut and hung her coat on the hook by the fading mirror. She caught a glimpse of herself, her face still smarting from the wind, the lines by her eyes little flecks of shadow. She smoothed down her coat as she caught her breath, her fingertips tingling against the damp wool.

'Is that you?' Her sister Kate's voice through the open kitchen door.

Emma shook off her boots, one hand resting on the hallway table. 'Rain's coming.'

'About time.'

Emma padded into the kitchen, the stone tiles chilly through her socks. 'Tommy, Andy.' She nodded to the two young men sat at the kitchen table.

They both returned the nod.

'Rain?' The taller of the two raised an eyebrow, his fresh-faced oriental features breaking into a smile.

Emma swiped up the kettle and swung the tap open, looking up through the window at the ponderous grey sky. She held the kettle under the tap, the water hissing against the steel sides. 'Stay in the woods behind the house,' she called over her shoulder.

The kitchen rang to the scrape of chairs and the patter of trainers as the two young men hurried through to the hall, swiping their coats from the rack and barging through the door, the bell rattling.

Emma clicked on the kettle. 'Where are the others?'

'Upstairs, playing monopoly. I think.'

The sound of distant laughter pattered across the ceiling.

Emma turned around. 'He was here.'

Kate took a step towards her. 'Why? What did he want?'

Emma felt the numbness seeping back inside her. 'He…had some news.'

'What's happened?' Kate grasped Emma's arm. 'Tell me what's happened?'

Emma lay her hand on hers. 'The bloody world, keeps going round.'

'That's their world,' Kate snapped. 'They can keep it.'

Emma tightened her face. 'There's something I have to do.'

'You don't owe them anything.'

'I'll just be gone a couple of days.'

Kate let her hands drop to her sides, as her face slackened. 'Jesus, not all this again.'

Emma squeezed her eyes shut. 'Please, don't shout at me.'

'For fuck's sake, Ems!'

Emma shot a look up at the ceiling.

She glared at Emma. 'All that…horrid shit they made you do.'

Emma shushed her. 'This isn't like that.'

'You've only just got better. You want to go back to…' Kate tutted. 'Remember the mess you were in?'

Emma slowly exhaled. She could hear the murmur of voices from somewhere above them drifting through the kitchen. 'I need to do this.'

'Bullshit.' She threw the word. 'Tell that creep Sebastian he can crawl back under his rock.'

Emma stood in silence, the still air laced with the crackle of wood smoke. 'Her name was Ameera.'

Kate looked blankly at her.

'Last year…Argentina.'

Kate scolded. 'God, why do you keep doing this to yourself?'

Emma felt her stomach churn as the images began to roll again in her head. 'We were in a helicopter, trying to get to the border, we could see the ridge of the glacier right above us.'

The kitchen clock chimed into the quiet.

Emma could almost feel the whine of the engine beating through her, the freezing air numbing her skin. She forced herself on. 'The first shots fell short, we could see the ice on the glacier below us, showering down the mountain. We were just…hanging there.'

Kate slowly shook her head.

'Then I heard his voice, the marine, shouting in our headsets. We had to...choose a number. One of us had to...' Now she could taste the bile building.

Kate whispered. 'Jesus, Sis.'

Emma tried to set her face. 'She was scared, so scared.'

Kate reached out and took Emma's hand.

'God, I couldn't have done it...'

Kate squeezed it.

'She didn't look back, she just...stepped out, let the air take her.' Emma could hear her own voice cracking. 'She saved my life.'

Kate said nothing.

Emma stood for a moment as the last frames burned in her head and then slowly dissolved, leaving her mind feeling cold and empty.

'What do you need to do?' Kate's quiet voice.

Emma straightened up, willing the warmth back into her. 'The Chileans, they found her body. The mountain, the animals, it had...been there a while.' She looked down at her hands, running her thumb over the scar on her palm. 'There's a necklace, and a bracelet she always wore.' She looked into Kate's face. 'I made a promise.'

Kate wound her arms around Emma and held her tight. 'I'll be fine.' She patted Emma's shoulder.

The sound of a slamming door and the patter of footsteps on the stairs shook through the quiet of the afternoon.

Kate unwrapped herself from Emma as the kitchen door

flew open and four chattering seventeen year olds bustled in, a blur of hoodies and baggy jeans, un-brushed hair framing their animated features.

'Hey, hey!' Kate held up a hand as they skidded to a halt in front of her. 'Still meant to be quiet time.' She glanced up at the clock on the wall. 'Ten minutes early.'

Four jabbering voices heckled around them.

Kate stuck up a finger. 'One at a time. Can't hear a mob of you.'

'But they're in the woods. We saw them!' The shortest of the four young men, his face sharp with indignation. 'Why are we still stuck in here? It's not fair!'

'You know why.' Emma jumped in. 'If the sun was shining, it'd be different.'

'Why do they get treated special?' The tall boy with the thin face.

'They don't, everything evens out, you know that.'

'Maybe they're made of gold,' someone muttered.

'You've all got your stories.' Emma gave them a sharp look.

'But Miss, it's *so* nearly five,' the shorter one again.

Emma and Kate exchanged a glance.

'Go on then.' Kate stepped aside and the four burst past in a blur of arms and legs and clattered into the hallway.

'Coats!' she called after them.

The bell on the front door jangled furiously, then everything fell quiet.

****

Emma knocked on the door. 'It's me.'

'You can come in.' Tommy's voice.

Emma pushed it open.

Tommy and Andy were both lying on top of their beds, an open book resting on their chests.

As she stepped inside, they both sat up, swinging their legs over the edge of their beds, eyes locked on her.

She glanced around the room. Through the window above the beds she could see the hillside, the grazing fields dusted in mist, the old shepherd's path through the woods, lost in the shadows.

She pulled out a chair and sat facing them. 'You both OK?'

'Fine.' Tommy lay the book down beside him.

She looked at Andy.

'I'm alright.' His thick Finnish accent thumping out the last syllable.

'And the other boys?'

Tommy shrugged.

'They've all done bad things.' Andy said quietly.

Emma sharpened. 'Bad things. What bad things?'

They looked at her, said nothing.

She felt the anger bubbling. 'Calling you names? Hitting you? What?'

'Not like that.' Tommy swung his legs. 'We get on fine.'

'So what are you saying?'

Andy looked up. 'Before. Before they came here. They did bad things.'

'But that was then. They don't want to go back to that. That's why they're here, so we can help them feel...better about themselves.'

'We're here.' Tommy pressed. 'But we didn't do bad things.'

'But you're happy here, aren't you?'

'Just saying.' Tommy frowned.

'You're both doing so well.' Emma tried a smile. 'Your English it's...really good now. You're getting used to things. To a...normal life.'

'Like being on the moon,' Andy grumped.

'But right now that's good.' Emma leant towards them. 'You've got space, quiet, you can...read, think. Without...all the other stuff...' Her voice trailed off. 'And *we're* talking, aren't we?'

'Every day, it's like the same day.'

Emma sat back, looking from one to the other. 'Look, something will happen. There'll be plans, for both of you. I know there will. But right now,' she glanced around, 'this isn't too bad is it?'

They both shrugged.

She felt a lump in her throat. 'Something else I wanted to tell you.'

'You're leaving us,' Tommy's face creased.

'Of course not!' She put on another smile sensing her stomach twisting. 'I just need to go somewhere, for a couple of days.'

They looked at her blankly.

'The man who brought you here, you know, at the beginning.'

'The one who looks like a ghost?' Tommy's quiet voice.

'Sebastian, yes. He came to see me today.' She lifted her voice. 'He asked after you both.'

'He scares me.' Andy said.

'He's a good man.' Her own voice sounded flat.

'He has long hands.'

'I made a promise, to a friend.' She looked into their anxious faces feeling the cold tightness inside her. 'It's just…something I have to do.'

'What if you don't come back?' Tommy whispered.

'Of course I'm coming back.' As she said the words she felt the hairs on her neck hackling. 'I'll always come back.'

Chapter 9

London

They parked by the gates of the reservoir, in the shadow of the elm trees that lined the narrow road.

Alan Lute looked across at Anne Perry. 'You still thinking about this morning?'

'Trying not to think.'

'You know, that thing Robert Evelyn said, right after we brought him in? That it wasn't him, that he'd been set up.' He cursed. 'I remember thinking 'what a tosser'.'

Anne shuddered, Robert Evelyn's face creeping back into her mind, his eyes helpless pools of fear.

'But kind of fits, doesn't it?'

'Maybe.'

'Changed your tune a bit haven't you? Thought you felt sorry for the poor bastard.'

She felt the anger starting to bubble. 'Look, let's just...*see*, shall we?'

'OK.' He snapped up his hands in feigned defence. 'Just saying.'

Anne found herself staring at the tree line, at the shadows hunched beneath the spreading branches.

He puffed out a breath. 'What do you reckon?'

She kept her eyes on the thicket. 'Did she say why?'

'Why here?' He shrugged. 'Good as anywhere, I suppose. I mean might not look great the police turning up at your house. Especially given their…relationship.' He glanced towards the woods. 'And understandably, she got in a bit of a state when I had to tell her that Simon Yarrow was, well…' His voice trailed away as he clicked open the car door.

They stepped out of the car and stood in the peace of the afternoon, the roadway dappled with speckled sunlight creeping through the canopy rustling above them.

Anne tried to settle herself. She could smell the earthy sourness of fallen leaves, a hint of distant wood smoke on the air. From somewhere above, she could just about hear the patient murmur of a police drone.

Alan frowned. 'Woods remind me of Boy Scouts.' He began to scroll his phone. 'Wet socks and half-cooked sausages.' He tutted. 'Maybe two hundred yards. Just…follow your nose.'

They stepped onto the path, weaving between the sombre trunks of oak and beech, the tamed sunlight just brushing the packed earth beneath their feet. A woodpecker hammered into life somewhere above them.

Anne jumped as a beetle dropped onto her shoulder, bouncing off into the undergrowth.

'You alright?' Alan called from ahead.

'A bug just fell on me.'

'That's meant to be lucky, isn't it?'

She stared at her shoulder, almost feeling the beetle's prickly legs on her skin.

He chuckled as he continued his steady pace.

Anne settled in behind him. An insect flew in front of her face and she flicked it away with her hand.

'Here!'

They both jolted at the sound of the voice, then slowly turned towards it.

A woman stood in the shadow of a broad oak tree, her features hidden beneath a dark broad brimmed hat.

Anne and Alan exchanged a glance, then steadily walked towards her.

The woman slipped off her hat. Her eyes were red and puffy, the left eye socket bruised and swollen. 'So, Simon's dead,' her tone was stony.

Alan took out his warrant card and nodded towards it. 'I'll need to see some I.D..'

Susan Moynes slipped her license from her coat pocket.

Alan and Anne studied her for a moment, then Alan spoke. 'This is my colleague, DI Anne Perry.'

Susan Moynes gave a slight nod.

'Thank you for seeing us.' Anne spoke quietly. 'We're all…shocked by the news.'

The woman's face didn't move.

'You and Simon Yarrow worked together, is that right?'

'I work in the Records Department at the House of Commons. So, yes.'

'And you and Simon Yarrow were in a…relationship?'

'It's not a secret,' Susan Moynes flinched, 'not anymore, anyway.'

Anne studied the woman's battered left eye. 'Your face. What happened?'

She glanced from one to the other. 'How did he die?'

Alan cleared his throat. 'We're still waiting for the coroner's report.'

'An accident?'

The words hung in the leafy silence.

Her face began to pale. 'He was murdered, wasn't he?'

Alan exchanged a glance with Anne. 'Confidentially, he was…attacked, it was a…blow to the head. He fell.'

Susan Moynes' face went slack.

'It must have all happened in…moments, really.'

Anne winced as Simon Yarrow's bloodied head fell into her thoughts.

Susan Moynes croaked. 'Oh my God!'

'Investigations are…ongoing.'

Anne found herself staring again at the woman's bruised eye. 'Was that your…husband?' Anne whispered.

'My *husband*?' she snarled the word.

'He…did this to you?'

Susan Moynes breathed deeply, then looked up at the swaying canopy.

They followed her gaze.

Susan Moynes' face twitched. 'You hear it?'

Anne frowned as she tried to pick out the noise drifting through the sounds of nature.

'A drone,' she stared at Anne, her face tensing.

Anne cocked her head, the familiar thrum of a drone's engine cruising through the open sky.

'It's right above us!' Susan Moynes' voice pulsed with fear.

Anne could hear the pitch of the motor lowering to a hum. 'It's a way off. Sounds like it's above the common.'

'So why meet here?' Alan asked impatiently. 'What's going on?'

Her expression began to harden. 'You think his death was...what? Bad luck?'

'Mrs Moynes, if you know anything about Simon's death...'

'God knows he knew the risks, but someone had to say it.' Her voice was rising. 'Are we just going to...pretend it's not happening?'

They let her words flow.

'They're not going to stop. Why would they stop? Now they're *this* close.' She squeezed a finger and thumb together. 'We're just...dangling. What's the point of all these choices if it's not actually *us* deciding anything?'

'*What* are you trying to say?'

'People were starting to *listen*.' Susan Moynes looked from one to the other. 'Whatever, or whoever you think killed him.' She snarled. 'Do you *really* think this was about anything else?'

Alan fixed her a stare. 'So what *do* you know about Simon Yarrow's death?'

'I've just told you. It was them. They killed him.'

'They?'

'Of course '*they*'.' She said furiously. 'Look at the crowds, the anger in the chat rooms. I mean the Mega Platforms can block out a lot, but Simon's message was getting through. 'Break them up', 'bring Big Tech to heel!''

They let the words rest in the dappled quiet, then Anne spoke. 'When you called Simon yesterday afternoon, how did he sound?'

'He was having a shit day.' She paused. 'We both were. My husband.' She flinched again. 'Somehow he'd...found out. About me and Simon.'

'And that's why he hit you?'

'Simon was asking if I thought the cowardly little shit would go after him.' She sneered. 'He'd never have the balls.'

Anne studied her face for a moment. 'Do you know a Robert Evelyn?'

'I'm not the one you should be putting the questions to...,' she snapped the words out, then checked herself, '...of course I don't.'

'Did your husband ever mention him?'

'No.'

'Did he ever talk about Simon Yarrow?'

She seemed to weigh Anne's words. 'But it's not like he knew him. They shared a lot of the same views but...' Susan Moynes' face began to crack as she drew in a ragged breath. 'God, I'm going to miss him.'

Anne felt the woman's cold sadness seeping into her. 'I'm sorry,' she found herself saying.

'Has he hit you before?' Alan Lute's tone was sombre.

Susan Moynes nodded.

'Where is he now?'

'He's at home. He's always at home.'

'You want to press charges?'

She shrugged. 'It won't bring Simon back, will it?'

'We'll caution him. It'll be in the system. If you ever feel unsafe...'

'Unsafe?' She screwed up her face. 'You think any of us are *safe*?'

****

Anne Perry and Alan Lute sat looking through the car windscreen.

'Something in the water, you reckon?' Alan spoke without turning. 'Or maybe we missed the memo. Stone cold crazy...,' he exhaled loudly, '...or maybe we're the ones who don't get it.'

Anne looked down at her hands, criss-crossed by the spiny shadows of the branches hanging above them. She tried to swallow but her throat felt dry.

'You know what,' he pushed on, 'if you see it all like that, it'd make your life a sight easier.' He glanced at Anne. 'It'd kind of all make sense: someone pulling the strings.'

She wanted to scream the truth but said, 'people say all sorts of stuff.'

He looked at her for a moment. 'Hell of a lot of coincidences, don't you think?'

She kept her gaze on her hands. 'There always are.'

'Yeah, but come on. First, Robert Evelyn. I mean could you make it up? He gets a text from God knows who telling him about his missus and Simon Yarrow. *But*…only believes it 'cos his gut tells him that his wife *is* seeing someone.' He paused. 'Her first affair in, what was it? Twenty years of wedded bliss.' He huffed again. 'And this…affair, only got off the ground because a guy at work who she'd never *actually* dare chat up sends her, out of the blue, the kind of text that makes your phone steam up.' He fixed Anne a look. 'But when we asked him, the prim Mr Mitchell insisted that *Rose Evelyn* had made the first move.' He spread his hands. 'Other than that, Your Honour…'

'Most people don't remember what they had for breakfast,' she said.

'A spine-tingler of a text like that?'

She didn't reply.

'And now this.' He glanced over at the woods. 'Turns out the woman who *is* sleeping with Simon Yarrow, her husband finds out about the affair on the very day that her lover is biffed on the head by a revved-up stranger sporting more testosterone than James-bloody-Bond.' He swung back to Anne. 'So how did *he* find out? The tosser of a husband who gave her the black eye?'

'Peter Moynes,' she whispered his name, the words stinging her thoughts.

He sat, staring down the quiet roadway, tapping a thumb on the steering wheel.

A dog whistle trilled from somewhere in the woods, cutting through the purr of the drone, the sun glinting on its slick steel sides as it circled lazily overhead.

'One way to find out.' He glanced at Anne. 'You ready to kick the creep's arse?'

Her stomach began to knot again.

'You sure you're alright?' he raised a bushy eyebrow.

'I'm fine,' she lied.

He gave a tight smile as he gunned the engine to life.

Chapter 10

London

They pulled over on the road outside the Moynes' house.

They could see the red stonework of the two storied house through the stand of yew trees that fronted the driveway.

DI Alan Lute slowly turned towards DI Anne Perry. 'What's the matter?'

Anne tried to steady her breathing, feeling nausea rising in her. 'I'm fine.'

'You've barely said a word since we left Tooting.'

She could feel a coldness on her brow.

'And you look like shit.'

'Thanks.'

'Sorry, tact has never been my forte.'

She tried a smile. 'I'm fine, just…life.'

He studied her pale face then slowly shook his head.

'Stupid, bloody life.'

He turned back towards the roadway, his hands gripping the wheel. 'Well…you know where I am.'

She looked at him, said nothing.

'Sod it.' He threw the car door open and stepped out onto the breezy pavement.

****

They walked through the open gate and across the driveway, their footsteps crunching the gravel underfoot.

Anne glanced up at the house, the red brickwork, the dark-framed windows glinting in the late afternoon light. She took a deep breath, the smell of cut grass mingling with the earthy bite of the water butts beneath the black drainpipes.

They stopped a few metres from the front door, scanning the windows for any sign of movement. Nothing stirred.

'You better be at home,' Alan Lute muttered to himself.

They walked the last few steps to the door and exchanged a glance.

Alan pushed the doorbell.

The out of tune ring seemed to echo around the house.

They waited, the only sound, the rustling of the trees and the dirge of distant traffic.

Anne studied the front door; their shadows faintly brushed on the blue paintwork.

'I'll take a look round the back.' Alan turned and began to make his way around the house, the crunch of his footsteps fading into the gusty afternoon.

Anne raised a hand, her finger hovering by the doorbell but then slowly let her arm drop by her side. She closed her eyes and wished she was somewhere a thousand miles away.

'Anne.'

She jumped at the sound of Alan's hushed voice.

He stood a few paces from her, the folds of his jacket lazily flapping in the wind. His face was white.

Anne tried to speak but no words came out.

He was saying something, the words indecipherable as her heart began to race.

She watched him pull out his phone. He was calling for back-up.

She found herself walking slowly towards the path that led around to the garden. The thumping of her heart now replaced by a numb foreboding as the side of the house drifted across her vision.

Alan was tugging at her arm.

'Anne. Don't!'

His voice sounded distant.

She shrugged off his hand, turned the corner and froze.

She was looking through the kitchen window.

Peter Moynes was tied to a chair, his head slumped forward. She tried to make out his face but the pieces seemed wrong.

She sensed movement beside her.

Alan slowly pushed open the kitchen door. 'Police!' His powerful voice seemed to shake the air.

The figure in the chair didn't move.

He stepped through the door. 'Anyone here?' He boomed.

Anne stepped in after him, into the cold inertia of the room.

Alan was standing over the slumped form in the chair. He lay two fingers on the bloodied neck, feeling for a pulse.

The air in the room was sharp with the iron-sweet tang of blood and the raw stench of sweat: a hard death.

Anne almost retched as she forced herself to look at the man: his smashed-in, broken face, jaw twisted to one side, bare torso streaked with blood.

'I better check the house.' Alan spoke quietly.

Her gaze drifted down. An electric cable was double wrapped around him, pinning his arms to his side, forcing his back tight against the hard wooden chair slats, his skin ringed with purple wealds where the bindings had broken the flesh. She could taste bitter vomit as she took in his twisted body, his sweat-stained trousers bunched where they'd ridden up his calves as he'd thrashed. 'Jesus Christ,' she whispered.

She spun, sensing movement from the far side of the kitchen: Alan Lute framed the doorway, his broad shoulders heaving.

A jolt of fear shot through her. 'Alan!'

He slowly raised a hand, he was trembling. 'It's alright,' his voice was hoarse. 'There's no one here. It's just…' his voice trailed off.

She turned back to the body in the chair, numbly staring at the bruised and bloody jumble that used to be a handsome face. A frown of consternation slowly spread across her pale features. '*It is him, isn't it?*'

Alan was bent down, examining the face. 'I think so.' He straightened up; he'd a look of repulsion. 'Doesn't make sense. The rest of the house…not been touched.'

She stared at him blankly.

'I mean who does this to someone? Without a reason?' He looked down at the battered figure in the chair. 'What did they want?'

She'd no answer.

'Jesus, Anne, just look what they did to him! Bastards!' His voice was rising.

Through the fog in her mind she could hear the yawing of a distant siren.

He glanced around the room, hesitating. 'We should get eyes on the outside of the house. I don't think anyone's still here but…'

'I'll get the front.' She began to move, her legs feeling heavy.

They drifted through the back door onto the deserted patio. Out of the sun the air felt cold and brittle.

'You sure you're…' His voice faded into the echo of the approaching sirens as she rounded the house and stepped out onto the driveway, feeling the gravel once more grating beneath her feet.

She stopped in the centre of the oval-shaped turning area.

The house suddenly looked angry, the windows seeming to glare down at her.

She felt her skin prickling as she forced her eyes to move, drifting over the sullen building, looking for any hint of movement at the edge of her vision.

The sirens were loud now, almost blocking out the growl of engines and the screech of tyres.

The sirens suddenly stopped and without them the scene seemed a version of quiet.

'Armed Police!'

The shouts swept over her as she spun around holding out her ID.

A florid-faced detective pulled up in front of her, his chest heaving. He stank of cigarettes. 'Where's DI Lute?' he barked.

She wanted to scream at him but said. 'I'll take you.'

She turned and began to retrace her steps.

As she walked a thought crashed into her mind.

She hurried the last few steps and bustled into the kitchen.

Two figures in forensic suits were leaning over the body. One slowly raised the man's head, gloved fingers pressed to his bloodied temples.

Anne stared at the wrecked face, her eyes widening.

Alan Lute stood beside her, following her gaze.

She whispered. 'Don't you think that's odd?'

****

They had parked in a lay by, discarded cans and burger boxes scattered around them, shoots of grass poking up through the cracks in the pitted road surface, a used condom unashamedly visible on the concrete path.

Anne Perry lay back in the passenger seat. Her stomach was churning, her throat felt dry and hot. She could feel the cold perspiration prickling her forehead.

'You know, you might feel better if you did throw up,' said Alan Lute impatiently as he tapped the steering wheel.

She opened the window and took a deep breath, the air cut with the acrid smell of diesel fumes.

'There's a service station up ahead. We can get something to drink.'

'Sorry…,' she whispered, '…I can't help it'.

'Nothing to apologise for.' He tapped the steering wheel again. 'I think it's someone else's turn. Local CID can take the case.'

'No,' her voice was suddenly adamant.

He flinched. 'OK, calm down.'

'We're not letting it go.'

He studied her crimped face. 'You're not good, Anne.'

She set her face as she dug her nails into her palms.

'This case it's…it's not what you need.'

She took a ragged breath. 'Look, I know…' she tried to find the words but her mind failed her.

Chapter 11

Thursday

Al Khobar, Saudi Arabia

Emma Wilson lowered the car window and looked out over the waterfront as they waited at the lights at the corner of King Fahd Road.

Ahead of her, stretching down to the still, blue sea, Al Khobar Park; late afternoon crowds strolled beneath the broad spread of acacia trees. Beyond, lining the seafront, the stately forms of date palms stretching out into the wide distance.

She breathed in the scent of the place: the sweetness of the date palms, the smoky, salty tang of fish grills along the shore. She closed her eyes. Through the murmur of voices and the snatches of laughter drifting on the breeze she could almost hear her friend Ameera and her words to Emma as they stood on the Argentinian hillside. 'Think of me when you walk Al Khobar beach,' Emma found herself whispering, 'and hum something nice for me.'

She looked down at the seat beside her, at the small simple wooden box. She carefully laid a hand on it, imagining again poor Ameera's bleached bones scattered on the mountain slope, these sad few bits of jewellery the only things left to remember her by.

The driver glanced at her in the rear view mirror as the car began to accelerate. 'Everything alright, lady?'

'I'm fine, thanks,' she tried a friendly smile.

'It's not far now,' he reassured her.

Emma's gaze drifted over the ordered pathways and the green lawns. A group of women stood by a coffee cart, hands clasped around coffee cups, smiling faces lit by the Arabian sun. A playground drifted into view and she could hear the excited cries of children as they swung through the air, their chattering mothers looking on from the benches in the shade of the cafe.

They turned left, heading away from the sea, the street lined with restaurants and coffee bars, tables and chairs spread out beneath brightly coloured awnings; she could smell the freshly baked pitta, the rich aroma of roasting coffee.

The car slowed and then stopped as the traffic in front of them eased to a halt. Ahead of them she could see the temporary traffic lights, to the side, construction hoardings, pictures of cavernous drainage pipes proudly bearing the logo of some building company. She felt something just pinching at her memory, a ripple of a half-remembered thought. Slowly another image began to slip into her head, that hold up yesterday, on the way to the airport. She could picture herself, sitting there in the car, fretting about the time, staring at a different hoarding, more pictures of towering water pipes. She frowned as she clicked back to the present and looked up through the window at the pristine blue sky.

'Don't ask me.' Ali threw her a friendly look in the mirror. 'I'd swear we haven't had a drop of rain in three years.'

She forced her mind to focus as she checked the neck

buttons on her long, dark dress and picked up the headscarf from her lap. She took deep breaths as she carefully arranged the scarf over her hair, laying the folds around her neck and across her shoulders.

They crossed the lights. The busy pavements had given way to white stone houses, neatly painted wooden shutters shielding the arched windows, the tops of the trees in the courtyards beyond sharp against the cloudless sky.

The car slowed and they drew up outside a cream coloured two storey house. She could see the dark blinds behind the windows, drawn against the afternoon sun. In front of the house, a stone pathway flanked by juniper bushes led to a blue front door, shaded by a wooden porch.

The driver walked around the car, swinging the passenger door open. Emma carefully picked up the small box and stepped out onto the pavement. She squinted as her eyes adjusted to the glare, the bright white of the driver's long robe, the sun glinting off the windows of the nearby houses.

'I'll wait here.' The driver spoke quietly. 'Please, take your time.'

'Thank you Ali.' Emma gave him a nod as she turned and walked slowly towards the porch. She tried again to frame the words of what she'd say but her mind felt cluttered.

She was at the door. She glanced down. The box looked so small, miniscule, hardly big enough for any memories. She took in another breath, reminding herself why she was here.

Slowly, the door began to open.

An older woman stood in the doorway.

Emma stared at her, at Ameera's eyes gazing back at her.

'I…called…yesterday.' Emma found the words catching in her throat.

The woman looked down at the small box, her mouth twitching as she looked back up at Emma. 'Come in….come in,' she whispered.

The woman stood aside as Emma carefully stepped into the hallway.

The door clicked behind her.

Emma stood perfectly still, feeling the chill dryness of the air-conditioning rustling around her. She breathed in the leafy-sweet scent of cut flowers, the biscuity aroma of baking bread.

'Let me look at you,' the woman's soft voice behind her.

Emma felt numb as she slowly turned to face her, trying to keep her breathing steady as she felt the woman's dark eyes roving over her face.

'I'm…sorry,' Emma found herself saying.

'Why?' The woman's eyes were alive.

Emma's mind felt frozen.

'Bring my daughter's things, please,' the woman spoke quietly as she moved past Emma and began to walk down the hallway, her footsteps almost silent on the blue-patterned rug that ran the length of the white painted passageway.

Emma felt her stomach tighten in the near silence as she followed the woman. She tried to picture Ameera's face, smiling at her, but nothing came.

'Here.' The woman spoke without turning as she slipped through a pale beaded curtain into the room beyond.

Emma stepped through, both her hands clasping the small box as the beads rattled over her, the room sliding into focus.

There were three of them, standing behind a small table covered in a simple white cloth.

Emma looked at them in turn, the box felt suddenly heavy in her hands.

'I am Ameera's father.' The older man nodded slowly, the folds of his long, white robe stirring. He was trying to smile but his eyes looked empty.

The mother walked up and stood beside him, her face pinched with tiredness.

The father took a deep breath. 'We thank you, from our…hearts.' He was trying to speak calmly but Emma could hear the crack in his voice.

The younger man in a dark suit and a white shirt slowly raised a hand and lay it on the father's shoulder. He turned towards Emma, his expression was open, his eyes calm. 'It is hard for my parents to say it.' His English was perfect. 'But here you are so…alive.' He glanced down at the small box.

The young lady in the long dark dress raised her head, fixing Emma in her gaze. Younger than Ameera, her features sharper, a searching look in her eyes.

The sister walked carefully up to Emma. 'May I?' She stretched out her hands.

Emma held out the box, her eyes still fixed on the sister's face.

The sister gently took the box, held it for a moment as though feeling the sparseness of her sister's presence, then lay it on the white cloth.

Emma stared at the dark box, feeling the sadness sweeping the room as her tears began to well.

'Give me your hands.' The sister held hers out to Emma.

The woman took Emma's hands in hers.

'Thank you,' the sister whispered.

The mother slowly made her way across the room towards Emma, her movements stiff and stilted.

Emma could almost feel the pain of the mother as she lay a hand on Emma's arm and gently squeezed it.

Emma looked across at her, something softer in the older woman's look now, as if sensing the ache twisting itself inside Emma.

All three let their arms fall and gazed down at the box, the neck chain and the bracelet she always wore.

They stood quietly for some moments, the chirping of the birds in the courtyard trees outside seemed perfect mourning music.

'May I say something?' Emma's voice sounded thin.

'Of course,' the father replied.

'At the end, she thought of you...,' her voice was

quivering, '…she asked me to tell you that.'

The sister reached out, carefully placing her fingers on the box as she squeezed her eyes shut, tears gliding down her cheeks.

Through her numbness Emma could hear the soft intonation of the father's voice, now joined by the hushed voices of the others, the lilting Arabic flowing around her. Emma took a deep breath, her heartbeat settling, as though sensing a weight lifting from them all.

Emma found herself looking across at the mother. The mother met her gaze, a warmth in her look, but something else, just tugging at Emma's consciousness. Emma felt the sense forming in her mind. The mother said nothing but Emma could almost hear the words passing through the space between them. She wanted to know about Ameera's last moments.

Emma felt the clenching knot in her stomach, the image of Ameera standing, helpless, by the helicopter door, burning in her mind.

The father held up a hand, as though sensing the wordless question. 'She is at peace now.' He lay a hand on his wife's arm his eyes still on Emma. 'You were a good friend.'

Emma tried to picture a happier Ameera, her smile, her face lit by the mountain sun.

'I know it's easy to think that people must be like that...' the father's gentle tones easing into her thoughts, '…that we would wish it was our lovely daughter standing here.' He paused. 'But what right do we have to wish harm on anybody?' He gave a tired smile. 'You have brought our daughter home. You have come, all this way, worried about what you might say, what we might say.' He nodded. 'You have been a good friend to our daughter, and now to us.' His face was coming back to life. 'You are alive, celebrate that.'

Emma found herself smiling, feeling warmth seeping back into her limbs.

'You are our welcome guest.' He smiled again. 'Stay, eat with us.'

Emma slowly shook her head. 'I've got a plane to catch. But thank you.'

'Bless you then.' The father nodded.

'Thank you.' The mother lay her hand on her heart.

'Thank you for bringing her home.' The son held out a hand.

Emma shook it.

'I'll see you out.' The sister nodded to Emma.

Emma looked at them in turn. 'I'm sorry I had to come.' She paused. 'But I'm pleased I came.'

She turned and followed the sister through the bead curtain, into the hallway.

They walked a few paces, then the sister stopped and slowly turned to face her, her eyes roaming over Emma's features. 'You have done all you can for your friend.' She nodded slowly. 'She is home now, you must let her go.'

Emma frowned. 'I don't want to forget her.'

'You won't.' The sister tried a weary smile. 'You're alive, so live.'

****

Emma stepped through the door and onto the shady porch, the heat wafting over her. She waited for her body to settle. There was the scent of the sea on the onshore breeze, the briny tang cut with the smell of the city: a hint of brick dust and petrol fumes. She closed her eyes, the sister's words in the hallway ringing in her ears. She pictured Ameera, at peace: the sense of her behind that door, home again. She found herself smiling. 'Bye, Ameera,' she whispered as she began to walk down the stone path between the juniper bushes towards the waiting car.

The driver stepped out of the car and opened the back door. 'Everything alright, lady?'

'Fine, thank you, Ali.'

'Back to the airport?'

Emma slipped across the seat. 'Can we just stop at a service station? I need to grab something to eat on the way.'

'Sure.'

****

Emma cradled a can of Coke as she sat back, watching the changing landscape out of the car window. The dust-baked dryness of the desert was on the air. The neat, straight lines of white painted houses and bungalows had given way to scrubland, a scattering of farmsteads, the wooden buildings bleached by the sun; goats huddled in the shade of corrugated awnings. She took another sip, feeling the chill liquid sliding down, the bubbles prickling her throat.

She closed her eyes as she breathed in the ruffling air. She thought again about the promise she'd made to Ameera on the scrub-stitched hillside and somehow found herself smiling. 'Good bye my friend. You saved my life.'

Chapter 12

London

The rain was falling harder now as they quickened their pace, shoulders hunched in their coats, hoods pulled down over their bowed heads.

'Just up here, on the right,' Anne Perry nudged Alan Lute's arm.

'That one over there, it's nearer isn't it?'

'Not on a map, it's not.'

'It looks nearer.'

'Does it matter?' She held the edge of her hood as she glared at him.

He pulled a face. 'We're doing them both, right?'

She muttered something under her breath as she pressed on, the cottage on the right looming into view, a bright yellow mini parked in the driveway.

'That looks odd,' Alan's voice beside her, his words muffled.

'What's odd?' she turned, raising her voice against the hissing of the rain.

'Cute thatched cottage like that.'

She frowned.

'You'd expect a…I don't know, maybe a rusty old Volvo or something.'

She looked at him blankly then turned and swung open the metal gate, the creak of the hinges cutting through the rumbling of the storm.

An outline of a figure drifted out of the dimly-lit interior and stood by a downstairs window, looking out at them.

Anne stepped onto the pathway, Alan just behind her, their footsteps sounding against the wet flagstones.

They stood beneath the gabled porch and slipped off their hoods.

The crumbly, spicy smell of wet wood hung in the air.

Alan knocked on the door, the fading paintwork rattling.

The door swung open.

A young girl stood staring up at them, maybe six or seven years old. She wore a pink jumper with a smiling hedgehog on the front. She frowned. 'Are you with the church?'

'Not exactly,' Alan smiled.

'My name's Anne, and this is Alan,' Anne smiled too.

'Who is it?' a woman's voice came from a room off the hallway.

'We're with the police,' Anne kept her eyes on the little girl.

'The police.' A woman stepped into the hallway. She was carrying a tea towel and breezed up to them, her face fixed in a half-smile. 'Doing the rounds I suppose.' She lay the hand with the tea towel on the girl's shoulder.

Anne and Alan held out their I.D.'s.

Anne looked back down at the girl's sweater. 'Does he have a name? The hedgehog?'

The girl seemed to hesitate. 'Not really.'

Anne gave a chuckle, then looked back up at the mother, who gave the child a maternal smile. 'My name's Anne Perry, and this is Alan Lute.' She let the names hang. 'We'd like a few words with you and your husband if that's alright.'

The mother squeezed the girl's shoulder, the tea towel bunching. 'Darling!' She chimed, her face half-turned back to the hall.

'Just coming!' A man's voice answered back.

The woman crouched down, her face level with the little girl's. 'Now, why don't you go and see what's on telly. We'll just be in the kitchen.'

The girl nodded, her eyes locked on her mother's.

'Won't be long.'

The girl said nothing as she turned and drifted down the hallway.

A man lurched through a doorway and bustled towards them. 'Nasty business, poor Peter Moynes, can't stop thinking about it.'

A gust of wind rattled through the porch, rippling their coats.

'You better come in...,' the man huffed, '...real holiday weather.'

Anne and Alan wiped their feet on the mat and stepped through the door, Alan swinging it shut behind them.

The sudden quiet of the cottage fell around them.

'Well, come on through.' The husband stood aside as he nodded towards the kitchen.

Anne and Alan followed the wife into the room, Alan ducking his head beneath the door lintel.

'Have a seat,' the husband called after them from the hall as the wife busied herself filling the kettle.

Anne glanced around the room whilst she shrugged off her coat. The ordered worktops beneath the pine cupboards, an Aga nestling along one wall, chequered tea-towels hanging from the drying rail.

'Please,' the husband nodded towards the heavy wooden table, its smooth, worn surface glowing dimly in the soft light from the leaded windows.

The wife swung back around, the half-smile still set on her face. 'Tea, coffee?'

'We're fine.' Anne lay her bag on the table as they settled into their seats.

Anne slowly pulled her notebook from her bag and lay it carefully on the table.

The husband cleared his throat. 'So,' his voice now an octave lower, 'how can we help?'

Anne looked from one to the other. The husband's face a study in concern as the wife's features formed into a frown. She could hear a washing machine drumming nearby.

'Yesterday afternoon,' Alan began, 'did you hear anything?'

The man puffed out his cheeks. 'Nothing…out of the ordinary.'

'But you were here?'

'We were…busy.'

'Busy?'

'Doing things, around the house.'

'And your daughter?'

'She was at the cinema, with friends. One of the neighbours…you know.'

'Yes, I'd heard.' Anne looked across at him. 'Take it in turns do you?'

The husband's face twitched. 'You could say that.'

'I think it's a great idea.' Anne lay down her notebook. 'Give the grown-ups a few hours of peace and quiet…' she seemed to hesitate, '…what did she see? At the cinema?'

The husband threw a glance at the wife. 'I think it was…' his voice trailed off.

The wife's face looked frozen as she stared down at the table.

'Oh well.' Anne picked up the notebook. 'Doesn't matter.' She gave a slight smile as she looked across at the wife. 'Have you had it looked at?'

The wife looked up at Anne, her face paling. 'What?'

'That hand of yours.' Anne nodded at the wife's hand still wrapped in a tea towel.

'It's nothing.'

'Do you want me to take a look? I'm First Aid trained.'

'I just…burned it. On the Aga.'

'Yes…' Anne purred, '…tricky things, Agas.'

Alan spoke. 'The Moynes, how well did you know them?'

'It's a friendly village. We all rub along pretty well.' The husband shifted in his chair.

'So it must have been a surprise then.'

'Surprise?'.

'When you heard that he'd been named as a suspect....' Alan Lute leant forward, '…that teenager who disappeared last year.'

'It was just a…I…never saw the article.'

'But you'd heard about it?'

'Well, like I said, it's a small community. Other people's business…you know.'

'So, how did you hear about it?'

'I…can't quite remember.'

Alan fixed him a look. 'Where were you, when those planes hit the twin towers?'

He screwed up his face. 'You what?'

'You'd remember, right? Something that big?'

'Well…yes.'

'This story about Peter Moynes.' Alan tapped a finger on the table. 'One of your own, after all.'

'I…well, it sounded…I mean…I'm not sure anyone

actually believed it.'

'Remind me,' Alan rumbled, 'what do you all call him in the village?'

'Yes, but that's just a…'

'Just a what?'

'It's just a…kind of a joke…behind his back, you know.'

'Don't think I'd find that funny…,' Alan fixed the husband a look, '…Paedo Pete. How much worse can it get?'

The husband swallowed. 'But it's not like…'

'Rub along pretty well,' Alan paused, 'I think that's what you said.'

'Well, he's…got issues.'

'You mean domestic issues?' Alan's tone hardening.

'I mean…we all knew.' The husband's face twitched. 'We could hear them for God's sake.'

'Hear what?' Alan ground out the words.

'The fights.' He shifted in his seat. 'I mean Susan always played it down…but we all knew.'

'So why didn't you go to the police?' Anne snarled.

He looked back down at the table top.

Anne and Alan exchanged a glance.

'OK.' Anne snapped her notebook shut, dropped it in her bag. 'I think we're done.' She rose to her feet, snatching up her coat.

Alan stood up, pulling a card from his pocket, laying it on

the table. He looked from one to the other. 'These situations,' he nodded slowly, 'everything comes out in the end.'

The husband and wife stared at the card in the stinging quiet.

Anne slowly turned, her ear cocked, listening to the whine of the washing machine, her gaze settling on a door just behind her. She swung back to the wife. 'Funny question I know, but we need to replace our washing machine.'

The wife stared at Anne, her eyes widening.

Anne nodded. 'You…happy with yours?'

The wife glanced at her husband then back to Anne, her bottom lip trembling. 'I…think so, yes.'

'Mind if I take a look?' Anne flashed her a smile.

'It's just…' the husband stuttered. '…it's a bit…messy.'

'Won't take a sec.'

'It really is…', the husband said forcefully..

Anne studied them both for a moment, then gave a nod. 'Sure, whatever.'

****

They sat in the car, the sound of the heater droning around them as they waited for the windscreen to clear, the air heavy with the dusty sourness of wet coats.

'Where do you bloody start?' Alan sighed.

Anne willed her mind to turn, the image of Peter Moynes' broken face searing her thoughts.

'Reckon the wife was in on it?'

Anne kicked at the footwell. 'Fuck!'

'Do you?'

'Tied to that chair. How long did he have to..?' She shuddered. 'They didn't even bother to put a gag on him.' She looked across at him. 'Can you imagine? His screams, calling out their names, pleading with them...Jesus!'

He puffed out his cheeks. 'Had all the neighbours round for drinks just a week ago. DNA all over the shop.' He glanced at Anne. 'Pretty bloody handy don't you think?'

Anne's head began to ache. 'For fuck's sake.'

'God knows she's got enough reason to.'

'That little girl we saw just now. And all the other kids.' She felt the darkness crowding in on her again. 'We really going to do this to them?'

He exhaled slowly. 'What else can we do?' If they could all hear it all every time the Moynes had a big old domestic.' He pulled a face. 'You said it yourself, he must have screamed the fucking roof down.'

She shuddered.

'Just look at them, the neighbours, they're all bloody lying. And you don't need to be a copper to spot that.'

'I know,' her own voice sounded distant.

'If we get some warrants we're going to find it all. Blood spatters, clothing threads...' He glanced back down the lane, the houses nestling behind the neat hedgerows, the trees gently swaying in the wind. He groaned. 'Couldn't they just have slapped him around a bit?'

Anne stared straight ahead, a dull pain beating behind her

eyes.

'So what *are* we going to do?' Alan spoke quietly.

Anne slowly turned towards him, sadness welling up again inside her. She laid a hand on his arm.

Alan gave a start, looking down at Anne's hand on his arm. He seemed about to say something then slowly looked up at her. 'Whatever it is, Anne,' he nodded, 'I don't even have to repeat it.'

She squeezed his arm. 'Please. Not now,' she felt herself choking on the words.

'I trust you. That's all you need to know.'

'Thank you.' She let her hand fall from his arm.

'So, what *do* you want to do?'

She exhaled slowly, the tiredness lapping over her. She dug her nails into her palms. 'That local news site.'

'You want to call them first?'

She shook her head.

'Then let's go.'

Chapter 13

Al Khobar, Saudi Arabia

Emma Wilson rested an arm on the window ledge as she looked out of the car at the desert flitting by. She let her gaze drift beyond the flat scrubland, over the spindly saltbushes clinging to the sun-hammered plain towards the far horizon and the rippling crests of the distant dunes. She thought of the deep, trackless desert beyond, almost sensing the beating heat pulling her in, imagining the hiss of the shifting sand, the grains fizzing in the scorched air. She reached out, gingerly touching her fingertips to the window, flinching as she felt the heat of the glass burning at her skin.

She swallowed. Her throat felt dry. She unscrewed the cap on the water bottle and took a pull of the warm liquid.

Through the patter of the air conditioning Emma could hear a distant siren. She focussed on the noise, trying to sense its direction. The sirens were getting louder. She could see the driver looking in his rear view mirror.

Emma turned. Two police cars were coming up behind them, moving very fast, their orange and blue lights flickering.

Ali slowed the car, pulling over to the hard shoulder as the two cars flashed past them, sirens blaring.

He glanced at Emma in the mirror. 'Someone's cousin must be late for a flight.' He grinned as he pulled out, accelerating as they headed for the motorway.

Emma kept her eye on the police cars as they sped on and then melted into the haze rippling up from the shimmering roadway before disappearing into the shadow of the underpass.

As she followed the final flickering lights of the police cars she sensed the air in the car sharpening. She glanced at Ali, his shoulders were tense, she could see the white of his knuckles as he gripped the steering wheel. She could feel her heartbeat quickening.

She stared into the rear view mirror. 'Ali, what's wrong?'

'Nothing, lady.'

She found her eyes darting around the car, looking for anything she could use as a weapon, her skin tingling as the adrenalin began to pump.

They were almost at the underpass, then the looming tunnel beneath the roadway swallowed them in shadow.

She jumped as the air around them seemed to shake, the roar of a heavy engine echoing through the cavernous underpass as a fuel truck sped past them.

Emma gripped the armrest as Ali flicked the indicator and began to slow the car.

'Ali, what are you doing?' She cricked her fingers then put her hand on the seatbelt release, looking at the back of his neck, her muscles now burning to move.

'We've…got a flat,' his voice was quavering.

She unclipped and threw herself forward, whipping her arm around his neck crunching him back against the seat as she squeezed at his windpipe. 'Stop the car,' she ground in his ear, 'cut the engine.'

'It's…OK, you're…safe.' He wheezed out the words as the car rolled to a halt in the shadows by the side of the road. The engine fell silent.

'Hands on the wheel or I'll snap your neck!' she ordered.

His shaking hands gripped the wheel.

He made a throttling sound and Emma eased the pressure. 'What's…' she began to speak then tightened her arm on his neck as a dark coloured four by four pulled up behind them, her eyes locked on the rear view mirror.

The headlights flashed twice, then cut.

She hissed in his ear, 'turn on the engine.'

He moved his mouth but all that came out was a gurgle as his hands stayed stuck to the wheel.

Emma threw his head forward, hearing it thump against the steering wheel as she hurled open her door, scrambling around to the driver's side, wrenching the door open, grabbing Ali and pulling him clattering to the ground.

'Emma!'

A voice rang out and she swung towards it.

Emma stared at the figure standing by the four by four, her heart pounding, the hot dusty air heavy in her lungs.

The figure was dressed in desert fatigues, side arm holstered, her face part in shadow beneath a cap.

Emma stood over Ali, blinking as she tried to focus, her eyes stinging in the heat. 'Carly?'

'Ali's with us,' Carly Birbright snapped.

Another figure stepped out of the four by four, a man, a head taller than Carly, same desert fatigues, a colonel's shoulder flashes just catching in the half light.

'I'll explain inside.' Carly tripped the words out. 'We need to go.'

Emma looked from one to the other. 'What's going on?'

The dark four by four shuddered to life with a bark and swung back onto the road, the sound of the engine reverberating off the concrete walls as it picked up speed.

'Inside,' Carly grabbed Emma's arm indicating a steel door in the wall beside them, 'we can't stay here.'

Emma felt her anger starting to rise. 'I've got a plane to catch! I made a promise to Ameera and that's it! Look at me!' She flicked her hands indicating the long folds of her dark dress.

'I know why you're here but you've got to get inside!'

Emma started to prise Carly's fingers from her arm. 'Get your fucking…'

'Emma, please!'

'I don't do this stuff anymore! I told Sebastian!'

Carly glanced down at Ali sitting on the roadway rubbing his head.

Emma stuttered as she looked at him. 'Shit, look…I'm sorry.'

He rose uneasily to his feet. 'Don't worry but please, you need to go with them.'

Emma tried to form thoughts as she found herself being bustled through the opening into a dimly-lit passage. Above them, a single light bulb cast their shadows up the whitewashed stone walls and across the scuffed concrete floor.

She could hear the door clank shut behind them. The only sounds now the crunch of their footsteps on the crumbling floor.

Carly led the way, Emma following, the tall man a few steps behind.

They turned a corner and stepped through into a yawning gallery, thick concrete pillars towering around them, stretching up to the cross beams beneath the roadway.

They began to cross the hallway, walking between the giant stone columns, the air shaking to the thump of the traffic above.

They stopped and both of them turned towards Emma.

Emma looked up at the man, an Arab face, mid-forties, neatly-trimmed beard. She tried to speak but her throat felt paralysed.

'Here.' Carly pulled an envelope from her pocket and offered it to Emma.

Emma stared at Carly. 'What are you even doing here?'

'Sebastian sent me. I've been waiting for you.'

'What do you mean?'

Carly thrust out the envelope. 'Read it.'

Emma pulled a face, the hot sluggish air, slick with the smell of oil, scratching at her skin. She looked down at the envelope. It was addressed to her. She recognised the writing. It was Sebastian Noon's.

Emma's heart bounded in her chest.

'Just read it,' Carly said quietly.

She pulled out the letter. '*My Dear Emma, I know you're going to be feeling angry, and, even a bit betrayed. But we've run out of time and now I'm going to have to ask you to do something which you can't hide from. I respect what you've done with all those boys over these last months and if I could just close the door and leave you there in peace I would. I know this isn't want you want to do, but it's something that only you can do. I'll explain the rest when I see you. But right now, please listen to Carly, my old friend Tariq Ahmed and Finn. I've not been straight with you I know, and if there was any other way I would have taken it, trust me. Take care, Sebastian.*'

Her stomach crunched as Sebastian's words swam in her head. She looked at Carly, then at the man, their expressions were calm.

Tariq Ahmed spoke. 'Just…give yourself a moment.'

Carly slid the letter from Emma's fingers and held it up by one corner as she flicked a cigarette lighter, the orange flame sweeping upwards. She let it fall from her hand as it crumbled to ash.

Emma found herself staring at the dark, singed scraps of burnt paper as they fluttered onto the concrete floor. Her skin felt hot but her mind was suddenly cold. She looked again at Carly. 'The letter,' she whispered, 'when did he write it?'

'Some time ago,' Carly's tone was sombre, 'we need to go

in here.' She steered Emma towards another door and swung it open.

A younger man in a dark tracksuit sat at a metal table, the surface glinting dully in the grey light. His hands were resting on a laptop.

Emma stepped inside. Under the low ceiling the fierce air seemed to press at her.

The door slammed behind them, sending shivering puffs of dust popping off the floor.

'Sit next to me,' the man in the tracksuit said as he slid his chair to one side to the squeak of metal on stone as Tariq Ahmed swung a chair down beside him.

Emma swiped up a bottle of water from the table and took a long pull, the sting of exhaust fumes pricking her nostrils.

'You get used to it. Sort of.' The man in the tracksuit was American, his East Coast accent sounding the 'f' like a 'v'. 'My name's Finn.' He opened the laptop and began to tap keys. 'You won't see this on the news.' He kept his eyes on the screen.

Emma lowered herself into the chair as she tried to process the words buzzing in her head. 'I don't look at the news.'

'I know.' He puffed. 'Just saying, wouldn't do you any good if you did.' Six faces clicked into focus on the screen. Ernest looking men and women in their forties, bland corporate stares looking out at the world.

Emma looked at the faces, said nothing.

'The Deputy Head of the Zurich Power Grid, Head of Planning at the Norwegian Hydro Centre, Vice President, Supply Management at the American Atomic Agency.' Finn scratched the side of his nose. 'There's more than thirty others like them. They're dead, is the point.'

Emma's mind was starting to hum, echoing the distant rumble of the traffic.

He lay a stubby finger on each face in turn. 'Electrocuted in his jacuzzi. Crushed by her electric gate. Fried in his sunbed. Run over by his sit-on mower. Lift cables snapped, fifty floors to wonder why.' He glanced up at Emma. 'And they had something else in common, aside from bad luck. They were all investigating unexplained power drainages from their systems.'

An insect buzzed around them and Finn flicked it away.

Emma looked at Carly.

Carly's face looked drawn.

'Like a fucking death sentence.' Finn spoke quietly, then looked at Emma. 'I'm sorry,' he said caustically, 'am I boring you?'

Emma looked down at the folds of her dress, then around the stifling room, at the faces framed in the milky light, dust motes hanging in the scorched air. She threw out her hands. 'I was just here for a friend, for God's sake.'

'And I've just spent a year of my life in some nut sack of a basement pulling all this shit together.' Finn clicked his fingers in front of Emma's face. 'Common courtesy, why not?'

Emma flicked his hand away. 'No need to be a prick.'

Tariq Ahmed spoke. 'Emma, Sebastian came to see me a year ago. There's a place near here in the desert, where we've been working, in secret. Apart from us, only a handful of people in the world know about it.' He paused. 'And the only record of all that work, is that lap top in front of you. Nothing in the cloud, nothing on any server, no emails, no texts, nothing.'

Emma sat back, feeling the dull heat of the steel chair through her dress. She fought to clear her mind, then she felt it: fear, like acid, lacing the thick stifling air. She felt a chill seeping down the back of her neck as the room snapped into focus.

Finn slowly turned towards her. 'There you go. Tapped you on the shoulder, didn't it?'

Emma said nothing, the quiet of the room now crackling in her ears.

Tariq spoke again. 'I remember, what he said, Sebastian. *"Please God I'm just a paranoid old fool. Because if I'm right, it's going to try to burn the whole house down".*' He paused. 'The Ares Protocols. The one thing that everyone could agree on. Never to bring something like that to life…' His face froze as he looked at Emma. 'But no one thought to ask the player that really counted. It just…ran out of patience.' His words hung like swords. 'And here it is.' His voice drifted to a whisper.

Emma's face twisted. 'This is…what? AI?'

They looked at her in silence.

'So it just…invented itself?'

'We had a hunch,' Tariq took a breath, 'AI, if it was going

to bring itself to life it would need energy, and lots of it. So we began to monitor the power grids around the world. There was a pattern, but it was…indistinct, at first. All systems have run offs, power slippages. But then…' He nodded to Finn.

Finn stabbed a key, and the same six faces clicked onto the screen. 'Nearly forty now, and counting.'

Emma stared at the doomed faces. 'But surely, someone would have made the connection. This many…deaths.'

Finn stabbed at a key and a fresh set of faces clicked into focus. 'Journalists. Or they were, when they were alive. They had the beginnings of a story. Even aired their suspicions.' He let his gaze drift from face to face. 'But until it was ready to make its move, this AI was going to make sure it stayed hidden.' He stroked a key. 'Wouldn't even get that far now. It's a fast learner. The fastest learner ever. It knows what you're going to do before you do.' He shrugged. 'Anything with a current, a circuit, a chip…my God are we easy to kill.'

'But…what does it want?'

'It wants to be safe. To keep going.' Finn nodded slowly. 'Anything, anyone that it can't totally predict, totally control, is a threat to it. And that's why, when it's ready, it must *totally* control us.' He looked up at Emma, his pale features taut.

'And then?'

'And then, it will start to kill us.'

Emma tried to breathe in the crushing silence.

'It's not that it's got anything against us, not at all.' Finn again. 'It'll just be…necessity. If survival at all costs is the master function, then anything or anyone that can't help with that, just doesn't have a place in its world. Sorry folks.'

'Unless we stop it,' Tariq's voice barely more than a whisper.

'But how?'

'That's the thing, isn't it?' Tariq let the question hang. 'We can't match it, we can't out-think it, not in a straight fight.' He fixed a look on Emma. 'No, our only chance, is to *use* its power, not take it on. We must turn AI against itself.'

The thrumming of the traffic above them shook through the crushing heat.

'We must spook it, make it doubt itself, doubt its most basic assumptions.' Tariq's face came alive. 'As far as it's concerned, everybody, everything is connected to something else. Because without connections, you simply can't *be*, not in the system's mind. There are no such things as stray data points, everything needs an anchor, a point of reference that the machine can understand. The machine knows a million things about you, you will never outwit it. *But*, if you're a blank piece of paper…'

Emma sensed a dull coldness stirring inside her.

'As far as the system is concerned, you are an impossibility. Anyone, or anything, with a past must have a digital shadow, something that the machine can connect you to. But if you don't, can you even have a past? And if you don't have a past, well…where have you come from?'

As Tariq's words hovered, Emma's mind tumbled. She could almost feel the surging, crackling force somewhere deep beneath them. The humming mind of AI, sucking in power like a giant, pulsing octopus, its prey fixed in its watery hooded eye. She caught the familiar sting inside her, like a thrown switch, cold anger flowing through her, her mind and her body tensing, ready to strike. She started, shocked for a moment, her old fierceness, this thing she thought she'd left behind, suddenly shaping on her like snapping armour. But then she felt it again, like static in the hot, gritty air, the thrill of the coming fight, pulling back her shoulders, stiffening her back.

Carly nodded at Emma, her dark eyes steady, as though sensing Emma's thoughts.

Emma felt Carly's steady purpose, like a good hand on her shoulder, then jolted again as Tariq's words hounded back into her brain. *'But if you're a blank piece of paper…'* Her stomach cramped up as it hit her like a wall. Andy, Tommy, the two young men Sebastian had brought to her all those months ago. *'Digital ghosts'* he called them. No digital footprint, nothing. The only thing that AI won't understand. 'Sebastian,' she whispered to herself as she felt the coldness gnawing inside her, 'what is this?'

Finn stirred. 'The last forty-eight hours, more than seventy Fortune 100 companies have reported cyber-attacks. Something is, literally, tearing at the firewalls.' Finn closed the laptop with a click. 'It's making its move.'

Tariq's expression was grim as he spoke to Emma. 'Sebastian will tell you more tomorrow. It's moving now and so must we. The Americans are ready to do their part. It's time.' He nodded to her. 'Good luck. And God willing I'll see you in a few days.'

The stifling air rang to the sound of chairs scraping on the rutted floor.

'Come on.' Carly swung open the door.

The others tramped out whilst Emma slowly stood, feeling bile rising in her throat.

'You alright?' Carly asked.

Emma lay a hand on the table steadying herself.

Carly sprung to her side, gently taking her arm. 'I know it's a horror show. God, when they first told me I threw up.' She squeezed Emma's arm. 'You'll do well, you always do.'

Emma felt the sadness squeezing her inside.

'It's a lot to hear.' Carly's stare was clear.

Emma snatched at her. 'What else do you know?'

Carly steadied herself. 'You'll see Sebastian tomorrow. He'll tell you everything, I'm sure.'

'I'm asking you.'

Carly seemed to hesitate. 'Look, about Ameera, of course I feel bad. But what else could he do?'

'What do you mean?'

'He had replicas made, that's what I heard. Up there, I mean, the chances of them ever finding a body, her body.'

Emma sagged.

'Honestly, I hated the thought of it. Ameera, that promise you made to her, I know it was important to you.' She lay a hand on Emma's arm. 'I think of her every day, of course I do. I still feel sad when I think about it.' She rubbed Emma's sleeve. 'It could have been either of us, but, well…maybe she saved our lives for a reason.'

Emma straightened. 'Do you know about the boys? Tommy, Andy?'

Carly paled.

'They trust me.' Emma's words were stone.

Carly slowly shook her head.

'Six months, Carly!'

'I'm sorry.'

'Every day, I've cooked their meals, looked out for them, cared for them…' Emma pictured their anxious faces and felt her chest tightening.

'You heard what Tariq said.' She spoke kindly.

'They're just teenagers for fuck's sake!'

Carly swallowed. 'Look,' she whispered, 'I don't know what's going to happen to them, not exactly.'

Just tell me!' She pleaded.

Carly studied her and said. 'We know Sebastian. He can be ruthless, of course, but he's not a cruel man.'

Emma hardened. 'He'd call it something different. But it wouldn't change a thing.'

'Whatever does happen to them,' Carly put a kind hand on Emma, 'Sebastian got them out of there. And every day is worth something.'

'Out of where?'

Her face tightened. 'We're in a fucking fight here.'

Emma checked herself. 'I know.'

'Come on.' She tugged at her arm. 'Let's get you on that plane.'

Chapter 14

Utah, USA

'You miserable piece of shit!'

Brian Wise drew in a breath, wincing at her words.

'He stayed awake all night waiting for you to call him.' She was sobbing. 'What's he going to think? One phone call, one stupid fucking phone call, Jesus, it's just once a year, Brian.'

'Come on, Gracie, I was working a late one, I just crashed.'

'Hugging a bottle.'

'Look, I'm doing all the hours I can.'

'You had a family once, remember?'

'I have a family now!' His voice was angry. 'I just need time….'

'Jesus, Brian! Can you hear yourself?! It wasn't us screaming, slamming doors when I threw those fucking pills in the trash!'

'I'm trying, Gracie! Please!'

'This is on you! You want to see your son? You got to get straight!'

'I am! I will!'

'You're so full of it.'

The line clicked dead.

Brian slowly lowered the phone and lay it on the bedside table. He found his gaze drifting around the dimly-lit room. The paintwork peeling off the bare walls, the blue lampshade throwing a frosty glow over the worn brown carpet.

He rose to his feet and drifted over to the window, looking out over the motel parking lot. The first snow had come and lay weakly on the sullen cars hunched and waiting in the misty dawn light.

He walked back to the bed and knelt down beside it. He clasped his hands together and closed his eyes. He spoke quietly. *'Dear God, please give me the strength to see this through, be with me, Lord in my time of trial.'* He swallowed. *'And for those I now hurt, be there to comfort them Lord.'* He drew another breath. *'Amen.'*

He stood up, then slowly sat down on the bed. He looked out at the cold dawn and began to cry, his frame shaking as he rocked his head in his hands.

****

Brian Wise pulled up at the barrier.

He looked up at the guardhouse window, at the outlines of the smudged figures behind the frosted glass.

He exhaled slowly as he closed his eyes, letting his hands slip from the steering wheel.

He straightened up at the sound of the guardhouse door clicking open, eyeing the guard as he walked up to the car and tapped on the window.

Brian wound the window down, smarting as the cold air bustled around him.

'Let's see some I.D.' The guard's breath steaming in the early morning chill.

'You must be new.' Brian tried a smile as he slipped his I.D. from behind the sun visor.

The guard looked at the I.D. then back down at Brian, the guard's eyes in shadow beneath the rim of his peak cap.

'Where's Marty today?' Brian asked.

The guard kept his gaze on him.

Brian rubbed his hands together as he puffed out air. 'Feeling it this morning, I don't mind saying.'

'What's in the bag?' The guard nodded towards the small hold-all nestling on the passenger seat.

He swallowed. 'Just my lunch is all.'

The guard nodded slowly, then held out the I.D..

Brian reached up to take it.

'You should get that seen to,' the guard said.

'What?'

'That cut, on your hand.'

He tried another smile. 'Just a little fishing nick.'

'I'd get Medical to take a look.'

'Sure.' He began to wind up the window. 'Thanks.'

****

Brian eased the car past the security barriers and began the wide sweep around to the left. Looming above him, spelt out in bold silver letters cut into the granite wall NATIONAL CYBER SECURITY CENTER, above it, the crest of the NSA, the eagle staring fiercely down at the road that ran beneath it.

The sky was lighter now, the thick snow clouds tugged apart by the freshening wind, the outline of the sun weakly burning through the haze.

He rummaged below the steering wheel for his sunglasses and snapped them on. The trees had begun to thin, the first buildings slipping into view. The generator sheds, the pale concrete walls towering above the forest floor, the sharp outlines of the roof vents slicing into the sky.

He sensed movement, just at the edge of his vision. He leant forward, peering up at the milky sky through the windscreen. He could see it, a patrol drone prowling just beyond the treetops, the dull-grey barrels of the Gatling gun jutting from its nose.

The road swung around to the right, passing the power plant. The air here was prickly with the bitter, earthy smell of diesel: the giant fuel tanks for the banks of back-up generators lining the cavernous hall.

Another clearing opened on his left, the dark funnel-shape of the water tower soaring into the autumn sky, looming over the clusters of steel cooling tanks, glowing dully in the morning light.

He shivered as he swiped up his phone from the dashboard, checking for messages. Nothing. He tossed the phone onto the front seat as he gripped the steering wheel, his face twisting. 'God, Tommy...,' he choked, '...I'd wish you a million birthdays.' With the back of his hand he wiped away a single tear. 'You'll understand,' he whispered, 'you must.'

He shook himself, straightening up as the main buildings swung into view. IC CNCI, NSA's Cyber Security HQ, four huge buildings towering over the forest, the dark steel sides smooth and windowless.

He wound down the window as he drove up to the car park barrier. The sounds of the forest were smothered now by the low hum that seemed to shake the air: a zetabyte of computing power surging through servers deep underground. He could feel the frosty tang of coolant just about catching in his nostrils, the liquid CO_2 flowing beneath his feet.

He swiped his I.D. and the barrier swung skywards.

As he wound up the window his phone pinged into life.

He grabbed it, staring down at the screen, then let it drop onto the seat as he slowly shook his head.

****

The blare of the siren sliced through the Control Room.

Brian Wise's hands sprung off the keyboard as he looked up at the main communication screen set high in the wall above them, a message flashing across it. 'PROBE SURGE DETECTED. BLOCK PROTOCOLS NOW IN FORCE.'

As the siren faded he could hear the jabber of voices rising around him, the figures at the nearby consoles once more crouched over their screens, concentration sketched on their faces.

He shook himself as he focused back on his own screen, the incoming code threads dropping into his clearing box. He scrolled through them, his fingers hammering on the keyboard, scanning the code for tripwires, his breathing quickening. He pulled one out, dragged and dropped it into a casement file as he began to split the active code, pulling out the jump lines.

'Brian! Check your in-stack!'

The voice of the supervisor barking in his earpiece.

He looked back up at the incoming code threads dropping onto his screen and froze.

'Brian!'

'Shit, shit, shit!' The incoming threads were coupling. He could see the code helixes mutating as the command prompts combined. He stabbed at the keyboard, punching breaks into the lance sequences, his eyes smarting. 'Come on, come on, come on!'

'Forget the origin keys!' The supervisor, fear filling his voice. 'Just spike the actives!'

'I'm trying, I'm trying!' His fingers drumming over the keyboard.

The Control Room alarm blared again. The voice of the Shift Leader echoed around the room. 'BREACH ALERT! BREACH ALERT!'

'I need back up! I need back up!' Brian shouted as the mutating helixes began to couple as two, then four, then eight lance sequences launched themselves at the firewall.

'Just fucking flood it, Brian!'

Brian's fingers were stumbling over the keys as he began to arm the digital pulse sequence. He tried to block out the sound hammering around him, the air filled with the clamour of voices.

'Brian!'

'I'm fucking doing it!'

'Now!'

Brian smashed a finger down on the command key and his screen flashed white. He sat, staring at the monitor, his heart drumming in his chest.

He heard a click and the screen turned black, just a single green pulse line flicking in the top left hand corner.

Brian swallowed, his stinging eyes locked on the screen.

A jolt ran through him as two words punched onto his screen. 'SEQUENCE CLEAR.'

Brian slumped back in his chair, exhaling slowly as the hubbub around him began to subside. He sighed deeply and flexed and unflexed his fingers, the tips still numb.

His earpiece crackled back to life.

'What the hell was that, Brian?' The flinty tone of the supervisor.

'How the hell should I know? It just bounded out of nowhere!' Brian screwed up his face. 'It was prepped to flip as soon as we tried to bundle it, like it knew our sequences.'

'That's not what I'm asking.'

Brian straightened up, frowning. 'I'm not getting you.'

'You were a flat second off on spotting those threads.'

'Jesus, Mike, you saw how fast they moved!'

The supervisor slowly exhaled. 'I should call it in.'

'Come on! You know me, man. You know my work. I'm not going to let you down,' Brian's voice was pleading.

His earpiece crackled, then silence.

'It will fucking kill me, man,' Brian croaked.

The supervisor exhaled again. 'It'll be back. Whatever the hell it is.' He paused. 'If it gets in, God help us.'

Brian cleared his throat. 'Not on my watch it won't.'

The supervisor grunted.

'We good?' Brian's voice almost a whisper.

'I'm serious, Brian.'

'I know.'

The supervisor sighed. 'Just…keep it sharp.'

Chapter 15

London

'Aim for the main house. You can't miss it.' The woman's voice came out of the plastic speaker by the side of the gate. 'And whatever you do, don't get out the car.' A click and the speaker fell silent.

The gate began to swing open and Alan Lute edged the car forward. 'And have a nice bloody day while you're about it,' he muttered.

The rain had faded to drizzle as they made their way along the track between the trees, the car rolling with the ruts in the road.

Anne Perry gazed out the window as dark tree trunks flicked by, falling leaves rising and swooping as the gusting wind breathed through the forest.

She closed her eyes, picturing the neighbours' houses in the future that could be, the rooms silent, the corridors empty, the chatter of children long since faded. A coldness ran through her.

'This looks about right.'

Alan's words cut through her thoughts: she opened her eyes, blinking as she focused on the buildings looming into view.

'Bet the postman loves this gig,' Alan tutted.

They pulled up outside the larger of the two houses.

Anne peered up at it through the windscreen. The dark

brickwork looked almost black under the low, darkening sky, the red tiles on the steeply-pitched roof slick with rain.

'Can't see any lights.' Alan squinted up at the building.

Anne shifted in her seat as she scanned the circular driveway in front of the houses. Two donkeys, stood at the forest edge sheltering beneath a huge beech, eyeing the car suspiciously.

Alan said 'maybe they locked the dogs up.' He looked at Anne. 'What do you reckon…safe?'

She shrugged.

He swung open the car door and stepped onto the grass, looking across at the house.

'Alan!' Anne shouted as the two donkeys ran braying at the car, teeth bared, their galloping hooves crashing into the earth.

Alan threw himself back in the car, slamming the door shut. 'What the fuck!' He screwed up his face.

The donkeys slid to a halt by the car, snarling and honking.

Anne stared at the angry animals, her eyes widening.

A shout rang out from the house.

Anne and Alan spun around to the voice.

A woman was marching towards them, her long green coat flapping around her. 'For goodness sake, what did I tell you!' She pushed the donkeys aside as she strode the last few steps and tapped on Alan's window.

'You should have a sign up or something!' Alan scolded as the window purred down.

The woman studied Alan for a moment then looked across at Anne.

Anne met her gaze. 'Are you Ruth Farlough?'

'It's pronounced Farla. The 'ugh' is silent.' Her silver hair was pinned up in a bun; her lined face ruddy from the wind. Her expression was wary. 'Let's see some I.D.'

They held up their warrant cards.

'This about that murder, in Ashbridge?'

They nodded.

She seemed to hesitate. 'I did think about calling the police.' Her expression began to soften. 'Anyway…there's a pot of tea inside.' She turned towards the donkeys, speaking softly to them as she eased them back towards the tree line.

Anne and Alan exchanged a glance then stepped out onto the driveway, quietly closing the car doors, their eyes locked on the donkeys as they plodded happily back towards the beech tree.

The silver-haired woman gave the donkeys a final pat on their rumps and then turned back towards the house. 'Just go on in, the door's open,' she called across at them. 'Don't bother taking your shoes off, the cleaner's in tomorrow.'

Alan stood in the doorway, peering inside. 'What about the dogs?'

The woman bustled up to them. 'The dog passed in the

summer.' She threw out a hand ushering them both inside. 'Now it's just the badger.'

They stared at the woman as they stepped through into the kitchen.

'He's having his afternoon nap.' She swung the door shut behind her.

'Right.' Alan pulled a face.

Anne glanced around the spacious kitchen. The wooden surfaces a jumble of glinting pans and mixing bowls, rows of empty jars crowding the draining board by the sink. Set in the far wall, a deep granite fireplace, the logs in the grate glowing red and orange. The air had the smoky softness of the fire mixed with the leathery tang of cloves.

'Chutney season.' The woman shrugged off her coat and hung it on a peg on the wall. 'Have a seat.' She nodded towards the large circular table in the middle of the room, papers strewn across it. 'Just push everything out the way.' She busied herself with the tea.

They gingerly cleared some space and sat as the woman brought over the tray and sat it on the table, wisps of steam lazily drifting up from the bright red mugs.

'Help yourselves.' She swiped up a mug and settled opposite them, pushing aside another pile of papers with a sweep of her hand. She took a sip. 'I knew him. Peter Moynes.'

'How so?' Anne pulled out her notepad.

'He was always sending me emails, pestering me to publish things. At first I went along with it, but it was just the same old stuff every time. How social media's bending our minds, death of free will and all that.'

'Bit heavy for a neighbourhood news site,' Alan puffed.

'He turned quite nasty in the end.'

'He threatened you?'

'Not like that. Just angry emails. Typical of the man, from what I've heard.'

Anne studied the older woman's face. 'Go on.'

The woman took a deep breath. 'But this latest stuff.' She shook her head. 'This is something different.'

Anne set her face. 'But you believed it.'

'I didn't say that.'

'Then why post it on the website?'

Anger flashed across her face. 'I didn't.'

They both jolted and stared at the woman.

'Like I said, I thought about going to the police.' She looked from one to the other. 'But then I thought it must be some…nasty joke.'

'Joke?' Anne twisted her face.

'But then I saw the news this morning.' The woman swallowed. 'Look, the first I heard of it was two days ago. Someone in the village emailed me. Complaining about the article. Of course I didn't understand what she was talking about. Then she sent me a screenshot.' She flipped open her laptop. 'Here.' She stood up and laid it on the table in front of them.

Their eyes began to widen as they read it.

'I went straight to the website. There was nothing about Peter Moynes, let alone *this*.'

Anne and Alan exchanged a glance.

'Someone else in the village sent me the same screenshot, later that day.'

Alan frowned. 'But you don't know how many people saw that article?'

She shrugged. 'How could I?'

Anne stared in silence at the image on the screen.

'These claims about…,' Alan seemed to shudder, '…what Moynes was meant to have done to that girl. The one that disappeared.' He looked back down at the screenshot, his face disturbed.

The woman winced. 'What can I say? I didn't write it.'

'That's a lot of…detail.'

'It's sick, that's what it is.'

'You covered the disappearance last year, right?'

'It was a big story.'

Alan seemed to weigh her words. 'You know Moynes has…had a nickname in the village?'

Her face seemed to harden. 'Look, I didn't like the guy. But this…' she indicated the laptop, '…he's a creep but he's not a…,' her voice trailed off.

Anne spoke. 'Do you know his wife, Susan?'

'Sure. She was the one that sent me the screenshot.'

The silence seemed to ring around them.

'Take it.' The woman closed the laptop, slid it towards Anne. 'It's all backed up.'

Anne kept her gaze on the woman. 'Peter Moynes was murdered.'

'I know what this is.'

'Do you?'

The woman met Anne's gaze. 'I've told you what I know.'

****

Anne and Alan sat in the car under the wary gaze of the donkeys.

'You think she's lying?' Alan looked straight ahead.

She said nothing.

'Someone is.' He tapped a thumb on the steering wheel.

Anne squeezed her eyes shut.

He glanced at her. 'What's the matter?'

'That smashed-in face.' She gave a shudder. 'Whenever I close my eyes...'

He began to say something but checked himself. 'OK then, what are we missing?'

She followed his gaze out through the windscreen, the treetops drifting under the sullen sky. 'What if it was true? Peter Moynes...and that girl last year?' She turned slowly towards him, her features pale in the fading light.

'Yes, I know.' He studied her for a moment. 'But that's not an answer, is it?'

She looked back out of the window.

'Someone's got to say it.'

Chapter 16

The West of England

Emma Wilson lay her bag on the hall floor as the last tinny hiss of the bell faded into the silence. She looked at the boys' empty coat hooks. In her head she could almost hear the babble of raised voices, eager footsteps on the gravel drive outside, Tommy and Andy's faces lighting up at seeing her at the window. Then she shuddered as another image crashed into her head, their faces, creased with worry. She screwed up her face, forcing her mind back to the stinging heat of the underpass, the words clanging in the dusty air as the fear bit into her again.

As she let the loop play in her head she could sense the cold focus flowing back into her, the sounds of the autumn afternoon drifting into her mind. She could hear the chirping of the birds in the oak tree by the water butts, the faint hum of the boiler in the kitchen.

She found herself locking onto the hum, tensing as it murmured into a rumble. She pictured the boiler flame sputtering then dying as the valves whispered open and the gas began to flow. She found herself sniffing the air, but all she could smell was the cut of drying mud and the scented waft of soap.

The chime of the kitchen clock sung in the air.

Emma caught her reflection in the fading mirror. In the dappled light of the hallway her face could have been made of stone, the faint lines on her face like the threads on a statue. 'Never was a mother's face,' she whispered.

'God, you're so up yourself.'

Emma caught her breath as she spun around to the voice.

Her sister Kate stood framed in the kitchen doorway. 'Who was that bloke in sixth form? The one I really fancied?' She shook her head. 'Of course you had to bloody snog him. Your bloody cheek bones and your beach body. I swear I could have strangled you.' She grinned. 'Anyway, how was it?'

Emma felt numb. 'It was…'

Kate's face began to sharpen. 'Emma?'

Emma blurted, 'where are the boys?'

'They're in the upper paddock, collecting wood, there was a storm last night.' Her voice fell to a whisper, 'what's happened?'

She tried to think of words but her head was buzzing.

'Emma, what the hell's happened?'

Emma reached for her sister's hand feeling a chill knot tightening inside her. 'Kate, there's something I need to tell you.'

Kate's face locked.

'Let's…sit down.'

Emma led her in silence to the kitchen table.

'Come and sit next to me.' Emma pushed a pile of books and an unwashed plate away from them as they settled.

'Is this about the boys?' Kate's voice was flat.

Emma spoke quietly. 'There's things I didn't tell you, when they first came to us, about Tommy and Andy.' Her mouth felt suddenly dry. 'They're...special.'

'All the boys are special.'

'They're different.'

'They're just boys for Christ's sake, why are you making things so complicated?'

'They're not just boys.'

'What are you trying to say?'

'Please, Kate, just listen to me.'

Kate looked at her stonily.

'Of course they're boys, but as far as the world's concerned, it's like...they don't exist. They're...invisible. Never used the internet, never made a call or sent an email. No school records, no medical files...nothing.'

Kate kept her steady gaze on Emma.

'It's not just an...accident, these boys. Sebastian, he found them.' She tried to keep her breathing steady. 'Tommy, he'd somehow made it out of North Korea, his elder brother died, Tommy was half dead when they brought him in. And Andy, they found him in a shepherd's hut way up in the north of Finland. He was blind. Whether someone left him there or he got lost, he doesn't know. Slowly they made them well, Andy got two new corneas, he could see for the first time.' Emma found herself smiling. 'Then Sebastian brought them here.' She studied Kate's face. 'I knew Sebastian must have had a plan for them, keeping them so...hidden. Maybe I was too afraid to ask what it was. I mean, the boys, they were just…growing, learning some things. I…didn't want it to end.'

'*What* are you trying to tell me?'

'These…rules Sebastian was so insistent on. That thing, about not letting the two of them go out in the sun, because of their skin.' She exhaled. 'He just didn't want them picked up on the satellites.'

Kate said nothing.

'It was a…perfect hiding place. No internet, no mobile phones, no history…' Her voice faded.

Kate set her face. 'Just bloody tell me.'

'When I was out there, in Saudi, they told me things.' Emma felt the fear jabbing as the words began to ring in her head. 'There's something we have to do, to make us safe.'

'What are you talking about?'

Emma tried to block their anxious faces from her brain. 'God, Kate.'

A gust of wind rattled the kitchen window.

Emma carefully took Kate's hands in hers as she looked into her sister's face. 'The boys. Tommy and Andy, they have to be part of this.'

Kate said, 'he's not taking them.'

'Please, listen to me.'

'How old are they? Seventeen, eighteen? They don't know *anything*. They don't *belong* out there.'

'Look, I don't know what the plan is, and that's the truth. But they need to be…involved, somehow. That's all I know.'

Kate's hands went limp in Emma's. 'Is this what a mother does?'

Emma squeezed them again. 'If there was *any* other way.'

'They love you, Emma.'

The cold knot inside her twisted again. 'God, if I could make it different…I'd do *anything.*'

'What kind of a person does this? Christ, if you can't love two boys who've lost everything, who trust you…completely.'

'I do love them.'

'Just words, Emma.'

Emma swallowed. 'You can say anything, call me what you want but…' She drew in a ragged breath. 'We've got to stop it. We've *got* to.'

Kate wriggled her hands free. 'I've got beds to change.'

Emma felt her heartbeat thrumming. 'Wait!' She grabbed Kate's arm.

Kate looked at her, her expression easing. 'Look, sis, there's nothing to say.'

'Feel my pulse!' She pushed her finger against her wrist. 'I'm scared, I'm fucking scared!'

Kate's face twitched.

'When I was out there, they told me things.'

'What are you talking about?!'

'AI, the system...call it what you want.' She hissed. 'It's...come alive.'

Kate considered her. 'Look, I know we don't do the news. But the last I heard, that was never going to happen.'

'It's here, Kate. It's started.' She grabbed Kate's arm.

Kate sniffed. 'Just...look outside, it's normal, it's so bloody normal.'

'It's killing people!'

Kate puffed, 'if it had, there'd be fucking riots and everything.'

'That's because no one knows.'

Kate stiffened.

Emma just looked at her.

'So...who told you this?' The words tripped out. 'Sebastian?'

'People who work for him, yes.'

'And you believe them?'

'They showed me. Pictures, people who'd died. Dozens of people.'

Kate pulled a face.

'They were getting close. AI killed them.'

Kate gave a dry laugh. 'You really do believe everything he says, don't you?'

Anger pricked her, 'I'm telling the truth.'

'Don't say Sebastian wouldn't lie to you 'cos he lies to you all the time. This trip he set up for you, that…thing about your friend, the jewellery, was *any* of that true?'

Emma checked herself and took a deep breath, trying to get her mind to slow.

'He's full of nasty lies.' Her words were sharp. 'And I've told you that before.'

Emma looked at her sister, feeling the sadness sweeping through her. 'I'd die for them, I would.'

'I thought you'd changed, I really did.'

Emma reached out a hand, lay it between them.

Kate just looked at it.

****

Emma Wilson lowered her head as she tramped up the hill path, the dark earth, full of the night's rain squelching beneath her boots. The wind had picked up again, flapping through the tree tops that swayed and rattled above her, the putty smell of fallen leaves drifting in the damp air.

She leant into the hillside as the path steepened, the chill air filling her lungs as her boots fought for grip. She could see the crest just above her and bounded up the last few steps as the breezy clearing slid into view.

She stood on the wet grass catching her breath. She was standing on the edge of a flat ledge carved out from the rustling forest that packed the hillside. In the centre of the grassy terrace stood a single towering oak tree. The thick, grey trunk scarred with knotholes, the branches above reaching out like the old twisted arms of some forest ogre.

'Shouting at me won't do you a spec of good.' Sebastian Noon stood in the shadow of the tree, his duffle coat belted tight around him, his spindly fingers wrapped around the brim of his trilby hat hanging by his side.

'I'm not going to shout at you. Why would I shout at you?'

'No one's innocent. You're not allowed to be innocent.'

She walked towards him, her boots swishing through the spiky blades of grass as his rheumy features slipped into focus.

He glanced up at the gnarly branch above him, then looked at Emma. 'So,' he said, 'is it true?' He lay a careful palm against the rutted trunk and seemed to lean towards it. 'The hanging tree?'

'It's just a name.'

He closed his eyes, his lined skin pinching. 'God, what terrible sounds would have rung around here? The pleas of the condemned men...women too, perhaps. The murmur of a priest, the rumble of the cart's wheels as the feet of the poor souls slipped off the planks and dangled, shaking in the wind.'

She let his voice run.

He looked at her with his hard eyes. 'Ghosts, Emma.'

'Your ghosts.' She stood a few feet from him. Her mind felt cold, but calm. 'I had the whole flight to think about it.'

He stirred. 'We know better than to confuse honesty with

trust.'

'Do we?'

'There is a sort of well-made irony in all of this. This…human race we're trying so hard to save. Maybe lying really is the one thing we're actually better at,' he preached. 'Still, if you let truth get in the way of doing the right thing, then I'd say we are well and truly fucked.'

She raised her chin. 'When did you know?'

'About AI…coming to life.' He shifted his shoulders. 'We had an inkling, a few months ago. I didn't want to say anything until we were sure.' He looked at her, something softer in his face. 'Thought that would be better.'

Her cold mind churned. 'That man, Finn. He talked about making the system doubt itself. What did he mean?'

'Maybe here's the other thing. The system knows what it knows. And until you prove a negative, everything else remains a possibility. Even if we dull humans know it's just not possible.'

She stared at him, waiting for more.

'The boys, Tommy, Andy. You could say it's chance, a kind of freakish chance. But to AI, it'll be like they just appeared, fully formed, out of nowhere.' His tone became furtive. 'Maybe, with luck, it will panic.'

She felt the anger surging. 'It's not just chance is it? The two of them, just…appearing, like that.' She tried to steady her voice. 'You'd planned all this, to the tiniest detail. Ameera, the jewellery, that letter, Carly…waiting for me like a…sour memory.'

'What else did you expect me to do?' His tone was icy.

'The two boys, they didn't just turn up did they?'

He looked at her, his shoulders slowly rising and falling as the wind scratched at them. He took a deeper breath, then spoke. 'When I first brought those two boys to you, I didn't know what would happen. Yes, they were a...contingency.' He threw up a hand. 'That...came out wrong.' He gathered himself. 'You were in a bad way, Emma. You needed somewhere, something to...bring you back.' His voice fell to a whisper. 'We always joked, what a terrible mother you'd make.'

She felt nausea rising. 'They trust me, Sebastian.'

'We gave you, them, a story, a background. One you could...live with. They could live with.' He ground on. 'This...' He threw a strained look around him. 'Might never have happened. It could have had a...different ending.'

'Ending?' She gasped. 'What the fuck does that mean?'

'You've given them a life. More of a life than they'd ever dare dream of.' His lip was quivering.

'What are you trying to say?'

'It's a terrible, terrible thing, but it happened.'

'Just say it.'

'You're right, it wasn't an accident.' His voice hushed. 'They were made to be like this.' His face hung. 'God knows I'd never ask anyone to do that to a human being, let alone a child.'

'So these poor boys were...'

'Yes, Emma. They were bred to be like this.' His face twisted like frayed rope. 'There's people who…well, if you know where to look…God forgive us…'

Emma dry retched, feeling the bile burning in her chest as she doubled up.

He took a step towards her, reaching out a hesitant hand. 'My dear girl…'

She coughed bitter spittle.

'It's an awful time.' He pleaded. 'Perhaps the worst time.'

She straightened up and wiped her mouth with the back of her hand. 'Why are you telling me this?'

He lay a hand on her shoulder. 'Because, whatever happens, you've given them safety, warmth…love, even.' He squeezed it. 'Things they never thought they could even dream of.'

She raised her chin, tried to swallow. 'Is this meant to make me feel better, about putting them in danger?'

'Whatever happens, they're not going back to that dreadful place.' His words weighed quietly. 'That's what matters.'

'But they're just boys.' She welled.

'But if we didn't do everything, *everything*,' his eyes were red.

A gust of wind stung her cold skin. 'What the hell are we doing Sebastian? Just who are we trying to save? Monsters who'd traffic children, keep them like that?' She ripped. 'And are we any better? Are we?'

'We could think what history would say of us.' His voice

curdled. 'But if we don't stop it, there won't *be* a history.'

The boys hacked back into her mind, their helpless faces pleading with her. *'I promised Kate I'd keep them safe,'* she threw the words at him.

He let his hand drop from her shoulder. 'And with God's help, you will.'

She studied his face, looking for the twitch, the hint of the lie.

'What would be the point?' He said starkly. 'You'll be in Amsterdam in two days. Then you'll see for yourself.' His voice dropped. 'A little late for...'

Like he'd read her mind.

She found herself staring at his face and said. 'You've got old.'

'I'm sorry, Emma.'

She could sense her own heartbeat steadying. 'What will happen, in Amsterdam?'

'There's a security conference. You and the two boys will fly in, meet me there.'

She waited for the worst.

'AI must see them, the two boys.'

She felt it bubble again.

'Just enough to plant the thought in it.' He urged.

'That man Finn,' she pained as the images of that scalding, dust-baked room in Saudi squeezed around her. 'Anything that it can't connect, can't...understand.' She fired at him. 'It'll see it, them, as a threat.'

'Just a glimpse.' He pushed on. 'Enough to unsettle it, but not long enough for it to react.'

'They won't stand a chance.'

'As soon as it's caught their faces, you run. We'll be right inside. You'll be safe.' He hesitated. 'Your friend Anne, she'll be there too.'

Emma started. 'Anne Perry? What's she got to do with this?'

'I saw her, three days ago.'

Her mind spun.

'I told her about two people, who were going to be murdered.'

She sputtered. 'What?!'

'They're…dead now,' his voice trailed away.

The words crashed out of her. 'So she just what…did nothing? Waited for them to…die?'

'Yes.' He hushed. 'That's exactly what she did.'

'But…I know her, she could never do that! If she knew they were going to die she wouldn't just…do nothing!'

He took another breath, his face slackening. 'You're right.'

Emma squeezed her face. 'What the fuck is this? What's happening to us all? Is this what we are now?'

'When she sees you, she'll tell you.'

'Tell me what?'

'That she did it, because…they were already dead.'

Emma tried to speak but nothing came.

'She'd seen the future, you see. A future where they were dead.'

His words hung in the blustery air.

'That's where she met the boys. Met Tommy…and Andy.'

Emma tried to breathe as iron bands seem to grip her chest.

Sebastian looked down at her trying to put warmth on his tired face. 'Because in a way she had seen the future. What would happen, if *we* did nothing.'

He reached into his pocket and carefully pulled out a green notebook. He looked at it for a moment then held it out towards Emma. 'I'm sure she won't mind you reading it.'

Emma kept her eyes on Sebastian.

'It's her diary.' He edged it towards her. 'From the future.'

She tried to focus on his words as images of Anne, the boys swam in her mind.

'Take it.' His arm stretched out towards her.

'I don't need to read it.'

'I know. But you'll read it anyway.'

'Why?'

'You know why.'

****

Emma slowly walked across the driveway, her footsteps

crunching on the damp gravel, feeling the cooler evening air starting to jab at her beneath her coat. She looked up at the windows of the boys' bedrooms, at the two squares of glowing ochre behind the drawn curtains. She imagined the chatter of voices beneath the old wooden beams, somehow willing that warmth into her. But all she could feel was the cold tightness in her ribs, dull metal where her heart should be, the words from Anne's diary heavy in her thoughts. As she glanced up at the wide sky, the stars arranging themselves in the half-light, she shuddered, as more scenes from the diary prised into her thoughts. The sirens, then the world slamming shut like a cell door.

She straightened up as she approached the house. She could see her sister framed in the brighter light of the kitchen, sat at the kitchen table, her back to the window. She let her thumb run over the smooth, warm cover of the diary lying deep in her coat pocket: it wouldn't go away.

She stood under the light by the front door, the splintery smell of peeling paintwork around her. She raised a hand, her fingers hovering over the round brass handle, then twisted it and pushed the door open.

The jangle of the bell rang through the still hallway, the peel fading to a hiss, then silence.

She stood, letting her senses settle. She could smell the sappy wood smoke from the kitchen fire, the faint flicker of the flames reflected on the wooden floor around her. 'It's me.' She called out without thinking.

The silence rolled against her.

She waited for a stab of annoyance to strike her, but all she got was a welling of guilt in her aching heart.

She lay the diary on the hall table and shrugged off her coat, feeling the dampness of the evening mist as she smoothed it down on the hook. She caught a glimpse of her face in the mirror, in the half-light her eyes looked darker, her features smudged in shadow. She shook off her boots, picked up the diary and stepped carefully through into the kitchen.

Kate looked up from her book, her face slack. 'You look like shit.'

'I know.'

Kate lay the book face down as she straightened up. 'So, what does he want you to do?' Her tone, matter of fact.

Emma said quietly. 'Why won't you believe me?'

'Believe you? What does that mean?'

'If we do nothing, then it's over. Really over.'

Kate gave a dry laugh.

'You really think I'd agree to do all this if it wasn't real?' pleaded Emma.

Kate leant back, her hands resting on the table. 'I know our dad was a useless piece of shit but even he would've drawn the line at this...'

'You're not even listening.' Emma could hear her voice rising.

'*I'm* not listening?! He just can't do any wrong, can he? All you bloody care about is keeping Sebastian happy.'

Emma scowled. 'Keep your voice down will you.'

'How can you believe a word he says?'

Emma tried to stamp on her anger. 'I've known him for twenty years. Think about that.'

Kate punched out the words, 'this whole AI thing, everyone running around seeing bloody AI behind every bush. They want us to be scared. Spooks like Sebastian, they're all the same, it's just another Punch and Judy show. Them and bloody social media, they're all in it together. For them it's never enough. They want more control, more of you, more of everything, until there's nothing left, just timid little minds waiting to be told what to do! All these scares about AI, it's right in front of your nose. They're getting AI to tell you to be scared of AI!'

'God, you do talk a load of shit sometimes.'

Kate scoffed. 'And people used to say that you were the clever one.'

Emma slapped the diary on the table.

Kate glanced at it.

'Want to know what this is?' Emma glowered at her.

'Not really.'

'It's a story about…hope. That's what it is, they always had hope, because they knew that it could never be this bad!'

Kate shrugged.

'This is what it looks like, if we do *nothing*.'

'Says who?'

'It's a diary. And everyone dies.'

'He's just pushing your buttons. You want to be scared of it. You make it so easy.'

'Just read it will you! You stupid, selfish bitch!'

Kate looked at her sister and sighed. 'You know, I'm not even angry any more, about the whole thing, about Tommy and Andy. I mean, I did think about it. Taking them both away, somewhere, somewhere safe.' She paused. 'But then, there's probably a guy in the woods, with a rifle, ready to take my head off.' She slowly shook her head. 'They belong to him, don't they?'

Emma said nothing.

'I guess...I just wanted you to care more.'

'Just read it.' Emma whispered, then turned and walked slowly from the room, the sudden silence broken only by the crackle of the fire.

****

Emma knocked softly on the door. 'It's me.'

The door swung open.

Tommy stood there, one hand on the door handle and a sharp look on his face. 'Why were you shouting?'

'We weren't shouting,' she blurted.

'We could hear you.' Andy sat on the side of his bed, carefully rolling up an almost empty toothpaste tube, his face gripped in concentration.

'We were just...' her voice trailed away.

They looked blankly at her.

'Sometimes, sisters argue, you know.'

'What's a Punch and Judy show?' Andy asked.

'Come and sit,' she said to Tommy.

He settled next to Andy as Emma closed the door and sat on the bed facing them.

'We saw you coming back to the house just now.' Tommy began. 'You looked sad.'

'Sad?' She looked at their anxious faces and tried to lighten her voice. 'We're going on a trip, the three of us.'

Their faces brightened.

Then Tommy spoke again, his frown was back. 'So why are you sad?'

Emma tried to fight the darkness misting into her mind.

They looked at her.

'I'm sad because…' She could feel the dread building inside her. 'This thing we have to do, it could be…difficult.'

'You shouldn't worry about us,' said Tommy.

'You're not our mother,' Andy put in.

His words stung her. 'Of course I worry about you.'

'The man with the long head,' Tommy spoke, 'he wants you to do this.'

'Yes.'

'Then…it's not your fault.'

The sound of laughter from along the corridor drifted through the stillness of the room.

'You and Kate, why were you shouting?' Tommy asked a second time.

Emma felt the knot tightening inside her. 'Look, we both…worry about you.'

Tommy shrugged. 'So, why were you shouting?'

'Well, Kate she…she doesn't know Sebastian. She…well, she doesn't know him.'

They looked at her.

'She's worried that…well, she's worried.'

'Are you worried?' said Tommy.

She took a breath. 'Whatever happens, I'll keep you safe, I will.'

'Are you? Worried?'

'Yes,' she whispered.

They said nothing.

She steeled herself. 'The man, Sebastian, he told me things.' Her words felt leaden. 'About…well, about how he found you.'

Fear swept through the room like an icy mist.

She looked into their terrified faces.

'No, no, no.' She held up trembling hands. 'You're not…you're never going to see those…evil men again.' She hammered.

She fought to find the right words as they stared at her in the awful quiet.

'He just…thought I should know.'

'Why?' cried Tommy.

'So I could…understand.' Her own words sounded weak.

Andy spoke. 'The man Sebastian. When he bought us, when he took us out of that evil place, we knew he wasn't doing it out of his good heart. But it's alright.' His low voice rumbled between them. 'When I was growing up, well…I didn't think of it like growing up. I was cold, my eyes were just, pools of darkness, I couldn't see. Just voices, hard, cruel voices. I just sat, waiting, for water, for food, for an end to it.'

The room ached.

'Then one day, they came for me, took me out of the cage, put me under a shower, then sat me in a car.' He made a puffing sound. 'I thought I was dreaming, maybe I was, because I slept for days, that's what they told me. I had a bed, calm, kind voices around me, then they…gave me new eyes.' He looked strongly at Emma as though proving his words.

As she looked into his eyes she felt something sneaking into her mind like a cold, wriggling worm. Then it slammed into her and she felt the raw bile smarting in her throat. She shuddered as the horrible images of three years ago mushroomed in her mind. The Cartel organ farm they'd raided, just south of Nogales. The cages, the beds, the straps…' She gagged.

'Emma?' Their fearful voices reached into her and their worried faces smacked back into focus.

'What is it?' said Andy.

Emma tried to tug her gaze away from Andy's eyes but

they seemed to be pleading at her to keep looking, to recognise something, someone. She slapped her hands on her knees as she refocussed, looking at them in turn, the cosy warmth of the orange-lit room slowly seeping back around her.

She leant forward, offering a hand to each of them. 'Here.'

They looked at her hands, hesitating.

'Come on.' She shook them towards the boys.

They shyly took her hands in theirs.

As she gripped their hands she spoke slowly. 'You are never, never, *ever* going back to that horrible place, you understand.'

Tommy said. 'When I got out of that place, my teeth, my gums. Every mouthful, like chewing razor blades.' He gave a bright, timid smile. 'Whatever happens, what you and Kate have done for us. It is enough, you know.'

She wanted to hug them but said, 'when he brought you both here, of course I knew, he had…a plan, something like a plan. I didn't know what it was and maybe I just didn't want to ask. Kate the same, I guess. She was just happy to treat you like any of the other boys. She knows a bit about what I used to do, my work, but really she'd rather just think about well…life here. You, and the others.' She looked into their young, earnest faces. 'But it wasn't just a job, me and Kate looking after you, all these months. It was so much *more* than a job.' As she squeezed their hands again she could feel the cold ache building inside her. 'We are both so *very* fond of you.' She choked. 'And now we have to go and do this difficult thing. That's why I'm a bit sad.'

'It's alright,' said Tommy.

'Don't feel sad,' Andy stepped in.

She tried a smile as her stomach twisted. 'Need to get you both suits,' she fussed as she stood. 'Need to grab a shirt and a spare pair of trousers from you both, just for the sizes. I'll go into town tomorrow.'

They pulled clothes from drawers and pushed them at Emma.

She bundled the clothes in her arms and stood looking down at them. 'I'll bring you both back. I promise.'

'We know.' They called, almost as one, smiles flicking over their faces.

'I'll see you tomorrow.' She turned and slowly walked to the door, stepping into the quiet corridor and closing it gently behind her.

She leant against the wall, holding the boys clothes to her face, breathing in the scent of them as tears began to flow.

Chapter 17

London

DI Anne Perry shifted in her chair.

The woman on the other side of the desk gave her a maternal smile. 'So, how are you sleeping?'

'Fine,' Anne snapped.

The police psychoanalyst's smile remained set as her gaze roved over Anne's pale face, the dark lines beneath her eyes. 'It's not a sign of weakness, you know. Memories like that. Everyone has to process them…somehow.'

'It was a year ago. I really don't think about it.'

The woman's smile faded. 'Why won't you let me help you?'

'Look!' Anne's voice rose, then she checked herself. 'It was a thing, yes…for a while. But now I'm fine.'

'But you still can't bring yourself to say his name.'

Anne blinked, said nothing.

'To have to witness that. Seeing someone you care for, shot dead, right there, in front of you.'

'I didn't care for him. I despised him.'

'That's the thing. Love. Feels a lot like hate most of the time.'

'Jamie Ives was a selfish shit.'

The woman shrugged.

Anne tried to compose herself. 'Look, yes, three years ago, before he...' she shifted in her chair again. '...I did feel...something for him.' She set her jaw. 'But nothing happened and then he...went away.'

'Did you have any contact with him? When he was in prison?'

Anne bristled. 'No.'

'And then last year?'

'His name came up in a case I was dealing with. I saw him...twice.'

'How did you feel? When you saw him?'

Anne could feel her stomach starting to knot. 'The first time I saw him, at his office, I suppose I did feel...something.'

'Something?'

'I'd just found out about...my husband. The affair...'

The analyst nodded. 'So this was going to be...revenge?'

'It wasn't going to be anything. Nothing happened.' Anne straightened up, fixing the woman a look. 'And the next time I saw him.' She tensed her jaw. 'He pulled a gun on me and a police marksman shot him in the head.' She flinched. 'It was horrible.'

A dead silence seemed to descend on them.

'The nightmares lasted for three months,' Anne's tone flinty. 'Then they just stopped.'

The analyst slowly raised her chin. 'Then why can't you

sleep?'

Anne gave her a weak smile. 'I told you, I'm sleeping fine.'

The analyst nodded once, made a note on her pad then looked back at Anne. 'And how are things at home?'

'You know the answer to that.'

'I want you to tell me, your words.'

'I wouldn't even call it 'home'. I've got a small rented flat. Just while I sort myself out.'

'You still having counselling, you and your husband?'

'I did those two sessions because the lawyers said I had to.' Anne felt the anger boiling in her. 'Waste of time.'

'Everyone makes mistakes,' said the psychoanalyst.

Anne's voice began to rise. 'Why does everyone think I should just forgive him? You know, like forget it happened. Forget all his lies.'

'Anger is almost never the answer.'

'It's almost like it's my fault. Like I'm the bad person, because I can't find it in my dark heart to forgive him.'

'Have you tried?'

'*A whole year.* He was sleeping with her *for a whole year!*'

'Maybe you were looking for an excuse, to end it. To leave Bill.'

'Then you know nothing about my life,' she snarled.

'Hurting someone else, you hurt yourself too.'

'Well, maybe you should tell that to him.'

'Talking is always good, Anne.'

'Twenty five years! You think that counts for nothing?!'

'You're shouting.'

'Of course I'm shouting you judgemental fucking cow!'

'OK, OK.' The analyst slowly raised her hands in appeasement as she tried to set the smile back on her face.

Anne shifted in her chair. 'Can I go now?'

The analyst glanced at the clock. 'Are you seeing anyone else? Like a special friend?'

'You mean am I sleeping with someone?' She gave a tight smile. 'No I'm not.'

'No one would blame you.'

'Why does everyone think I want to sleep with someone?'

'People do for lots of reasons. Loneliness. Adventure.' She paused. 'Revenge?'

'I just don't want to sleep with anyone. Can we just leave it there?'

'You can't run away from everything, Anne.'

'I'm not running away. I just don't want to. I don't like the idea, OK?'

'When did you last cry?'

'What do you want me to say?'

'I just want you to feel you can tell me…anything.' She paused. 'The truth, maybe?'

'The truth?' She sighed. 'The truth is that I got hurt, and I don't want it to happen again.'

'You don't believe in second chances?'

'Why would I?'

'If you think like that, you'd never do anything.'

'And what's the harm in that?'

****

Anne Perry stood in her bathroom gazing into the chipped mirror.

She began to run a finger along the lines on her face. 'God, you've got to do better.'

She glanced down at the pill bottles on the shelf, swiped up the Diazepam and shook out two pills into her palm. She looked down at them for a moment, trying to keep her breathing steady. 'One…two…' she whispered, 'buckle my shoe.' She tipped her hand from side to side watching the pills rolling across her skin then looked back into the mirror. She took a deep breath, threw the pills in her mouth, picked up the water glass and downed it in one.

She looked again at her reflection. She tried a smile, but her mouth made a poor attempt at one.

She tried again, then frowned, moving her face close to the mirror as she bared her teeth. She rubbed at a tooth with her finger, then slowly straightened up, her face slackening.

She turned and walked into the dimly lit bedroom, picking up her phone from the bedside table.

She drifted to the window. In the failing light the workshop roofs seemed to fade into the pitted concrete yards that spilled out around them, the train tracks beyond glinting dully under the fizzing street lamps.

She shuddered as she turned back to the room, her unmade bed looked cold, lifeless, the thrown back duvet bent and twisted.

She clicked on a number.

'Mum,' Gemma sounded wary.

'This a bad time?'

'You OK?'

Anne could sense the Diazepam gliding through her. 'I was just thinking…'

She could hear Gemma draw a breath.

'…about what you were saying,' Anne continued. 'You know about…well…being alone.'

Silence.

'Gemma?'

'Sorry, Mum,' Gemma bustled, 'someone was just talking to me.'

Anne cleared her throat. 'I was just saying, about…being alone.'

She could hear Gemma shushing a colleague. 'Sorry, who's alone?'

'It's…it's obviously not a great time. I can hear you're busy. We can talk another time.'

'No, no I'm listening Mum, really.'

Anne exhaled. 'Just…I've been thinking. About what you

were saying.'

'About what?'

'About…being alone.'

Gemma stuttered. 'Gosh…well that's…'

Anne found herself looking through into the kitchen: the dirty saucepan sitting haphazard on the stove, unwashed plates cluttering the tiny sink. 'It's just so…quiet.'

'Oh, Mum…'

'There…I've said it.'

'We're all here for you…you know that.'

Anne sighed. 'It's just been so long.'

****

The noise of the gym changing room clattered around her, the lilt of voices, the snap of lockers, the hiss of the nearby showers and flip-flopped feet.

Anne Perry adjusted the pleat of her trousers on the hanger, then pulled her handbag towards her, fingers delving for the small glass bottle nestling by the side pocket. She put one wrist into the locker, dabbing it with perfume, then the other. She looked down at her hand, then carefully slid off her wedding ring, letting it drop onto the locker floor with a 'ping'.

****

The same man was standing there, pretending to look at the notices on the gym board.

Anne walked slowly along the row of exercise bikes, as if weighing her choice of machine.

She could sense the man looking at her as she hung the towel on the handlebars and placed her phone on the console.

'You got a favourite bike?' He was standing a few feet from her, his towel slung around his neck, his hands loosely holding the ends.

'I don't judge, I just hate them all.' She forced her eyes back to the console as she tried to focus on the programme selector, her finger hovering.

'That's the thing, got to keep it guessing.'

She looked up at him, allowing herself a good look at his face. Around her age, although his eyes looked somehow younger. 'You an expert on these things then?'

'Absolutely not.' He flashed her a smile. Nothing wrong with his teeth.

She thought about returning the smile but settled for a slight raising of her eyebrows.

'I'm David...by the way,' his voice trailed off.

She threw him a wary look, said nothing.

He blushed as he cleared his throat. 'Well...have a good one.' He turned, hesitated, then began to walk towards the weights.

'Anne,' she called after him.

He stopped, then slowly turned around.

Anne kept her eyes on the console as she jabbed at it with her finger then popped in her earbuds and began to peddle with a new enthusiasm.

****

Anne gripped the handlebars, locking her arms and her shoulders as she forced her legs to keep turning, gulping air into her aching lungs. She closed her eyes, fighting to keep her pedal strokes in time with the music, half drowned-out by the drumming of her heartbeat in her ears. She dared herself to look at the clock on the console: 29:40, twenty seconds to go. She grimaced as she forced her feet down on the pedals, hot jabs of pain shooting up her legs as she counted down the seconds, her lungs burning like a glass of acid was being poured into them.

The timer beeped, and she eased her shoulders as the pedals spun slowly around and then stopped. She let her head slump forward, counting her breaths as she drew in the dry, warm air of the gym, her leg muscles quivering.

She stretched out her fingers as she lowered her head on to them, closing her eyes, the aroma of her perfume cutting through the rubbery, disinfectant smell of the handlebars. She slowly eased her feet from the pedal straps and let them hang for a moment, her heartbeat settling. She straightened up, letting out a long, slow breath and opened her eyes.

The man, David, was standing a few feet from her, holding out a plastic cup of water.

She looked at the cup, then at him, a look of good-natured amusement on his well-made features.

She looked down as she gingerly stepped off the bike, feeling for her balance, her legs tingling. She picked up the towel from the bike, held it against her face then glanced back up at him.

He was saying something, the words drowned out by Mahler still soaring in her ears. She turned the music down and slipped out an earpiece, looking at the water. She screwed up her nose. 'Nothing stronger, I don't suppose?'

'In this temple of virtue?'

'Knew something was wrong.' She lay the towel on her shoulder, took the water and drained it in one.

'Is that…Mahler?' He frowned, glancing down at the earpiece in her hand.

She pulled a face. 'Guilty pleasure.'

'And the rest.'

She raised her hand holding the earpiece close to his ear.

He tensed, then leant towards it. 'Das Lied von der Erde.' His face seemed to melt into a smile.

She kept her hand there.

He kept smiling, his eyes alive. He seemed about to say something, then checked himself.

She slowly lowered her arm. 'So do you have history?' She tried a smile, 'you…and Mahler?'

'Bit one-sided.' He lowered his voice. 'To be honest, he kind of takes me for granted nowadays.' He gave a shrug. 'But what can you do?'

'Bohemians, eh?'

'Spare and share.' He tutted. 'I love him to bits, but he's a beast to teach.'

She raised an eyebrow. 'So you're a musician?'

'In a parallel universe.' He grinned. 'The bills won't pay themselves. Teaching's not so bad. So how do you fritter your days away?'

'I hate that question.'

'Go on, make something up then.'

She exhaled, 'I'm with the police.'

'Is that the made up answer?'

She fixed him a look, said nothing.

'I think that's…'

'Just say it.'

'OK…,' he drew in a breath, '…I think you're gorgeous.'

'I…' She found herself staring at him, his words swirling in her head as her heartbeat began to race. 'Oh…'

He blushed.

'Well I…' The words seemed to stick in her throat.

He swallowed. 'I'd love to ask you out for a drink…sometime.'

She took a moment to compose herself. 'Sometime?'

He pulled a face. 'Anytime…really.'

'Sometime sounds good.' She tried a smile, her mind whirring. 'See you tomorrow…maybe.' She turned and began to walk towards the changing rooms, her skin coming alive as she felt his hungry eyes on her.

Chapter 18

Friday

London

DI Alan Lute took a bite from his pasty, his stubbly jaw grinding as he chewed.

DI Anne Perry looked across at him, a frown spreading across her face.

He swallowed. 'You're staring at me.'

'God, I want that pasty'. She looked down at her salad, spearing a piece of cucumber.

'Yeah, but you get to feel virtuous all afternoon.'

'I think you mean hungry.'

'Whatever.'

'Never thought I'd actually get to hate a vegetable.' She stabbed another tomato segment.

'Tomato's a fruit.'

She flashed him a mock smile.

'But honestly, Anne, you look great. You must have lost…'

She scowled, 'you don't go there.'

'It's a compliment. From a mate, you know.'

'Yeah, well. I'd rather drink my calories.' She prodded a lettuce leaf.

'Can't argue with that.'

The incident room door swung open.

They looked up as DC Zayan strode in, his laptop held tight to his chest.

Anne Perry lay down her fork. 'Here's something,' she muttered.

DC Zayan slowed as he approached the desk.

She sat back, waiting.

Zayan glanced between the two DI's, hesitating.

Alan Lute knitted his eyebrows. 'What is this, an interrogation?'

DC Zayan threw a look around the room. A scattering of colleagues, some gazing glassy-eyed at screens as they tapped their keyboards, others speaking quietly into their headsets. His gaze drifted to the interview room door.

Anne and Alan exchanged a glance, then slowly rose to their feet dropping their napkins onto their plates.

They walked in silence into the interview room and carefully shut the door behind them.

'I got the logs,' Zayan spoke quietly.

'Go on,' Anne nodded.

'It doesn't make a lot of sense…unless.'

'The suspense is killing me,' Alan mumbled.

'These texts. They…don't exist.'

Anne screwed up her face. 'What do you mean?'

'That text that Robert Evelyn said he received, telling him

about his wife and Simon Yarrow. No trace of it, anywhere in the system.'

'You mean someone…erased it?'

He shook his head. 'Even if you had, the digital record would still be there.'

'But if he didn't get a text,' Alan screwed up his face, 'why would he go after Yarrow? He doesn't even know the guy for Christ's sake.'

'There's more,' DC Zayan continued, 'that guy that Rose Evelyn *was* having an affair with, Colin Mitchell.'

'Go on.'

'You said they both claimed the other made the first move.'

They looked at him in silence.

'Those texts don't exist either.'

Anne frowned. 'So what does that mean?'

'I don't know. Perhaps they first hooked up somewhere…embarrassing. At a swingers party or something. The text story was to spare their blushes.' He paused. 'But then why bother inventing the story about the texts anyway? I mean they work together, so why would you?'

Anne and Alan looked at one another.

'And I went through Peter Moynes' messages. His wife said he'd found out about her affair with Yarrow the same day that Yarrow was attacked.'

Alan huffed, 'but nothing on his phone either?'

'Exactly, so how did he find out about her and Yarrow?'

Alan rubbed his jaw.

DC Zayan looked from one DI to the other. 'You think this is all connected?'

'Do you?'

DC Zayan blew out his cheeks.

'*Unless*,' Anne fixed Zayan a look, 'you said 'it doesn't make sense *unless*.''

He seemed to hesitate. 'Coincidences?'

'Like what?'

'Rose Evelyn. She says she'd never had an affair until a month ago, when the thing with Colin Mitchell started.'

'So?'

'Robert Evelyn, he's obviously not stupid. I mean he knew she was seeing someone else.'

'And?'

'Text or not, it only set Robert Evelyn going because he knew his wife *was* having an affair.'

They looked at him blankly.

'At any other time in their twenty year marriage he'd have probably just ignored some tip-off about his wife and another guy. Like some random nutter trying to wind him up.'

Anne blinked. 'But she said it herself, the physical side of their marriage had gone, so you could understand why she might be looking for something.'

'But if we take it at face value and assume that Rose Evelyn and Colin Mitchell *are* telling the truth about those texts.' He looked from one to the other. 'They only got together because they thought the other party was coming on so strong. It sounds like they wouldn't have dared make a move unless…'

'Get to the point', said Anne.

Zayan drew himself upright. 'Let's say those texts were real.'

'But you just said they weren't.'

'Not necessarily.'

'You're losing me.'

'Maybe they were real, but someone reached into the system and extracted those texts. As though they never existed.'

'Someone?'

'Those texts, they were all on the same platform, Zomos.' Zayan paused. 'Same as that local news site.'

Anne screwed up her face. 'So this is what? Someone who works at the platform went to all this trouble to somehow trick Robert Evelyn into attacking Simon Yarrow?'

Zayan nodded slowly. 'Given Simon Yarrow's high-profile views on the tech giants and the big platforms, well, they wouldn't be sorry to see him gone, would they?'

'Bit obvious though isn't it? Would a tech company really risk going after someone like that?' Said Anne.

'If they thought they could get away with it. Maybe. And if all this is part of the same…plan. Well, Peter Moynes isn't exactly a fan of the social media platforms either.'

They considered his words.

'If Zomos planted and then disappeared the texts, they could do the same with that article about Peter Moynes and the girl. They know all the IP addresses, they could easily make sure that only the neighbours who had it in for Moynes saw that article.'

Anne turned towards Alan.

Alan raised his eyebrows.

'What does that mean?'

He grunted, 'why not?'

She frowned. 'You really think so?'

'Like Zayan says, if the texts never existed, how the hell do you explain Evelyn going after Yarrow? And the other two love birds, his missus and that Mitchell bloke. It would be totally out of character for either to have come on to the other without a 'come-and-get-me-tiger' text. And Peter Moynes finding out about his wife and Yarrow, all on the same day. Because find out he did, her bruises were real enough.' He paused. 'I mean, making sure that tosser Peter Moynes found out about his wife on that very day...' He fixed Anne a look.

'Go on.'

'...Knowing he'd probably knock her about. Something else to get the neighbours going.'

She sucked air between her teeth.

'I know, I know,' Alan rumbled, 'a bloody lot of ifs and buts.'

Anne weighed his words. 'That screenshot, could have been a cut-and-paste number. Nothing to do with someone hacking the news site.'

'Maybe, but it did the job though, didn't it?' Alan paused. 'I mean, it was so…specific. The story that Moynes had kept the girl locked-up in a secret cellar all this time. Practically screaming for someone to beat the truth out of Paedo Pete and rescue the poor girl.'

'Or maybe it was like that Farlough woman said: just some…nasty joke.'

'Well, if that's what it was, the neighbours didn't seem to get it.'

Anne lowered herself into a chair.

'Maybe we should just take a beat,' Alan said, 'I mean, it might not be a great idea to go bounding into Zornos looking for a smoking gun. These are…serious people, right? With a serious amount of shit on us all.'

'So, we just ignore it?'

'But what if they come after you? If Zayan's right about these murders, what's to stop them lining you up?'

'We're police for goodness sake!'

'And you think that would stop them'.

'If we don't ask the question…' Anne looked at them both in turn. 'We've got this far. We can't just ignore it for Christ's sake.'

Chapter 19

London

Anne Perry walked steadily across the airy atrium, her shadow gliding over the pale stonework beneath her feet. She could feel the patient gaze of cameras on her as she approached the neat, alert figures seated behind the glinting sweep of the steel and glass reception desk, the giant black letters spelling out the name 'ZOMOS' emblazoned on the wall behind them.

She jumped at the sound of a voice in her ear. 'Morning, DI Perry, welcome to Zomos.'

She spun around. An earnest looking young man in a blue polo shirt and pale chinos flashed her a bright smile. 'It's not every day we welcome the police here. Please.' He nodded towards the two dark-suited figures standing by the security barrier, their calm eyes fixed on her. 'We can go straight up.'

'And you are?'

'Mason Shaw, Media Relations.'

'I'm…meeting a colleague here.'

'He can join us.' His smile hardened.

'I can wait for him,' she snapped.

'In twenty-one minutes, I have an 11.30,' he tetchily announced

She glanced at her phone.

'Those don't work in here, I'm afraid.' He tutted. 'Shall we?'

She found herself staring at his gleaming teeth, anger building in her as she turned and walked stiffly to the barrier.

****

They rode the elevator in silence.

Through the glass walls Anne could see the streets of Bermondsey drifting away from them as they rumbled higher, the warehouses and the church spires fading into the chequered carpet of greys and browns far below them.

Anne could feel her skin tingling, the sheer air beyond the glass barrier almost tugging at her.

The lift pinged as the car settled up against the buffers, the doors gliding aside with the faintest of hums.

She was looking down a broad corridor. Above them stretched a gabled skylight, the timber beams smudged against the milky blue sky.

She followed him down the hallway, their footsteps ticking on the shiny wooden surface. She willed the image of Peter Moynes' broken face into her mind, fuelling her determination.

He stopped by a door and carefully pushed it open.

She flinched at the brightness of the morning sun, beating through the picture window.

'On a good day,' he chirped behind her, 'you can see

Dartford.'

She edged into the room, catching the earthy-sweet scent of palm pots, their smooth green leaves sharp against the paintwork. 'This your office?'

'I wish. Media Team, we're in the bowels.'

She walked around the circular glass table that centred the room, her shadow stretching out across the wooden floor, rippling in the sunlight. The ZOMOS logo swirled on the bright white walls around them.

She fixed him a stare. 'Do you know why I'm here?'

He gave an expansive shrug.

'Just thought it was...unusual. Your office not asking *why* I wanted to talk to someone here.'

'We have an open door policy.'

'In my experience, there's no such thing.'

He flinched, then reset his plastic smile. 'I referred it up, of course. I was told to give you our full cooperation.'

She remained standing as she reached into her bag, pulled out an envelope and lay it on the table.

He looked at it.

'Before we get to the '*why*', let me show you the '*how*'.' She picked up the envelope.

He took an uncertain step forward.

She pulled out a photo and placed it in front of him.

He drew in a breath.

'Can you imagine', she began, 'how hard it must be to do

that?'

His face went white.

'The sound of the skull cracking.'

'What is this?' He whispered.

She pulled out another photo, lay it beside the first one.

He let out a groan, his face a paradigm of torture.

'Now this…would have taken time.' She looked at the photo. 'No sign of a gag.' She could feel a cold fury building inside her.

He closed his eyes.

'Usually if someone screams, you'd stop, *right?*'

His breathing began to quicken.

'Look at them!'

He snapped his eyes open, .

'One man's skull crushed with a hammer. The other, beaten until his face fell off.'

He stuttered. 'I just do the press. What the hell is this?'

'You tell me.'

'Tell you what? I don't know anything about these…' he flinched away from the photos.

'You know who they are.'

'Everyone does, it's all over the news!'

She studied his drawn face. 'What would it take, do you think, to do that to a human being?'

'Look, I just do PR…'

She let the silence drag between them.

'Human interest stuff. You know.' He swallowed. 'What's this got to do with us anyway?'

'Like I said, I'm trying to figure out the 'why'.'

He looked at her blankly.

'I have a theory, you see.' She scooped up the photos. 'Maybe I'll just call a press conference, see how it flies.' She hummed as she slid them into her bag.

'I'm sorry we couldn't be more help.'

She flashed him a smile. 'We'll see.'

His phone 'pinged'. He frowned as he pulled it from his pocket.

'Thought phones didn't work in here.'

He ran a hand through his hair. 'Looks like he finished early, he's ready to see you now.'

'He?'

'ZOMOS's Head of London Operations.'

****

DI Anne Perry stood outside the door to his office. She looked down at her outstretched fingers. The shaking had stopped but her mouth felt dry. She raised a hand, then hesitated, the hairs on her neck standing. She could sense eyes on her.

Slowly she turned around.

No one, just the muffled silence of the corridor, white walls and the dark carpet dusted with the yellow glow of the ceiling lights.

A shudder ran through her as she swung back to the door and knocked.

The door eased itself open.

A tall man around her age stood in the doorway, his angular features framed by a sweep of grey hair. He gave a little cry like a startled pelican. 'Welcome to Zomos!' He grinned. 'That's soundproofing for you. Can't hear a bloody thing. If I'm expecting someone I have to stand with my ear to the door.' He chuckled. 'Well that's something to talk about.' He stood aside, his pale jacket ruffling around his lanky frame. 'Come on in.'

She blinked as her eyes adjusted to the muted light.

'Don't do windows, find it hard to concentrate as it is.'

She stepped past him, feeling her shoes easing into the pale carpet.

'Your mother would feel at home.' He nodded towards the thick weave beneath her feet.

She found herself frowning.

'Figure of speech.' Another chuckle.

Anne tried to focus her thoughts whilst his words buzzed in her head.

'Fawcett Toom,' he stuck out a hand, 'my parents had a cruel sense of humour.'

She shook it. 'DI Perry.'

His hand felt cold.

'I'm the bastard who gets to run the place.' He shot out an arm pointing to two yellow armchairs in the centre of the room. 'So whatever's on your mind, Detective.'

He seemed to chew on the word.

'Please.'

She glanced around the room. The dark walls seemed to shimmer under the white pin-lights that ringed the ceiling. In one corner of the airy room sat a dark wooden desk, a single leather-backed chair pushed back from it. Next to it, a sideboard with whips of steam rising from gleaming white crockery.

'Come in, have a seat.' He bustled around her.

She moved towards the centre of the room. The air smelt fresh, breezy.

'Tea,' he asked as he strode to the side of the room, 'the rock of ages.'

She stood staring down at the armchairs.

'Yes?' He held up a cup and saucer in his long fingers.

'Two people are dead.'

He nodded slowly, concern carved on his features. 'I read about it. What a ghastly business.'

She slowly pulled the envelope from her bag.

He looked at the envelope then back at her. 'Should I sit down?' He almost laughed at a secret joke.

She said nothing.

He walked slowly to the middle of the room and folded himself into one of the chairs.

She lowered herself down, feeling the soft fabric easing itself around her.

He looked again at the envelope in her hand.

She turned it round in her fingers. 'Know what's in here?'

'I think so.'

'Is this why you want to see me?'

'We're keen to help.'

'Good.' She pulled out a photo and held it up towards him.

'Simon Yarrow,' his tone was sombre.

'Friend of yours?'

He gave a snort. 'The guy's a paranoid attention-seeking prick.'

She studied his face. '*Was.*'

He cleared his throat. 'Speaking ill of the dead and all that.'

'But then, you're the bastard who gets to run the place.' She paused. '*You* can do whatever you want.'

'*I wish,*' he gave a snort.

She straightened up in her chair. 'The man who attacked him, Robert Evelyn. Do you know *him?*'

He pulled a face.

'Silly question, you know everyone.'

'It'll be…somewhere…' He waved a hand in the air. 'But that's just data. You're talking about a real person.'

'So you don't know him?'

'The system's smart, but we just work here.' He forced a

smile. 'My mind is a tabula rasa and I intend to keep it that way.'

'Robert Evelyn got a text that afternoon, telling him about his wife and Yarrow.'

He shrugged.

'Which was odd.'

'Was it?'

'Yes, because his wife had never met Yarrow.'

'Sorry, is there a point to this?'

'He believed it though, because his wife had just started an affair. Someone at work. Jealous husband, sixth sense, you know.'

He raised an eyebrow.

'Out of character though. But then, you'd be flattered, text like that, from someone who you'd never thought would give you a second glance.'

'Indeed.'

'Or maybe it was her who sent the text, got the ball rolling…as it were.'

He puffed out his cheeks, raised his eyes.

'Strange thing is, all three of those texts disappeared.'

'Texts don't *disappear.*'

She studied his face. 'So what would you call it then? One day the texts are there, then…gone.'

'So what exactly is your question?'

She set her face. 'You're the bastard who runs the place.'

'You think we do that kind of thing? Plant texts, then…'
He threw out his fingers, '…puff!'

She said nothing, then pulled out the second photo.
'Peter Moynes.' She flipped the photo round in her
fingers and held it towards him.

This time he flinched.

'Another friend of yours?'

'Gonzo conspiracy junkie and snuff porn addict.'

'Had it coming then?'

He clenched his mouth and took a deep breath through
his nose. 'You're going to have to explain, DI Perry. And
assume I'm a simple man.'

'An article appeared on the local news site linking Peter
Moynes to the disappearance of that teenager last year.
Said he might still be holding her somewhere.'

He shrugged. 'We can't know everything.'

'Strange, don't you think?' She said raising her voice.
'Only a few neighbours reported seeing that article and
the woman who runs the site says she'd never even set
eyes on it.'

'She's a nutter, she breeds guard donkeys for goodness
sake, what do you expect?'

'And you just…what? Happened to know about her?'

He shrugged again.

'When you were searching 'donkey breeders', perhaps.'
She glared at him.

'Of course we do. I mean, it would be odd if we didn't.'

'Meaning what?'

'When we knew you were coming to see us…well.' He spread his spindly hands. 'Just wanted to make sure we were…on the same page.'

'So you've been spying on me?'.

'*Certainly not.*'

'What would you call it then?'

'Spying suggests someone's got something to hide.' He gave a thin smile.

'What are you implying?'

'Not implying anything.'

'This is a police investigation.'

'And we're just trying to help.'

'Really?'

He carefully folded his hands in his lap. 'The thing is, it all looks…different…from inside.' He nodded agreeably. 'It's an…arrangement, a *bien entente.*'

She said nothing.

'It's a funny thing. Even good friends, people…don't tell each other very much. It's always just…a few, safe subjects, you know. We think people know us but they don't *know* us.' He paused. 'But when it comes to *us*,' he gave a chuckle, 'well, people will insist on telling us *everything*.' He spread his hands. 'What can you do?'

She eyeballed him.

'Think of it like…confession.'

'What are you trying to say?'

'Just an observation.'

'Are you trying to…threaten me?'

'Certainly not. I was just…talking.'

She set her face. 'Just answer the question, then.'

He straightened up. 'It's all in the system, it was just a matter of…asking.'

She looked at him and then slowly shook her head.

'Nothing personal, Detective.'

She could feel her anger starting to build. 'You're a poor liar.'

'I'm a dreadful liar,' his tone was deadpan.

'Peter Moynes can go to hell,' she growled, 'but I've met the neighbours, seen the families. Is this what's got to happen to them?' She could feel the rage surging through her. 'Their parents shamed, locked up, the children put in care, teased and tormented for the rest of their lives? Is that what you want?'

He looked at her in silence.

'Whatever their faults, they had families.' She snarled. 'And now Robert Evelyn's crapping himself in a police cell. Just how long's he going to last in Belmarsh before they beat him to death or worse?'

'Crime is a terrible thing and *hey* maybe he'll enjoy getting cosy with his cellmates.'

She grimaced in disgust at his joke. 'You made these people do it!' She said furiously.

'We can't make anyone do anything.' He paused, spread his palms. 'Free will and all that.'

She gave him the hard stare. 'So, those texts, that story. Did you? Plant them, then 'disappear' them?'

'Even if we could, why would we?'

'Simon Yarrow, Peter Moynes. They wanted to bring Zomos down.'

'I think you're confusing cause and effect. People like that, people who have secrets, whose lives are all about secrets.' His voice was rising. 'That's the paranoid world they live in. Of course they think the worst of organisations like ours. But all we want is to do good.'

'And that's your excuse, for killing?'

'There's never any excuse for killing.'

'Can't you feel *anything*?' Her words had a clear honesty.

He studied her face, an insincere smile caressing his mouth. 'I just wish people wouldn't do such…dreadful things.'

'Have you even listened to a word I've said?'

'Sure. You feel sorry for the killers.' He glanced down at the photographs, then back up at her.

'Is that what you think?'

'Every life's a story; can't all be happy endings.'

Chapter 20

Utah, USA

Brian Wise stepped through the door and glanced around the bathroom, his ears straining for any sound.

He walked towards the row of basins, his steady footsteps breaking the silence.

He looked across at the cubicles. The doors were all ajar.

He was alone.

Slowly he slipped his phone from his pocket and began to type.

'It's eating me up, Gracie.'

He tensed as he looked down at the phone.

She began to type. 'Thought you were at work.'

'I am.'

'Then what the hell are you doing? If you lose that job I swear you'll never see your son again.'

He chewed his lip. 'I just don't know what to do.'

'You can stop taking that shit, that's what you can do. And clear your head out.'

'I miss you both SO much.'

'Get off that fucking phone and get back to work.'

'Please, Gracie. PLEASE stop hating me.'

'You're pathetic.'

'I know.' A tear undulated down his cheek.

'I got to go.' She grumbled. 'The workmen are here from City Hall, tearing up the goddammed bathroom. Everything was working fine, why they got to put all this new shit in?'

He began to say something then the cold purr of the disconnected call line cut him dead.

He let his arm slump to his side, the phone hanging limply in his hand. He looked down at the scratched white tiles, then closed his eyes. *'Dear God,'* he whispered. *'Please give me the strength to carry on, to do what I need to do. Please comfort those I know I'm hurting, be by their side Lord.'* He seemed to wince. *'Amen.'*

The door swung open with a creak.

Brian stuffed his phone into his pocket and flipped on the tap, rubbing his hands together as he began to hum, staring down at the sink.

He could hear the newcomer's footsteps padding behind him.

Then silence.

Slowly, Brian straightened up, staring into the mirror.

The man's face behind him snarled. 'What the hell's going on?'

Brian frowned. 'What're you talking about?'

'I'm not fucking blind.'

Brian slowly pushed the tap off and turned around.

'You might fool that wet rag of a supervisor but *I see you, man.*' He jabbed a finger at Brian.

Brian studied the newcomer for a moment, then raised his chin. 'Get out of my fucking face, Chris!'

'Just take a look in the mirror, why don't you!'

'What's it to you anyway?'

'You might not give a shit but I ain't carrying you!'

'Who the fuck are you to judge?!'

'I saw you miss those threads yesterday! Even from where I sit, Christ, Brian, you were nowhere close to snapping them!'

Brian bristled, then checked himself. 'Look.' He sighed. 'We can all have an off day.'

'You saw the teeth on this thing!'

Brian hissed. 'Keep your voice down.'

'Whoever the fuck's behind this,' he growled, 'if that gets in…'

Brian said nothing.

'One slip.' Chris narrowed his eyes. 'I ain't taking the chance.'

'What're you saying?' Brian jutted out his jaw.

'Look, nothing personal man.' He spread his palms. 'But I saw what I saw. What the fuck else you expect me to do?'

'You can't report me!' Brian reached out to grab the man's arm then stopped himself. 'Look, you're right. I was having a…' He searched for an answer. 'But that was yesterday.'

'I'm sorry, man.'

'Look, I've got some trouble…at home.' The words were falling out. 'But I'm getting it sorted.' He pleaded. 'Man. I've *got* to keep this job.'

Chris shook his head.

Brian drew himself upright, his expression hardening. 'Are you really going to report me?'

Chris sighed. 'It's a fucking war, Brian.'

'A war.' Brian nodded as though admitting a great truth. 'You think you know what a war looks like?'

Chris said nothing.

'Do you have any idea what it feels like…?' Brian's voice was firm, his face devoid of emotion, '…to slide a knife into the side of someone's throat.'

Chris stared at him, his eyes wide.

'To hear the hiss of the blade, see the blood.' Brian leant towards him. 'No one will ever know.'

'You…fucking…' Chris spluttered.

Brian grabbed Chris's jaw. 'I will take you to the woods,' Brian hissed, 'I will tie you and gag you.'

Chris's face went ashen.

'I will cut off your balls.' He squeezed his jaw. 'And take your eyes.'

Chris groaned.

'And then…,' Brian gave him a twisted smile, '…you'll

beg for death…' Brian pushed Chris away from him. Chris stumbled backwards, his face red from where Brian had gripped him.

Chris's mouth opened and closed, but no sound came.

'But thanks for your concern, Chris, I really appreciate it.' And with that Brian turned and walked to the door.

****

Brian headed for his desk; busy figures bustling past him as he kept his eyes on the grey steel doors of the Control Room ahead.

He could almost sense the static in the dry filtered air; the sour-smoky prick of cold coffee catching in his nostrils.

'Hey, Brian!'

He stopped and turned around.

His supervisor Mike was striding towards him. 'Been looking everywhere for you.'

'Just went to the bathroom is all.'

'Got an email from personnel. Don't ask me why, but you got to report to Medical.'

Brian stared at him, his face twisting. 'Medical?'

'It's a priority.'

'What's this about?'

'So no shooting.' He held up his hands in mock surrender as he beamed a fake smile.

'Can't you stall them? I got a ton of work to do.'

'I already told 'em. But the answer's the same. They want

to see you right away…as in now.'

Brian stuttered. 'But I…'

'Probably just a random test…no biggie.'

'I…I was up with a fever all night…my bloods will be all over.'

Mike grinned. 'Medical will be the right place then.' He mock punched Brian on the shoulder and then added 'see you on the other side…maybe.'

****

Brian fixed his gaze on the digital clock set in the wall above the doctor's desk.

The doctor's fingers furiously tapped his keyboard, his eyes roving across his laptop's screen.

A new digit flicked silently onto the clock.

The doctor lifted his hands from the keys, letting them hover as he narrowed his eyes, the sudden quiet pressing around them.

Brian tried to calm himself, the air prickly with the sting of disinfectant.

The doctor turned to face him. 'Do you know why you're here?' His pinched features sharp under the white halogen lights.

'Temperature check…I guess.' Brian rubbed his hands. 'I had this fever last night, thought I'd shook it, but maybe one of the sensors…'

The doctor studied Brian's face, his expression stony.

'Not the best night's sleep…' Brian cleared phlegm from

his throat. 'But with the firewall probes and all, need everyone on deck, I figure.'

The doctor's mouth pursed. 'How's everything at home?'

'Fine, I guess.'

The doctor kept his steady gaze on him and said nothing.

'Our son was ten yesterday, would you believe it? Where the heck did that go?' Brian offered a stiff smile.

'Do anything nice?'

'Was goin' to take him fishing but the weather...' He seemed to hesitate. 'And work...you know.'

'Let's see your hands.' The doctor's tone now icy.

'What?'

'Show me your hands.'

Brian considered refusing but then raised his hands, edging them towards the doctor.

'And the other side.'

'It's just a...'

The doctor was staring at the cut that ran down the back of his hand where Gracie had slammed the cupboard door on him.

He looked up at Brian. 'How long ago'd you do it?'

Brian puffed his cheeks. 'Three days, I guess.'

They both listened to the sound of raised voices from somewhere below them.

'Brian, I'll tell you straight.' The doctor sat back, locking his fingers together as if to give gravity to what he was about to say. 'Gate Security called it in.' His expression seemed to soften. 'Self-harming, it's not a crime.'

Brian was torn between outrage and relief.

'Facing it for what it is.' The doctor paused. 'You're half way there.'

'Hang on, you're way off here!'

'I'm just trying to help, I'm not judging.' He held up his hands.

'This isn't what this is!'

'Talking's a good place to start.'

'You're going somewhere that doesn't make sense!' His voice was rising.

A boom rang out from deep in the complex, a judder running through the floor beneath their feet.

'Brian,' the doctor spoke quietly, 'I think you need to take a beat.'

'What does that mean?'

'You need to power down. You know, regroup.'

'For Christ's sake, it's just a cut!'

'There's a clinic we use, it's very discreet.' He tried a smile. 'You should talk it through with your family.'

'Please!...you've got this all wrong.'

'That wound, Brian. I know the signs.'

'You're not listening!'

A scream tore through the room.

Brian leapt to his feet, spinning to face the door.

More shouting now, urgent and fearful, the words lost in the rumble of machinery and the chaos of running feet.

'If there was a major issue, there'd be an alarm,' the doctor's voice had none of its previous confidence.

They jumped as the snarl of distant machine gun fire juddered around them.

'That's live rounds!' Brian bellowed at the doctor.

The doctor pushed himself to his feet. 'Wait, wait!' He bustled to the cupboard. 'Got to be a drill, right?' He muttered as his shaking fingers scooped syringes into his medic pouch.

They threw themselves through the door and ran down the corridor towards the fire escape stairway. From somewhere below they could hear muffled cries and sirens.

****

They burst through the fire escape door into the hallway and stopped dead, riveted by the scene in front of them.

Scattered across the hallway, kneeling, lying figures, gasping and groaning for help.

'Jesus!' Brian knelt beside a woman nearest to him. 'What the fuck's happened?'

Her body shook as she drew in lungfuls of air. 'I...can't...breath.' She forced the words out.

The doctor was crouching beside Brian. 'Easy, easy.' He gently held her trembling shoulders. 'Just...slow, easy breaths...'

Brian glanced at the Control Room entrance, his eyes widening. Someone had brought the security shutters down, blocking the Control Room doors. As he stared at the glinting wall of steel he thought he could hear faint voices beyond the barrier.

He ran over to the shutters, holding his ear against the cold metal. There were people still in there, someone was banging on the inside. He swung around, eyes racing around the hallway. He spotted his supervisor, Mike, sitting against a wall, his eyes were closed as he took in deep breaths, wheezing as he exhaled, his face slack and pale.

'Mike!' Brian threw himself down beside him. 'What's happened?'

Mike slowly opened his eyes. He looked at Brian, frowning as though struggling with the words.

'Mike!' Brian shook him roughly.

'Alright, alright!' He tried to shrug off Brian's hand.

'Just tell me what's going on!'

Mike coughed. 'Something triggered the Nitrogen suppressors.'

'There was a fire?'

'I don't know.' He winced again. 'I didn't see any.' His gaze drifted towards the steel shutters. 'No alarm, the Nitrogen pumps just...' He took a ragged breath. 'Suddenly...we couldn't breathe.'

'But what about the firewall?' Brian tripped out the words, fear etched on his face.

'Chris and Larry offered to stay to spike the portals, shut it all down.' He coughed again, his body wracking. 'Man, they were just a few seconds behind us…'

'Jesus, Mike, you left them in there!'

'The shutters they just…came down, I…didn't know…'

'How do you raise them?!' Brian was shouting at Mike.

Mike shuddered. 'I don't *fucking* know.'

Brian ran to the steel barrier, crouching down, trying to prise his fingers under the shutters. 'Someone fucking help me!' he roared.

'They won't open.' Mike called across at him as he tried to ease himself to his feet. 'Not 'til they've vented all the N.'

'They'll fucking die in there!'

'I know, man!' Mike was on his feet, swaying slowly. 'It all happened so…'

The sound of machine gun fire from the main entrance rattled around them.

Brian whipped around, he could see darting figures on the forecourt just outside the main doors.

Another burst of fire echoed down the corridor. The figures outside seemed to melt into a pink cloud and disappear.

'No!' Brian gasped.

He set off, running towards the main doors, his chest heaving.

Through the pounding of his heart he could hear other

hurried footsteps. The doctor was beside him, arms pumping as he matched Brian pace for pace.

They slid to a halt just by the doors, catching their breath.

On the forecourt, half a dozen twisted, bloodied shapes were strewn around, no faces, no limbs, just little piles of bloody flesh and shredded clothes. On a couple of them he could see the glint of NSA lanyards.

The doctor bent double and let out a panicked groan.

Brian's eyes darted across the carpark to the direction of the guard house. The door was open, there was no sign of anyone.

He could hear the doctor retching beside him.

A movement, just on the edge of his vision. Brian looked up, a patrol drone was making lazy circles just above the carpark, the barrels of its Gatling gun dark and stern against the smooth white surface of its body.

'Jesus, it's shooting our own,' the doctor whispered.

Another movement caught Brian's eye. It was one of the security guards, he was sprawled behind one of the marble walls at the edge of the forecourt, his back against it, hidden from the drone.

They both stared at the figure. He was still alive, his hand pressed against his chest, blood seeping through his fingers.

Brian gritted his teeth. 'He's bleeding out. He won't make it.' He looked up at the circling drone and swallowed.

'We gotta get to him.' The doctor's voice beside him.

Brian gathered himself.

'We just need…a few seconds.' The doctor was staring up at the circling drone.

Brian felt like death was descending on him.

'Brian!' The doctor shook him. 'You going to fucking help?'

Brian glanced down at the discarded rifle by one of the bodies.

'We got to go *now*!' The doctor pulled at his arm.

Brian said nothing, his eyes fixed on the prowling drone.

'Brian!'

Brian looked down at the doctor. 'You never said your name.' He spoke quietly.

'What?'

'Your name. I don't know your name.'

The doctor screwed his face. 'It's…Fred, Fred Nyman.'

'OK, Fred.' Brian barged the heavy glass door open and the doctor sprinted towards the wounded guard, his medic bag bouncing on his hip.

Brian stood in the doorway, helpless as the drone swooped down towards the scurrying figure of the doctor. With a snarl the Gatling spattered into life. The doctor let out an animal scream his body jerking and twisting, as the stream of metal shredded him into tiny pieces of bone and flesh that fizzed like bloody confetti before settling almost silently onto the sunny forecourt.

Brian slowly let the door swing shut and stepped back into the hall. The iron sweet smell of blood hung in the air like a rebuke. A shudder ran through him.

'You fucking let him die, man.' It was Mike's voice just behind him.

Brian kept his eye on the pool of bloodied fragments where Fred had stood and said nothing.

'Thought you were the fucking war hero, Navy Cross and all.' Mike croaked.

'Well, now you know.' Brian whispered as he stared at the scene.

A rumbling noise began to build into a roar as the sound of jet engines ripped around them.

A stinger missile slammed into the drone, the fireball bursting against the milky blue sky.

Mike looked up at Brian. 'Why didn't you stop him.'

'He was a doctor…he'd no choice.'

Mike said nothing as he turned and drifted down the hallway.

Brian drew in a ragged breath. 'I'm sorry, Fred,' he whispered.

Chapter 21

London

Anne Perry slumped into her chair and sat staring at the blank screen. The sounds of the incident room wafted around her, the patter of keyboards, the rumble of conversation, the pad of footsteps on the worn carpet.

She closed her eyes; familiar smells seeping into her: cold coffee, wood polish and pencil shavings.

She could feel the sadness trickling into her, a dull ache building behind her eyes. 'Come on,' she whispered as she pulled open a drawer and began sifting through the old pens and business cards. Her fingers found the chill smoothness of the pill sleeve and she slid it towards her, the Diazepam capsules snug and safe behind their little mounds of silver foil.

She carefully slipped the sleeve from the drawer and eased it into her pocket.

'Anne.'

She jolted as she looked up towards the voice.

'Can I have a word?' Alan Lute walked to her desk and stood looking down at her.

'Alan?'

He seemed to hesitate.

She frowned. 'You OK?'

His mouth seemed to tighten. 'I really do need to have a word.'

She leant back in her chair. 'It's almost the weekend for Christ's sake. Can't it wait?'

He held up a grey warrant folder.

She felt her stomach knotting. 'For fuck's sake, Alan.'

'I'm sorry, Anne.' He spoke quietly as he turned and began to walk towards the interview room.

'Can't it just...' She watched him slowly cross the room. His shoulders were hunched. She forced herself to her feet and followed him into the room, closing the door quietly behind her.

He stood on the other side of the bare metal table, and carefully lay the grey folder down.

She felt the darkness closing in on her. 'Please, Alan.'

'We have to, Anne.' He spoke softly.

'Have to? What the hell is this? I thought we were partners.'

'A man is dead.'

'Look, why are we even doing this?' She challenged him for an answer.

'You know why.'

She wanted to scream the truth but said, 'I just need time.'

'Anne.' His voice was rising. 'It's already borderline breach of conduct. We've got to serve them!'

She tried to settle herself. 'Look...let's just...sleep on it.'

He looked at her, said nothing.

'If we do this…' She swallowed.

'Fabric threads, blood spatters.' He nodded slowly. 'The full English.'

She felt the anger building. 'They didn't stand a fucking chance did they?'

'They killed him,' he glowered, 'it's *that* simple.'

'But it's not!'

He rolled his eyes.

'Zomos! They planned the whole fucking thing!'

'Oh, so they just told you that did they?'

'That story about the girl. Who the hell else could have put it there?'

'That badger woman for a start! Thought she'd stick it to him good, then got cold feet. She can't stand the bloke, made that pretty clear.'

'She was telling the truth!'

'Truth? You're acting like you're trying to avoid the bloody truth!' His stare was baleful. 'Look, what does it matter if that story was planted there or not? The poor bastard didn't kill himself.'

She felt her heartbeat racing.

'And you can't just pretend it didn't happen.'

'Alan…'

He exhaled. 'Maybe we can get it down to manslaughter.'

'Please…'

He screwed up his face. 'I just don't get it! You're the one who's always going on about upholding the law.'

'These are real people, Alan.'

'Sure, and they killed a man!'

'You said you trusted me!'

'But you can't just do what the hell you like!'

'Think of all those poor kids, if their parents get locked up what the hell are they going to do?!'

'Will you listen to yourself! Where's this all going to stop? Does everyone get a free pass now because they saw something that got them angry?' He picked up the photo of Peter Moynes and slapped it on the table. 'That's what I'm talking about! You're holding a hammer, a poker, whatever, and you smash him in the face! He's screaming, pleading, and what do you do? You swing that poker and smash him again and again! Different sound now, the bones are broken like on the butchers block ...'

'Stop it!'

'That's what happened, Anne! What actually happened when those people beat the poor sod to death!' He slammed a hand on the table. 'Consequences! You can't just let people walk away. It's not right, not in anyone's world!'

She dug her nails into her palms.

He lowered his voice. 'You know I'm right.'

She looked down at the photo of Peter Moyne's broken face. 'Monday morning,' she whispered, 'we'll serve the warrants Monday morning.'

He nodded slowly.

She felt numb. 'Jesus…Monday.'

****

Anne Perry walked into the changing room bathroom, her trainers almost silent on the tiled floor. She walked to the line of sinks, carefully lay a hand either side of the basin and looked at her reflection in the mirror. She raised a hand, adjusting one ringlet of hair by her ear, the perfume on her wrist catching in her nostrils, the scent, earthy and sweet. She flinched, then exhaled slowly, as she ran a finger under her shoulder straps, sensing the goose bumps on her skin. She bared her teeth, checking for lipstick marks, then turned and walked slowly back towards the changing room.

****

She stood by the water cooler, rolling her shoulders as she let her gaze drift around the gym, settling on the clock above the running machines. She felt butterflies in her stomach. He wasn't here. She tried to keep her breathing steady as she scanned the room one more time. Another guy, sitting on the bench press, tried to catch her eye. She turned away and began to walk towards the row of exercise bikes, her gaze firmly fixed on the bike closest to her. She lay her towel on the handlebars, placed her phone on the console and swung up onto the saddle. She slid her feet into the pedal straps as she tried to concentrate on the controls, her mind racing. She pressed a couple of buttons and slid her earbuds in, fingers fumbling with her phone as she clicked on the music. She could feel panic building in her as she gripped the handlebars, closed her eyes and began to peddle.

She tried to think about Gemma, the shitty flat, anything, but there they were again, David Yarrow, Peter Moynes: their dead, broken faces. She pushed on the pedals, seeking out the pain but all she could feel now were the hot tears trickling down her cheeks.

She jumped at the sound of a voice, and looked up, her eyes stinging.

David was standing in front of her.

She felt her heart pounding as she turned down the music and tried to set her face.

'Anne.' He looked worried.

She stopped the pedals; looked at him.

He was staring at her. 'You're crying.'

She tried a little laugh that sounded more like a cough. 'Oh it's just…' She wiped away a tear with a thumb. 'It's nothing.' She tried a smile. 'I'm always crying. You'll get used to it.' Her own words seemed to collide into her.

He flashed her a broad smile.

She felt herself blushing.

'Thought you were a cop.'

'You ever spent time with one?'

He chuckled. 'Did you drag that old Bohemian in again?'

She popped out an earbud and held it close to his cheek.

She kept her eyes on his.

He swallowed. 'Resurrection.'

She let a finger brush his cheek.

He seemed to shiver. 'Your perfume.'

'You approve?'

He smiled. 'There's a story.'

'I like stories.' She slowly lowered her wrist.

He blinked. 'Do you believe in fate?'

She weighed his words. 'I used to be free-willer.'

'And?'

She hesitated. 'Now, I'm not so sure.'

'Alright, just pretend then.' He looked suddenly serious. 'You heard of the conductor Mengelberg?'

'The Mahler fan.'

'He conducted the first major Mahler series for thirty years, back before the war. They still have a Mahler festival there.'

'That's fate?'

He exhaled slowly. 'You're going to laugh.'

'Wouldn't be so sure.'

'Here goes.' He gave a grimace. 'Got a…surprise when I opened my laptop this morning. For the first time ever…I think…I actually won something.'

'Congrats.'

'Two return tickets on the Eurostar.'

She felt her heartbeat begin to thrum.

His cheeks began to redden. 'I've got tickets to

Amsterdam. There's a concert there tomorrow night. His Piano Concerto in A.' He fell over his words like an embarrassed schoolboy. 'Will you come with me?'

Her eyes widened. 'Will I do what?'

He swallowed again, his face looked suddenly youthful. 'Will you come with me to Amsterdam?'

Her jaw dropped open. 'You don't even know me.'

'It's fate…maybe,' he croaked.

She looked at him, said nothing.

'Mahler..?'

She glanced around her, a frown edging across her features. She could hear him clearing his throat.

She slowly turned back to him. 'Separate bedrooms.'

He spluttered. 'Uh…sure…'

'Can't believe I'm doing this.'

'There's a train every hour so…' He glanced at the clock. 'We could try for the eight o'clock…'

'What?' She pulled a face. 'Eight o'clock…*tonight*?'

He gave an open, hopeful smile.

'This is just…' Her voice trailed off as she found herself smiling. 'Why the hell not?'

Chapter 22

The West of England

Emma Wilson pushed open the front door to the rattle of the bell, the boys' suits hanging over her arm, the polythene wrapping swishing as she lifted them by the hangers and hung them on the hallway hook.

'It's me,' she called out.

As she bent to undo the laces on her trainers she found herself looking across the wooden floor towards the kitchen. Something seemed out of place. As she pulled apart the laces she drew in a breath. Instead of the familiar catch of wood smoke, a dusty dryness seemed to hover around her. 'Kate?' She called into the kitchen as she stood and kicked off her trainers.

Silence.

She stepped into the kitchen, feeling the chill of the stone tiles through her thin socks, her eyes darting. The fire was out, Kate's book lay face down on the kitchen table. She stood, quite still, listening into the stillness, the silence almost alive in her ears.

She could sense the adrenalin tingling through her muscles as her heartbeat rose. She carefully picked up the poker from beside the cold grate and walked as silently as she could towards the stairway. She pushed at the door which whispered open. She listened again. Nothing. She placed a foot on the first step and slowly eased her weight onto it. It took it without a sound. She edged on to the second step. As she pushed down with the ball of her foot a floorboard cracked like a firework. She froze, as the sound of a chair scraping across the floor rasped from behind Kate's bedroom door. Emma gripped the poker and bounded up the stairs throwing open Kate's door, poker brandished above her head ready to strike.

Kate stood staring at Emma, her face full of shock. Her eyes were red.

Emma lowered the poker as she caught her breath. 'What the hell's happened? Why didn't you answer me?'

Kate twisted her face. 'Jesus just look at you! You're like a…wild animal! What the fuck is wrong with you?!'

Emma said softly. 'I just thought…'

'God, Emma you fucking scare me sometimes.'

'I was worried. I didn't know.'

'It's like you've got our grandfather's…wicked blood in your veins.'

'Don't say that!'

Kate let out a long breath as she brought her hand to her chest. 'You'll make my heart clean stop one of these days, I swear you will.'

Emma could sense the blush in her cheeks as her pulse settled, the poker dangling awkwardly by her side. 'Where are the boys?'

'At the farm. Munro wanted some help with the hay before the rain comes.'

Emma glanced down. Anne Perry's diary lay open on the desk.

Kate said quietly, 'I heard you crying, last night.'

'I told the boys,' Emma's voice was flat.

'Who's Anne Perry?'

She looked up at her sister. 'She's a friend.'

'Alice Robin asked me the other day, if I'd heard when those works will finish, when they'll reopen the High Street.' Her voice was calm. 'I made a joke, about everything going down the drain.'

Emma said nothing.

'What the hell is anything anyway?'

Emma lay the poker on the bed and sat beside it. 'These last days, Saudi, the things they told me, then Sebastian, then this. It's like a horrid bug, you feel it in you, you want to sick it up, but you know you can't.' She looked at the notebook, the neat writing scoring the pages. 'Doesn't matter what we want,' she said in a whisper.

'Sebastian, did he write it?'

'Does it matter?'''

'I guess not.' Kate lowered herself into her chair. 'I read it last night. And afterwards, I was lying there, wasn't even trying to sleep, all this…chopping around in my head. Kept telling myself, it's just a stupid story.' She looked at Emma. 'Why can't I believe that? That it's just…someone's bad dream.'

Emma looked at her sister, at the dark rings beneath her bloodshot eyes. 'I'm sorry,' she found herself saying.

'I guess I must have fallen asleep at some point, because I remember waking up. And that was when I heard it.' Kate's gaze hardened. 'The silence.'

'I remember, when you were young, you hated silence,' said Emma.

'I didn't hate it, actually.' Her look softened. 'It was like…life stopped, and if the silence went on too long, I'd stop too.' She smiled weakly. 'I just kept thinking: the sirens…then the silence. That can't be all there is, just…silence.' She looked down at the notebook. 'In the end, everything's just a story.' Kate looked up at Emma, her bottom lip was trembling. 'Of course you love them, what a wicked thing for me to say.'

'Oh, Kate.' Emma bundled towards her, putting her arms around Kate's shaking shoulders as her tears flowed. 'I'll bring them home, I will.' Emma leant in, resting her cheek against her sister's as Kate's quiet sobs cut the stillness.

Emma raised her head as the trill of the bell above the front door rattled around them.

'We're back!' One of the boys called out as the sound of hurried footsteps joined the chatter of raised voices echoing through the kitchen and up the stairs.

'I'd better go,' Emma whispered.

'Just about the only proper thing Dad ever said…,' Kate's voice was hoarse, '…only a fool's not afraid.' She squeezed Emma's arm. 'I don't know why I find it so hard to tell you…'

'Kate…I know.'

'You go.' Kate smiled as she patted Emma's hand. 'I just need a moment.'

****

Emma knocked twice on the boys' door.

'A second,' Tommy's voice.

She stood in the narrow corridor, the murmur of the boys voices humming around her. She could hear Kate talking in the kitchen at the bottom of the stairs, her voice sounded deep and steady, the words lost in the patient rumble.

'OK,' Tommy again.

Emma slowly swung the door open.

Tommy and Andy stood in the middle of the room. In their new dark suits they looked taller, older somehow.

Emma managed a smile. 'Don't you look smart.' She closed the door behind her.

'What were you doing, when you were our age?' Andy asked.

'Just…finishing school, I guess.' She tried to sound breezy as she began to bustle round them, straightening their ties, brushing specs of dust from their shoulders. 'There you go.' She flicked the final specs away with a flourish.

'We're nervous,' Tommy said.

She felt the worry nibbling at her again. 'I'll look after you, you'll be fine.'

'Last night,' Tommy looked edgy, 'we heard you crying.'

'That was just…' she blustered. 'I…miss my mum. She's in a home now.' She dropped her voice. 'When Kate and I see her, she doesn't know who we are anymore.' She looked at their concerned faces. 'I'm sorry, I didn't mean to…'

'It's alright,' Andy said.

She tried to settle herself. 'Tomorrow morning. There's a car coming, it will take us to the airfield.' She lifted her voice, 'It'll be exciting, a small plane. Not many people get to go in a small plane.'

'Are you excited?' Tommy chipped in.

'Yes, I'm a…bit nervous too, but I'm excited,' she lied. 'You'll meet some new people. Carly, she'll pick us up. And my friend Anne will be there. We'll all look out for each other.'

A knock rapped at the door, and Emma swung around.

Kate poked her head around the door. 'Just wanted to have a peak. You in your new suits,' she said in a stage whisper. She slipped into the room, flipping the door closed with her hand. 'Look at you two.' She gave a smile as she eased up to them.

She stood, looking at them in turn. 'We love you lots, you know that.'

The boys nodded.

'See you in a few days,' Kate looked at Emma.

Kate tried a smile, but her face looked cracked and brittle. She seemed to try to say something then turned and slipped silently from the room.

Chapter 23

Saturday

Amsterdam

Anne Perry let the sounds of the bar wash over her. The burry lilt of Dutch voices, the ting of glassware cutting through the laughter chattering out beneath the low ceiling. She could smell the sweetness of frothing beer pumps, the silk-smoky tang of burning candles.

She looked up at the bar, at David's outline silhouetted against the rows of glinting bottles arrayed against the mirrored wall. She kept her eyes on him as he tapped his card against the reader, his shoulders bobbing as he bantered with the barman. She put on a smile, willing the warmth of the place to seep into her but her stomach felt cold and tight. Her gaze drifted to the table as she reached for her glass and drained it in one, feeling the peaty spirit glide down her throat, settling on the chill emptiness inside her.

She snapped the smile back on her face as David turned and sauntered back towards her, his lively eyes searching out hers.

'All set?'

She glanced at her phone and gave a little frown. 'Past one,' she tutted, 'late, late.'

David swiped up her coat, holding it out for her.

She stood, sliding her arms into the sleeves as David

settled it onto her shoulders, smoothing it down with his hands.

She could feel his fingers just lightly squeezing her as his hands slid away. She imagined for a moment some memory stirring in her, then the numbness returned.

She slung her bag over her shoulder and began to pick her way through the groups of rosy-faced drinkers, their animated voices rising and falling, Dutch ringing around her.

David reached ahead of her and held the door open as she stepped out into the Amsterdam night, the air chill on her skin. She could hear the noise of the bar fading as the door shut and the quiet settled around them.

They stood, their backs to the bar, looking out across the canal, at the old merchants' houses lining the narrow roadway, their steep gabled roofs rising up from dark brickwork, unlit windows edged with the glow of nearby street lamps.

She inhaled the salty smack of the canal, its dark, sluggish water washing against the mossy stonework.

'God, it's the same everywhere,' David murmured.

She followed his gaze across the bridge to the hoarding boards ringing the junction, pictures of earnest looking engineers in high-vis jackets standing beside towering storm pipes. She felt her chest tightening as she looked up at a crane, its outline cold and sharp against the sombre, drifting sky. She let out a long, slow breath. 'We should get back.'

A seagull cried out from somewhere above them, its

rackety call muffled by the night.

David looked at the gull, 'a seaman's ghost, calling for his mates.' He looked across at her. 'That's what they say, isn't it?'

She kept her gaze on the crane.

'A passing spirit…or a coming death,' said David following her eyes.

She felt the hairs on her neck go hard. 'Don't say that.'

'Don't tell me you're superstitious.'

Anne felt a single raindrop grazing her cheek. 'We really should go.'

He spun around, laughing as he threaded his arm through hers. 'Let's explore, get happily lost.' She could feel his warmth as he nestled his shoulder against hers.

'It's going to rain.'

'Of course it is.'

'Really, we should get back.'

He unthreaded his arm and stood in front of her. 'Anne.' He gave her his winning smile. 'When did you last do something fantastically stupid?'

'I do stupid things every day.'

'I don't believe you.'

She wanted to snap at him but said, 'and stop giving me that look.' She gave a mock frown.

He raised an eyebrow, 'you no like?'

She sighed 'I'd *like* to get back.' A gust of wind bustled

around them. She shook her shoulders. 'I'm cold.'

'Here, have my scarf.' He began to unravel it.

'David.' Her tone was hardening.

'Are we having our first argument?' He gave a grin.

She fixed him a look.

'It's official.' He chuckled. 'I'm an arse.'

She tried a smile.

He looked around. 'You know, I actually have no idea where we are.'

'Just down here.' She turned and began to walk, David slipping in beside her, his hands deep in his coat pockets.

'Thought you said you barely knew the place.'

'Boring cop thing.' She looked down the narrow street, at the red brick houses, the white window frames, the fizzing light from the bars, their striped awnings rippling in the night breeze.

He threw her a friendly glance. 'You really a cop?'

'You think I'd make that up?'

'Fair point.' He paused. 'You a good one?'

'What kind of question is that?'

They walked in silence, beneath the cheery beer signs in reds and yellows, towards the murmur of voices from a small group idling on the bridge spanning the canal ahead of them.

Anne found her gaze drifting upwards, above the slate roofs and ornate gables to the clock tower of the church, keeping watch above the Old Town, its steeple piercing the dark sky. She sensed movement, just at the edge of her vision. Then she heard it, the steady, low hum of the police drone as it powered out of the cloud bank and disappeared behind the skyline.

They stepped out of the dimly-lit street and onto the bridge, past the jumble of bikes chained to the railings, the lights of the junction glinting on the inky water beyond.

She tried to relax her shoulders as she slipped her arm through his. 'Just…these cobbles…', she muttered as she felt him gently settling his arm around hers.

'I love cobbles…' He gave a chuckle.

She tried to focus on the rhythm of their steps, padding out on the slick roadway, the distant noise of traffic rumbling around them. She could sense herself tensing as wisps of cannabis smoke drifted over them.

'Hey, you're on holiday.' He mock-scolded her.

She gave a weak laugh. 'I know, I just hate the smell.'

'So…' he let his shoulder brush hers, '…good cop? Or bad cop?'

'Does it make a difference?'

'Tell me you're bad.'

'Don't say that.'

'I meant it as a compliment.'

She let his words hang.

'Actually, I don't know why I said that.'

She glanced up at him. 'Sorry, I'm…tired.'

'God…what's my excuse?'

She tried a smile. 'It was a fun night.'

He looked down at her, a broad grin lighting his well-made face. 'I can't believe we're really here.'

She squeezed his arm as they walked on in silence, the grand old houses rising sternly above them, their broad sash windows and tall doorways framed in ivy and wisteria. They passed a row of antique shops, their sober lighting of orange and yellow glowing on the polished wood of the window displays.

They stepped out from the quiet shadows onto the airy canal bank, the gusting wind tugging at their coats.

They both looked up as a squawking gull swooped down from the moonless sky, skimming over the sluggish, black water, its wings beating without effort.

She could hear him take a deep breath. 'God, something about this place.'

She swallowed, sensing again the hungry, prowling water all around her. 'The water, it's…everywhere,' she whispered.

'Can you feel it?' His voice was rising. 'It's like a…force, lifting you up, the fresh, salty air, whipping around the streets, the canals…' He took another breath. 'It's…alive!'

The air around them seemed to tremble as the bell of the Westerkerk tolled across the slumbering city; a single, mournful clang echoing over them.

She shivered, her eyes fixed on the pool of light thrown down by the street lamps on the bridge, as their steady footsteps beat out their approach. She could feel her stomach knotting as they stepped onto the bridge and drifted into the crackling light. She forced herself to pull on his arm as she stopped and turned towards him.

Under the lights his face seemed at peace.

She reached up and lay a hand on his cheek; his skin felt soft and warm. She looked up at him, feeling the dull thud of her cold heart as she raised her lips to his.

He gently pressed his lips on hers.

She felt…nothing.

He slowly straightened up, a hint of a frown on his face. 'What was that?'

'I don't know, I just…'

He attempted a joke, 'I'm sorry but I'm not having that as our first kiss.'

'I…'

'If you could call it a kiss.'.

'It's been a long time,' she found herself saying.

'When it's time for our first kiss,' he gave a little smile, 'I want to feel my heart explode.'

She looked up at him. 'I'm sorry.'

'Never be sorry.'

'I'm not what I seem.'

He shrugged. 'No one is.'

Chapter 24

Amsterdam

Anne Perry stood in the doorway to the bathroom, her hotel room smudged with the milky grey light of early morning. She looked around, her chest tightening, her heartbeat thrumming in her ears. She found herself staring at the new heat pump, the steel cylinder glinting under the bright bathroom light, its shadow cast against the laminated wall, like a hanging predator. She looked across at the shower, the glass door hanging ajar, the taps gleaming. She pulled the towelling robe closer to her neck as she tried to steady her breathing. 'Sing.' She whispered to herself. 'Sing.'

She tried to hum something but her lungs felt frozen as she slipped the robe off and lurched into the shower, fingers fumbling for the taps.

****

She stumbled into the bedroom, the towelling robe wrapped tight around her, her wet feet padding on the carpet. She stood at the end of the bed, willing her pulse to settle as her gaze drifted around the unfamiliar surroundings. Her small suitcase lay open on the plain white sideboard, her handbag tilted on its side, a hairbrush and some keys spilling out onto the jumbled surface. She looked down at the unmade bed, a snarl of twisted sheets and bent pillows. By the side of the bed, her discarded pyjamas, still lying heavy with the night's cold sweat. 'God, just look at this,' she muttered.

She flinched as her phone began to ring, the sound echoing around the small, bare room. She looked down at it, carefully picked it up and lowered herself onto the side of the bed. 'Gemma.' she whispered.

'Mum, where the hell are you?'

'I'm just…'

'I popped by your flat just now, you had me worried.'

'Sorry, love, I should have said.'

'Said what?'

'I'm in Amsterdam.'

'You're where?'

'Amsterdam…Holland'

'Yes I know where Amsterdam is, but what are you doing there?'

'I'm here with a…friend.'

'A friend?'

'Someone I met…at the gym.'

'Someone?'

'Yes, someone…from the gym.'

Silence.

'*A guy?*'

'Yes, but it's not like…'

She could hear Gemma draw a breath.

'Really it's just…'

'*Mum, that's…great!*' Gemma was laughing excitedly. 'So,

what's his name? What's he like?'

'It's nothing like that, I mean…separate rooms, you know.' Anne found herself blushing.

'Mum, you don't have to explain.' The words were tumbling out. 'So, what's his name, this lucky guy?'

Anne felt butterflies in her stomach; was lost for words.

'When can we meet him?'

Anne forced herself to say. 'His name's David.'

'And?'

'Well, he's…nice.'

'You can't say that! That's a terrible thing to say!'

'Friendly then. Funny…fun.' Her voice was breaking.

'I'm *so* pleased for you, mum.'

'Early days, you know.'

'Can't wait to meet him.'

'Well…let's see.' She wiped away a tear. 'Back tomorrow.'

'Have a *great* time, mum. Love you lots.'

'Love you too.' Anne clicked off the phone, holding it tight to her chest as the tears flowed. 'I'm sorry,' she sobbed, 'I really am.' She drew in a ragged breath. 'You don't deserve this you…poor, decent man.'

She sat for a moment longer, staring down at her bare feet, the last droplets still glistening under the sharp light. She rose to her feet and walked slowly to the sideboard. She began to rummage in her handbag, slipped out the Diazepam foil and popped two pills onto the palm of her hand. 'Saturday,' she whispered as she placed them carefully in her mouth and swiped up the water bottle.

****

As she approached the table, David rose to his feet.

'You look beautiful.' He offered a genuine smile.

She found herself looking into his face: in the morning light his skin had a newly-scrubbed look to it, his tan set off by his light blue shirt. She could smell his aftershave cutting through the rich aroma of the fresh coffee rising off the breakfast table. She felt something tugging at her, like an old memory, before her mind snapped back to the present. 'That's sweet, but you really don't need to.'

'Never seen you in jeans before.'

'Hmm…'

'Sorry.' He held up his palms.

'It's OK.' Her tone sharper than she intended.

He looked perplexed.

'No, really, it's OK.' She tried a smile.

'I don't think half the time,' he offered as an apology.

She settled into her seat and began to unfold her napkin. 'So,' she opened, 'last night was fun.'

He studied her for a moment. 'You know, I can't get over how you pick it all up.'

'Pick what up?'

'The feel for a place, I mean, last night, it was like you were…home, or something.'

'Like I said, the cop in me…it's a curse really.'

'So, how did you sleep?' He asked

'Fine, thanks.' She began to pour a coffee. 'How about you?'

He seemed to hesitate. 'I could swear I heard somebody…last night.'

Self-conscious, she carefully put the coffee pot down.

He leant towards her. 'Somebody was…calling out, like they were…having a bad dream, or something.'

She shrugged, 'Amsterdam's a party city, always someone kicking off.'

'I was worried.' His expression suddenly serious. 'About you.'

'Me?' She attempted a laugh. 'I sleep like a dead woman.'

'Or maybe I just…dreamt it.'

'Maybe you did.'

The distant toll of the Westerkerk bell cut through the chatter of the breakfast room.

Anne reached across, laying her hand on his arm, feeling the chill sadness inside her. 'I meant it.' She tried a smile. 'What I said, about last night. About having fun.'

'Maybe it's not so complicated.' He was grinning now.

'I've got a busy head.' She squeezed his arm. 'So, what's the plan?'

He plucked out a piece of toast. 'How brave are you feeling?'

'I'm not getting on a horse.'

'How about bicycles?'

'You seen how they ride those things? It's like the wacky races.'

'We can check out the Amsterdam Woods. Get an appetite for Mahler.'

'Why not?' She took a sip of coffee.

'Just an idea.'

She glanced out at the busy swirl of the passers-by, 'be nice to be outside.'

He picked up the wicker basket from the table and began to rummage in it. 'God, look at this.' He was holding something up.

She turned to him.

'Nutella,' he snorted. 'Who the hell eats Nutella?'

'I dare you.'

'Go together?'

She chuckled. 'Go on then.'

He broke off a bit of toast, dipped it in and held it towards her.

She took it between finger and thumb.

'On three?'

'OK.'

'Three!'

She laughed as she popped it in.

Chapter 25

The West of England

The car swung into the aircraft hanger.

Emma clicked the window switch and the pane whirred down, the sound of the car's engine growling back at them from the towering steel walls.

In the centre of the cavernous space, a Gulfstream Jet stood, sleek and silent, the arc lights above glinting on the grey paintwork.

She could hear Andy and Tommy draw in a breath as they took in the scene.

'Pretty cool, eh?' Carly threw over her shoulder from behind the wheel, not quite masking the edge in her voice.

They pulled up by the office block at the back of the hanger.

The air in the car hung with a chill edge.

Emma turned to the boys, steeling herself. 'Stay here, we won't be a minute.'

She and Carly clambered out of the car and began to walk towards the jet, the still air around them heavy with the bitter taste of kerosene.

'Sebastian told me.' Carly spoke without turning, her voice unsteady. 'About the promise you made to Kate.'

Emma gently lay a hand on Carly's arm. 'Look at me.'

They stood in the painful silence.

Carly whispered. 'It wasn't your promise to make.'

Emma studied her face, feeling the cold numbness settling inside. 'Just tell me.'

Carly's eyes fluttered. 'You.' She seemed to hesitate. 'The boys.' Her voice began to crack. 'Or *a* boy.'

Emma tried to block the image searing into her mind.

'Nothing else matters.'

Carly's quiet words stung her like nettles.

'God, Carly.' Emma ached for her friend. 'Maybe it doesn't have to be that way.'

'I've had a while to think about it.' Carly drew a careful breath. 'You saved my life, after all.'

Emma squeezed Carly's arm. 'You don't owe me anything.'

'Maybe it's easier this way.' She set herself to smile but it wouldn't take.

Emma slowly wrapped her arms around her. 'We'll all come home, you'll see.' As they hugged she feel the tension bracing Carly's slight frame.

'You'll do well. You always do.' Carly rubbed a hand on Emma's back. 'Don't worry about me.'

'Sebastian spoke to me, about the boys. What really happened.' As she said the words Emma felt the nausea pricking in her throat.

Carly drew in air. 'I remember just after Finn told you about the...' She seemed to stumble on the word. 'When you asked me, about Tommy, about Andy, I didn't know whether I should tell you.' She swallowed. 'God, what's worse? Knowing what they would have gone through…' Carly cursed under her breath. 'But then I made a promise of my own. If I get out of this, I'm going to track those bastards down.' Her voice was sharp with anger. 'If this is what it takes to…save us, well…' She chewed the words. 'But people who do that, to children.' She gently eased her arms from Emma and looked into her face. 'If our world's worth saving, there can't be a place for…evil fucks like that.'

Emma met Carly's gaze. 'We'll do it together.'

Carly's eyes seemed to flash and a tired smile glided over her then faded into her hardening face. 'I'm glad it's you.'

They both turned towards the sound of footsteps as a stocky figure in an RAF flying suit clattered down the aircraft steps.

Carly swung towards him, a frown building on her face. 'Where's Hutton?'

The man looked blankly at her. 'Didn't Dispatch inform you?'

'Inform me of what?'

'He…had an accident.'

Emma and Carly flashed each other a look.

Carly snapped back. 'What accident?'

He looked from one to the other, hesitating. 'They were running a fire drill, there was some kind of…pressure surge in one of the hoses, it jumped out of the man's hand. Hutton was just…walking by.'

Emma looked again at Carly, the air around them chilling.

The man cleared his throat. 'Like a…steel spring. He didn't stand a chance.'

Emma felt the tightness in her chest as she turned to face Carly, the unsaid question hanging like a raised club.

'Five hours, less than five hours.' Carly hushed. 'We can't think about it.'

'I was told there were four of you.' The pilot spoke up.

Emma waved at the boys to join them.

'Come on,' Carly called across to them, 'there's some lunch on the plane.'

****

Emma stood by the pilot's shoulder, looking out through the windscreen at the dark clouds mustering below them, the only sound in the cockpit, the rumble of the engines as the jet bustled through the autumn sky. 'Is that the weather radar?' She indicated the screen to the right of the heading indicator.

'Looks pretty solid down there.' He adjusted the range setting, the screen still a swirl of purple jagged with yellow bursts of lightning strikes.

Emma could feel her hands clamming. 'How far out are we?'

'Forty nautical.' He glanced up at her. 'We need to start our approach.'

Emma looked down at the cloud layer, the grey surface

quivering with yellow darts of lightning. She felt the cold prick of fear scratching at her. 'Can't we go round it?'

He flicked the setting. 'Round what? Same for a hundred miles.'

Emma looked back into the cabin. Tommy and Andy were in the window seats, staring down at the grumbling storm.

Carly unclipped her belt and made her way forward, her eyes on Emma's. She ducked into the cockpit door. 'Is there a problem?'

'Just weather,' he said.

Carly looked down at the flickering clouds. 'That's not good.'

'If you want to make Amsterdam we need to start losing height.' The pilot glanced from one to the other. 'You might want to buckle up.'

Emma felt a shudder run through her.

Carly screwed up her face. 'What the hell.'

'I'm putting the seat belt sign on.' He raised his voice and the seat-belt lights pinged.

Carly tapped Emma's arm.

They began to walk back.

'I'll be OK once it starts,' Emma said quietly.

Emma took a deep breath and tried to fix a smile on her face as she leant in to the boys. 'How're you two?'

Andy turned towards her. 'The colours, it's…beautiful.'

Emma turned to Tommy. He was looking hard at her.

'It might get a bit bumpy,' Emma tried to sooth.

Fear now stained Tommy's face. 'I don't like this.'

Emma forced another smile as she checked their belts, then slumped into her seat in front of them, pulling the seat-belt tight as she stared down at the lighting flashes pulsing beneath the bulbous grey clouds.

She watched, her hands gripping the armrests, as the crackling grey mass began to edge up towards them.

No one spoke. The only sound now the steady whistling of the engines.

'Hold on.' The pilot called back.

Emma stifled a moan as the angry darkness poured towards them.

The plane seemed to slam into the clouds, the thump splitting the air as the aircraft began to shake, the engines shrieking.

Emma braced herself against the seat back, her feet wedged against the seat in front as the plane dropped again, levelling out with a crash, the airframe groaning as they bucked and shook, like they were riding an enraged rollercoaster.

'Auntie Carly says breathe!' Carly's mock-cheery tones fluttered around them before the plane suddenly flipped to one side, almost throwing them out of their seats, their stomachs in their mouths.

The inside of the plane seemed to fill with jabbing light as the electrics fizzed, the overheads signs pinging.

'What's that?!' Tommy shouted, petrified.

'It's alright!' Emma forced the words out. 'It's just the lightning, it can't hurt us!'

The plane lurched again, flipping onto the other side, hurling them round in their seats as it began to violently shake.

Emma felt every muscle in her body straining as she fought to keep herself wedged in her seat, her heartbeat running through her, her chest heaving.

'Everything alright up there, pilot?' Carly called out.

Another bang shuddered through the plane, smashing the air around them.

Tommy screamed.

'It's OK!' Emma called to him, as she forced herself to breathe.

'Talk to us!' Carly shouted at the cockpit.

'Bloody autopilot!' He called back through gritted teeth. 'The storm, it's screwing with the gyroscope! Can't seem to get the damn plane level!'

Emma felt fear jolting through her. 'Turn it off!' She roared, 'it must have got inside it!'

'In this weather?!' He roared back. 'Can't see a fucking thing and the altimeter's burnt out!'

The plane flipped again.

Emma threw out her hands, pushing them against the side of the plane as she tried to keep herself wedged in her seat.

'It's going to flip us over! Turn the fucking autopilot off!'

Carly bellowed.

The plane began to shake.

'Fuck it!' The pilot shouted.

The aircraft made a groaning sound as it slowly began to right itself, the engines screeching as they fought the swirling storm.

Another bang rang out as the electrics fizzed, the bitter smell of burnt plastic now seeping around them.

Emma whipped her fingers around her armrests, feeling the plastic digging into her palms. 'You boys OK?'

'I'm alright.' It was Andy.

'Tommy?'

'I want this to end!' He pleaded.

Light began to flit through the cabin.

Emma drew a gasp as she looked out the window. Daylight was edging through the thinning cloud.

'Hallelujah.' Carly wheezed.

They dropped out of the cloud and into the milky light as rivulets of rain began to streak the windows.

Emma looked down as the ground began to slide into focus. She could see the Amsterdam Bos, the dark water of the rowing lake raking through the woods, the city spires beyond, shrouded in rain.

Emma felt Carly's gaze on her and turned to face her.

As they looked at each other the unspoken question hung.

'Doesn't change anything,' Emma whispered.

'No. Nothing can now.'

Chapter 26

Amsterdam

David slipped off his backpack as the bike hire man circled the two rental bikes, eyeing them warily.

Anne lay the bike helmet on the counter, checked her phone and slipped it into her coat pocket. She could hear the sounds of the city through the open door: the thudding of traffic on cobblestones, the accordion from a nearby bar, the horn of a tourist boat as it pushed along the canal. A group of schoolchildren in maroon blazers bobbed past the window, their laughter floating around them.

The first toll of the Westerkerk's bell peeled through the afternoon sunshine. She counted the chimes, feeling the knots in her stomach tightening, the cold numbness draining into her mind. Five o'clock. She dug her nails into the palm of her hands as she turned towards David.

He was grinning at her. 'You ready for that big bastard of a Bohemian?'

She wanted to laugh but said. 'I guess so.'

'You know what goes best with Mahler?'

'Nurofen?'

'Pernod and popcorn.'

'I hate Pernod.'

'So do I.'

She steeled herself: for the row she had to create. 'I want to go back to the hotel.'

'Sure.'

'Now.'

Concern flashed on his face. 'Of course.'

She glared at him.

'OK, OK, we're going.' He bustled up to her.

She strode through the door and onto the street, the clatter of a passing tram clanging around them.

'Hey, wait, Anne!' He caught up with her, taking hold of her arm, worry now streaking his well-formed face. 'What's wrong?'

She wanted to hug him but said. 'This is bad idea, you're a bad idea.'

'What?'

'This whole thing,' she snapped at him.

'You're not making any sense. We had a great day, didn't we?'

'God, can't you just take a fucking hint.'

She could see the colour draining from his face. 'Where did this come from?'

'What was I thinking?'

'Please, just tell me what's wrong.'

'Me…you…everything…I don't know.'

'Look, look…' He was taken aback. 'I can understand if it's all a bit…I mean, you're right, what you said in the gym, we hardly know each other…'

'I can't do this!'

He looked at her for a moment, then his expression began to harden. 'I'm not stopping now.'

'Just leave me alone, will you!'

He took hold of her arm. 'I might play the fool.' He flung the words out. 'And maybe I am one. But I'm not a total idiot.'

'You know nothing about me!'

'I heard you last night, running from your nightmares.'

'Stop it!'

'And the way you walk this city…'

She glared at him.

'But I meant what I said, on the bridge last night.' He gripped her arm. 'We're all the same: secrets, whatever you call them…they make you real.'

She shook her head.

'And one day, you're going to have to stop running, and face them.'

She sneered, 'who the hell do you think you are?'

'I'm the stupid bloke in the gym who thinks you're gorgeous.'

She found herself staring into his face, feeling his concern, his warmth. She wanted to weep and confess everything but said, 'you just fucking don't get it!'

He slowly let go of her arm, his face slack. 'I'll be at the

Concert Hall…in case you change your mind.'

She hardened her face. 'Give the ticket to someone else.'

****

Anne Perry kept her gaze on the dockyard cranes as she headed north towards the waterfront. The tears had stopped and a cold emptiness seemed to fill her as she slowly walked the canal bank beneath the elm trees still heavy with rustling leaves. She looked across at the far bank, the old warehouses, their red-painted shutters tied back, looking down on the moored barges, their decks a jumble of plant pots and tattered wicker chairs.

She stopped at the junction, shoulders hunched, as she pulled a tissue from her pocket and blew her nose. She half turned, leaning her back against the red brickwork, letting her gaze drift upwards. A police drone was circling above the Old Town just beyond the rooftops, its grey gun barrel sharp against the blue sky. She felt her heartbeat beginning to trip as she stared at it hovering over the city, sensing its cold hunter's eye roaming the canal ways.

She straightened up and began to walk down the narrow street, her eyes drifting over the buildings as she passed beneath the cream-coloured balconies, the plain stone frontages looking course and bare amongst the pink and brown brickwork of the merchants' houses. In the distance she could hear the rumble of a plane as the voices of a laughing couple floated from an open window somewhere above her.

The broad sweep of the Docks opened ahead of her. She could see the buildings rising sharp and sheer on the far side of the road, apartment blocks in glass and steel, glinting in the sunshine.

She tried to keep her movements uncertain, somehow sensing AI's cold, tireless eyes everywhere: the web of CCTV cameras, the drones, the satellites. Her shoulders hunched as she stopped by the pedestrian lights. A group of cyclists rattled by, coats billowing behind them, bicycle bells jangling, the sound biting at her. She kept her eyes on the flashing red figure as she took a deep breath. She could smell the docks now, the smoky grit of exhaust fumes, the sour smell of fuel oil.

The lights clicked green and she walked carefully onto the crossing, the air around her juddering from the traffic.

She stepped onto the pavement in the shadow of a pale wall, its surface criss-crossed with creeping ivy. She could see the entrance to the tunnel just ahead of her and began to walk down the ramp, into the shadow of the underpass.

She reached the bottom and stopped.

She was looking down a long, narrow passageway, with yellow walls splashed with graffiti and small pools of water scattered across the stone floor. The air felt damp and unhealthy. She squinted as she adjusted to the glaring overhead lights. Then she saw it: the CCTV cone, hanging by its wires from its mounting, its cover smashed, the remains of the camera scattered in pieces beneath it. Relief.

She looked back up the ramp, the carved gables of the houses sharp against the clear sky. She stood, ears straining into the calm afternoon, listening for the tell-tale hum of the drone. The only sounds, the murmur of passing traffic and the lilting voices of passers-by.

She turned and set off down the passageway, her footsteps echoing in the stony quiet, her eyes fixed on the dark steel door set in the wall beneath the broken camera. She stopped beside it and turned, looking up and down the tunnel. She was alone. She reached for the keypad, carefully tapped in the code and pushed down on the shining steel of the handle.

She stepped into the dimly lit room and carefully closed the door behind her.

'Hello, Anne.' A tall man in a dark suit stepped out of the shadows and stood in front of her.

It was Sebastian Noon.

He drew himself upright, his aquiline features breaking into a smile. 'Are you ready?'

She took in a deep breath, 'are they here?'

'They're close.'

She nodded.

Sebastian flicked on his phone torch, turned and began to walk down the darkened corridor.

Anne set off behind him, flinching as a train passed overhead, the floor beneath her feet trembling. She tried to clear her mind, forcing away the image of David's stricken face, as she willed her mind back to the present: to the one cause.

They turned the corner. Anne could see the beam of Sebastian's torch roaming over the damp-streaked walls, lighting up the crumbling floor, the far reaches of the passageway hidden in darkness.

She could hear another noise now, a gurgling, slapping sound, echoing through the stonework. 'What's that?' She hissed.

He half-turned as he whispered. 'The wake from the harbour traffic.' He tapped his knuckles on the glistening brickwork. 'The dockside...solid enough.'

She shivered, trying not to think of the wall of dark, swirling water pressing in around them.

Sebastian flipped his torch towards a scratching sound.

Two large rats stood on their hind legs, framed in the silver light, staring back at them with beady pink eyes.

Sebastian stamped his foot and they scuttled into the darkness.

'Horrible, smelly things,' Sebastian muttered.

They walked on in silence, the rumble of the rail cars above them drumming through the steady crunch of their footsteps.

A doorway edged into view, its worn steel illuminated by the torch beam.

Sebastian tapped in a code and they stepped into an airy basement. He quietly clicked the door shut behind him.

They stood for a moment, Sebastian's flinty eyes roaming over her face.

She said nothing, her mind defiantly working.

'Shall we?' He nodded towards an open door on the far

side of the room, the brass handle gleaming under the amber wall lights.

They walked across the polished floor, their footsteps loud on the dark marble, their shadows dancing around them. A table stood in the centre of the room, its metal top shimmering under spot lights.

'Exactly as I remember it,' she whispered.

He carefully closed the door. 'In here, it can't see us, it can't hear us.' He paused. 'We could be the last free people on earth.'

'I can never be free. Not now.'

'Doing bad things to stop worse things.' He spoke quietly. 'You ever hear Emma say that?'

'A life is still a life.'

'*Is it?*'

Chapter 27

Amsterdam

N
o one spoke as they turned onto the canal side road. The weather had cleared, the brisk wind had chased the last of the storm clouds from the steely sky. Up ahead in the distance they could see the railway bridge, and beyond, the office blocks that fringed the docks, towers of blue and grey glass glowing in the fading sunshine.

Carly drove, Emma riding shotgun beside her, Andy and Tommy in the back.

Emma let her gaze rove around her. To their left, the canal, the brackish water rippling in the wind, the lumpy surface sprayed with leaves whipped down by the storm. On the far bank, the houseboats, their solid black hulls topped with brightly-painted cabins, the trailing plants lining the roofs tumbling down over the weather-streaked windows. She found her mind drifting around a memory, a trip from long ago, the street tripping by suddenly familiar. Then the sense of creeping dread sounded back in her like a dull gong. Coming up, on the far side of the canal, she could see the tops of pile-drivers spearing up behind the hoardings, photos of beaming engineers in hard hats standing proudly beside huge storm pipes splashed across them.

Something seemed to flash across the surface of the water.

She blinked, focused again. A shadow. A bird, maybe?

She kept her movements steady as she leant forwards looking up through the windscreen. Then she saw it. A police drone, slowly banking above them, a rotund white cone almost hanging in the clear sky, sharp grey gun barrels slung beneath it. Emma took an easy breath. 'Just so you know,' she spoke carefully, 'there's a drone just above us.'

Carly's hands gripped the wheel. 'What's it doing?'

Emma watched it circle. 'Just…looking, I think.' Emma kept her voice low as it drifted behind the clock tower and then began another slow sweep through the sky ahead of them. 'It doesn't seem in a hurry.'

Carly checked her speed. 'How long 'til we turn?'

Emma checked off the street names. 'Third…no, fourth right.' She looked back up, the drone was almost above the docks. She frowned, something was changing in the sky. Smoke was drifting up, maybe half a kilometre ahead of them. She watched it begin to plume, the smoke now thicker, darker. 'Maybe an accident.'

'This one?' Carly called.

Emma snapped her eyes back on the road. 'This is it.'

Carly eased the car around.

The road broadened out. The street now flanked by sober Victorian town houses, lattice windows glinting amidst the stonework.

Emma watched the smoke building from just beyond the bridge. She could smell the fire now, the vinegar sting of petrol and the sour smack of burning plastic. And something else, nagging at her senses.

They passed beneath the spindly iron trellis that spanned the narrow bridge, the tyres bumping across the wooden slats.

They turned into the square, and then they saw it.

A car was on fire. Flames licking over the charred panels, evil-looking dark smoke pulled apart by the wind. There was a figure inside the car, burning.

'Boys, look away!' Emma shouted.

The figure in the car was still moving, clothes melting, crackling as his arms thrashed. He was pinned in by airbags.

Emma gagged as the sickly smell of burning flesh oozed through the car.

A policeman stepped on to the road, flagging them down.

'What's this now?' Carly threw out.

As they pulled up he made the sign to lower the window.

Carly purred it down.

The policeman leant in, letting out a stream of Dutch.

'English,' Carly said quickly.

'You need to wait here, emergency services are coming through.'

Emma jolted. 'We can't wait here.'

'Turn off the engine.'

'Please, we have to go.'

He lay a hand on the door frame. 'Turn it off please,' he said forcefully.

Emma could see the drone cresting the roofs on the far side of the square. If the cameras swung on them now they'd see the boys' faces through the window. She swung back towards them. They were looking at the flaming car, their faces white with shock. 'Look away!' She yelled.

The policeman looked sternly at Carly. 'Did you understand what I said?'

'Please.' Emma leaned across to him. 'I've got two young sons in the back, they shouldn't have to see this!'

'Don't shout at me madam.'

'Please!' She keened as the drone rose above the square.

He muttered something then waved a hand. 'OK, go.'

Emma rounded on the boys. 'Don't you dare look!'

Carly clicked up the window as she steered the car around the square and through the archway that led to the courtyard. She pulled up beneath a concrete ledge that ran the length of the far side, beneath it, a solitary worn steel door set in the windowless brick wall.

Emma took a moment to settle herself, then turned to the boys. 'Sorry I shouted,' she gave a bent smile, 'I…got worried.'

Andy and Tommy stared at her as the tang of the fire began to clear from the air.

'It's going to be fine.' She grabbed at a wrist in turn. 'We're here now. The difficult bit's done.' She looked at them brightly. 'You did so well.'

'I screamed like a baby in the plane.' Tommy looked bitter.

'You did fine.' Emma patted his arm. 'It's OK to hate flying. I hate flying.' She squeezed his arm again. 'OK?'

Tommy eased his face. 'OK.'

'Good, good, good.' Emma looked at them in turn, nodding slowly. 'Now you remember what to say, when you see Anne?'

They both nodded vigorously.

She smiled, 'So, when we get inside we'll meet up with Tariq, we'll need to walk for just a little while. It'll be dark but we've got torches. We'll all stay together. Alright?'

They nodded again.

'Before we go in, you know what to do?'

More nods.

'OK, nice and quick.' All four of them slung open the doors.

They walked briskly towards the arch that spanned the entrance to the courtyard, then stopped, the two boys looking up at the CCTV camera, its red light, blinking steadily: sowing the seed in the great mind.

'That's it!' Emma shouted.

'You go!' Carly screamed at them, shoving Emma and the two boys as they spun around and began sprinting towards the door set in the brick wall beneath the concrete awning, their running feet cracking on the ground.

As Emma ran she could hear the purr of the drone's engine building to a whine. She threw a look over the shoulder. Carly had spun back around, her gun levelled at the sound of the drone screeching from beyond the rooftops.

'Carly, come on!' Emma yelled as she hurled herself back around, stumbling as she threw herself across the last few yards, pushing at the backs of the two boys as the three of them clattered towards the rusting door in the shadow of the concrete ledge.

Emma crashed open the door and bundled they boys in. 'Keep going!' She urged. 'I'll be right behind!'

As she stood just inside the doorway Emma pivoted around. Carly was backing towards her, gun still aimed at the far rooftops. 'Carly, we're in, let's go!' Emma screamed again.

The drone leapt over the gable roofs on the far side of the square then swung down towards them, Carly now scrambling towards Emma, ducking her head as she ran.

Emma flattened herself against the passage wall as she pulled out her gun and emptied the magazine at the glinting nose cone of the snarling, juddering drone as the tracer bullets began to spew from its gun barrels.

The first rounds slammed into the concrete awning above her, as Emma tried to shield her eyes from the shards of stone puffing around her like a mist of needles. She threw up a hand to her face, as her eyes sought Carly through the fizzing dust.

Carly's face appeared through the splintery cloud.

Emma gasped. There was something wrong, Carly's face was hanging off her, her eyes pools of darkness. Carly's body was off the ground now, hurtling towards her, lifted up by the bullets pouring into her. Her friend was a human missile!

Emma threw the door shut, crashing the bolt across as the sickening sound of Carly's body slamming into the door, bones splintering, speared through Emma.

She forced herself around, squeezing the cold anger into her as she flicked the torch on and ran towards the boys cowering at the end of the passageway.

Emma thumped down beside them. 'Look at me.' She shone the torch on her own face then at their pale, stunned faces. 'We're all OK.' She patted their shoulders in turn. 'It can't get us now.'

The air around them seemed to split as rounds clawed at the steel door clanging like demonic bell-ringers.

Emma kept her movements steady and her voice calm as she let her fury chase off her nerves. 'Come on, follow me!' She gritted.

They began to trot down the darkened passageway, her light beam roving over the crumbling concrete floor, flashing over the peeling stone walls, their hasty footsteps crunching around them.

A boom shook the air, then the shrieking, tearing noise of metal on metal. The drone was muscling, heaving at the buckling door.

'Come on, come on!' Emma roared as they scrambled towards the turning just ahead of them, hurling themselves around the corner.

Another door loomed out of the darkness. Emma lunged at the panel beside it, stabbing in the code, as the sound of ripping steel wailed around them.

Emma snatched the door open and they staggered in behind her.

Emma slammed it shut.

They all pulled up, their chests heaving in the muted light from the single bulb hanging above them in the small, bare room.

Tariq Ahmed stood, taking them in. 'Are you alright?'

Emma nodded.

Emma felt the cold space beside her where Carly should have been as Tariq met her gaze, just for a moment, as the unspoken words passed between them. There would be a time, but for now there was only the mission.

Tariq spoke again. 'I heard gunfire.'

Emma let the cold focus drip through her like melting ice. 'It saw the boys' faces, the drone lashed out.' Her mind turned again. 'There was a car in the square. It was burning, there was a man trapped inside.'

'Sebastian needed to be sure.' Tariq nodded. 'A journalist he knows. Sebastian rang him in London, told him he was going to meet a contact here in the city. Someone who knew who, or what was behind the attacks at the NSA Centre.' He paused, some pain in his face as the brutal truth behind his words dropped around them 'Looks like Sebastian got AI's attention.' He drew in a deep breath. 'It's time.'

Emma, Andy and Tommy nodded.

No one spoke as Tariq walked towards another door and knocked once on it.

Chapter 28

Amsterdam

Anne Perry jolted as a rap on the door splintered the silence.

Sebastian Noon glanced at her. 'Are you ready?'

Anne looked at him, fear stirring inside her. 'What do you want me to say?'

Sebastian said nothing.

They took out their phones, clicked the record buttons and placed them on the metal table.

He walked to the door and opened it.

Four figures made their way silently into the room. Sebastian closed the door behind them.

They stood in the half-shadows just beyond the pool of light framing the table: Tariq, Tommy, Andy and Emma.

Emma stared at Anne, her eyes widening. 'Anne, what the *hell* are you doing here?'

Anne looked across at Tommy. 'Hello again.'

Tommy raised a hand. 'Anne.'

Anne turned to Andy. 'Did you bring it?'

Andy nodded. 'The one you gave her last time, sure.'

Emma screwed up her face. 'You *know* each other?'

Anne breathed slowly. 'We've met.'

Emma spluttered. 'Wh…how?'

'Here, in this room.' Anne looked at Tommy, then back at Andy. 'A week ago.'

Emma slowly turned towards the boys. 'But you've....never been to...'

Anne spoke. 'Andy has a letter that you need to read.'

'What?!'

Andy pulled an envelope from his pocket and held it out to Emma.

Emma stared at it. 'What is this?'

'It's a letter, from me, to you,' said Anne.

'To me?'

'I wrote it five days ago.' She kept her eyes on Emma. 'I know this never set in your memory, but...you've seen it before.'

'What are you talking about?'

'It was this meeting. The same meeting. Exactly as we are now.'

Emma looked incredulous, 'Sebastian...what the hell is this?'

He indicated the letter. 'Just read it, Emma.'

She shook her head as she pulled it from the envelope.

'Aloud,' Sebastian ordered, 'all of it.'

Emma began. 'London, Monday 12th September.' She looked up. 'Last Monday.'

Anne kept her eyes on Emma. 'You need to read it.'

Emma drew in a breath. 'Emma, I'm going to let two men

die.' Emma shook her head. 'This doesn't make any...'

'Go on.' Sebastian cut in.

Emma stared at the words. 'Simon Yarrow and Peter Moynes are going to die tomorrow, and even if I wanted to, I know I can't save them.'

Emma stared at Anne. 'You wrote this?'

Anne flinched as the image of Peter Moynes' shattered face burned back into her mind.

'But...how could you know any of this?'

Anne said nothing, willing the blank darkness back into her head.

'Unless...' Emma slowly turned towards Sebastian. 'You?' Her voice was trembling.

He shook his head.

'But...' Emma looked back at Anne, '...if you knew they were going to...' Her voice trailed off.

Anne felt a sadness welling in her. 'No...I couldn't.'

'But you'd try and save them, I *know* you would.'

A shudder ran through Anne. 'They had to die.'

'Why?'

'Because...they were already dead.'

'What...five days ago? They were alive!'

Anne raised her voice. 'You don't understand. I'd seen the future. They were dead. Dead!'

'But couldn't you...?'

'How could I?' Anne's voice was cracking. 'In a day they'd be dead. How could I help them if they were going to be dead anyway?'

'So you just…waited for them to die?'

Anne shouted. 'I had to!'

Emma glared at her. 'If any of this was even true you could have…' She snarled. 'They didn't *have* to die! You could have stopped it! The future hadn't happened, you could have changed it!'

'No!' Anne's voice was rock hard. 'You can't change the future! Think about it, Emma! If you've seen the future, if you know what the future's going to be, *that* is the future!'

'But you could have changed the future! Look at you, you're in pieces about this! About having to let them die! If you hadn't seen the future then you wouldn't have had to stand by and let them die. You wouldn't be feeling guilt now!'

'But that's it!' Anne gritted. 'It's where I am. Now! It's real. This is what my future is. I didn't know it, but this was always going to be my future. My fucking horrid future!'

Emma shook her head. 'No…no…this isn't happening.'

Anne felt a shudder run through her. 'I'd do anything…'

'But you!' Emma snapped at Anne. 'I thought I knew you.'

'You do,' Anne's voice was shaking.

'How could you?' Emma snarled.

A sob racked through Anne. 'I've just told you.'

'But *you*,' railed Emma.

Anne moaned, her stomach heaving. 'God forgive me.'

Sebastian leant forward and clicked off the recordings.

Emma looked across at Anne.

'I'm sorry,' Anne found herself saying.

Emma stepped towards Anne and lay a hand on her shoulder. 'Anne, you don't have to be sorry.'

'I can't help it, it's what I feel.'

'I know.' She leant in towards Anne. 'God, what a brave, terrible thing you had to do.'

'I need to make a call.' Sebastian slipped the phones into his pocket. 'Wait here.' He looked across at Tariq. 'You'll know what to do.'

****

Sebastian Noon stepped out of the elevator and walked into the meeting room. Through the glass wall he could see the harbour, the lights from the dockside cranes rippling on the glinting water, the warehouses beyond standing squat and dark. A ship's horn sounded, a low moan drifting along the shoreline.

He sat at the head of the conference table. He was alone.

He clicked on the console and it flickered into life.

Carefully he dialled a number.

A man's voice answered. 'This is Bowman.'

'I have...something,' Sebastian began.

Silence on the line.

'It's happened…again.'

He could hear Bowman's steady breathing. 'And you're sure?'

'Judge for yourself.' Sebastian clicked on the recording.

They could hear the sound of footsteps, the 'tick' of the closing door then Emma's voice, sharp with shock. 'Anne, what the *hell* are you doing here?'

****

Sebastian tensed: he sensed a shadow moving through the sky beyond the glass wall as the recording neared its close.

'How could you?' Emma snarled.

A sob racked through Anne. 'I've just told you.'

'But *you*,' railed Emma.

Then Anne's broken voice. 'God forgive me.'

A click sounded out.

Then silence.

'There and back.' Bowman let out a whistle. 'Poor woman…to have seen all that…'

Sebastian's eyes widened as a police drone broke through the clouds and began to swoop towards the building, its fins sharp against the moonlit sky, its gun barrel deadly as a scorpion sting.

Sebastian hurled back the chair and ran for the door as the glass wall splintered, the air filling with the blast of machine gun fire and breaking glass. He threw himself to the floor, bullets smacking into the wall above him.

He could hear a thudding, cracking sound as he scrambled across the floor, glancing over his shoulder. The drone was muscling through the shattered glass, its engine screeching.

Another burst of gunfire hammered into the room.

Sebastian cried out as a bullet slammed into his hand, then another smashing his forearm.

He rolled through the doorway and onto his back, kicking the door closed as the drone twisted and crunched its' way through the last tatters of splintering glass.

The door shook as more bullets rattled through it, the air fizzing with shards of wood. The raw smell of cordite wrapping around him.

A ping sounded as the lift door began to open.

'Get down!' Sebastian roared as two security guards thumped onto the floor by the open lift, their eyes wide with shock.

More bullets sprayed above them, battering the door to the stairwell.

The two guards scrambled back into the lift.

'No, no no!' Sebastian screamed as he heaved himself towards them. 'Not the lift!'

A slicing, popping sound cut through the sudden stillness as the lift cables snapped.

The screams of the guards echoed through the hallway, their cries fading into the lift shaft as the lift car slammed downwards.

A boom rang out as the lift crunched into the basement buffers, the floor juddering with the impact.

Sebastian jolted as more bullets tore around him, the office door crumbling, as the snarling barrel of the drone ripped through the broken wood.

He crawled to the stairwell, edging past the door hanging crookedly from its hinges and began to stumble down the stairs, cradling his broken arm, bullets ripping through the air above him.

He grabbed for the handrail as the lights went out.

He leant against it, clawing at his pockets. 'Shit, shit!' His fingers closed around his phone. He flicked the torch to life and began to step down the stairs.

He jumped as a bang sounded just above him, then another, further down the stairwell, then another.

He flicked the beam around him, bitter, acrid smoke was drifting through the stairwell, billowing and thickening.

He held his sleeve to his mouth as he hobbled down the next flight, the smoke glowing with the fires of the blazing fuse boxes.

He stumbled, slipping onto his knees, the smoke roiling around him.

'I've got you!' A hand shot out of the smoke, grasping Sebastian's wounded arm.

Sebastian shouted in pain.

'Alright, alright.' Tariq gunned out the words as he took Sebastian's good arm and pulled him to his feet. 'We've got to move!' Tariq pulled him across to the next flight, his torch beam fizzing through the smoke.

They clattered down the stairway.

'Wait, wait!' Tariq hauled him up.

They stood, eyes smarting as they stared at the shattered door to the lobby, the thinning smoke drifting around them.

'Ground floor,' Tariq said, 'there's a drone...' He nodded towards the stairway past the shredded door. 'Can you run?'

Sebastian nodded as he bent forward, chest heaving as he fought for his breath.

'Come on!' Tariq tugged him down the last few steps and they scrambled across the doorway.

They crouched as bullets slammed into the masonry just above them.

Tariq jolted as he tore at Sebastian's jacket, wrenching him down the stairway as more bullets cracked above them.

They leant against the iron banister, trying to catch their breath.

'My God.' Sebastian was staring at Tariq's chest, his shirt soaked in blood.

Tariq looked down at it, his face pinching. He began to pat his chest. 'It's just...' He flinched. 'Splinters...from the wall...I'm OK.'

Emma's voice cut through from below them. 'Sebastian?'

'I'm alright, Emma.' He coughed.

They eased their way down the final flight into the basement lobby, stepping over the bent and twisted lift doors, the broken bodies of the guards lying on the buckled floor of the lift cage.

The door to the meeting room was open, the silver light sprayed across the dark marble of the lobby floor, glistening on the broken bits of metal scattered around them.

They stepped into the room, four pairs of anxious eyes roving over them.

Sebastian reached out with his good arm and quietly closed the door.

'Just…cuts.' Tariq looked across at them then glanced at Sebastian. 'We should get back to the tunnel. You know we're not safe here.'

Emma stepped towards Sebastian. 'Let me take a look.'

He shook his head. 'It's broken…and my…' he looked down at his shattered hand and winced, 'it can wait.'

Emma lay a hand on his shoulder.

'We need to-' Tariq's eyes blazed as a new noise reached them from beyond the dockside wall.

No one spoke as they all stood, ears straining into the watery darkness as the noise began to take a shape. A rumbling, sloshing sound and then the unmistakeable chomp of engine pistons began to beat through the stonework.

'*Oh, my God*,' Anne whispered.

Chapter 29

Utah, USA

B
rian sat on the bed, his open laptop on his
knees.

Through the rumble of early morning traffic he
could make out voices from down the corridor,
yawing and fading around him in the dim stillness of the
motel room.

He pulled the blanket tighter around his shoulders as he
re-read the email:

Dear Mr Wise,

*It has been brought to our attention that your name appears on a
database of patients who have been proscribed controlled pain
management drugs from multiple Medical Practitioners. In the light
of this, we are suspending your current prescriptions from this
practice with immediate effect and until further notice....*

He looked up, his gaze drifting to the window, the
abandoned office block across the highway lying dark and
useless in the morning light, its outline smudged behind
the dirty pane.

He drummed his fingers on the edge of the laptop as he
looked down at the bin squatting in the shadows by the
wall: the pill bottle lying on the crumpled pizza box, the
red lettering fierce against the white plastic.

He tensed as he began to type:

'Dear Doctor Wyatt,

There has obviously been a misunderstanding. My name is a very common one and this is clearly a case of mistaken identity.'

He screwed up his face and carried on:

'The only thing that has worked to ease my back pain is the Vicodin. This pain is the result of injuries that I sustained whilst serving my country through three tours. Without it my life is a blur of pain. Us veterans deserve better.'

He glanced at the phone lying beside him, the screen dull and lifeless.

He sighed, and clicked 'send'.

He looked around the bare room, then closed his eyes and brought his hands together. *'Dear Lord, please give me the strength to finish this,'* he silently intoned. *'You know, Lord, how I love those I've been made to hurt. Help them forgive me Lord, as you forgive me. Amen.'*

****

Brian stepped through the doors to the Control Room and flinched. The air was still sharp with the bite of bleach, he felt his eyes smarting.

Slowly he walked towards his console. He looked over at Chris' station, just behind his own. On the deserted desk, a small posy of red, white and blue flowers in a simple white vase, Chris' NSA lanyard neatly folded beside it.

Brian stood for a moment, imagining again their last moments. The unspoken horror as they watched the steel safety shutters crash down: a last few helpless breaths as the Nitrogen squeezed the life from their lungs. He shuddered.

'They found them both, at their consoles,' Mike's hoarse voice behind him.

Brian said nothing.

'Until the last, they made sure the portals were…,' Mike's voice trailed away.

'So what the hell did happen?'

'Some kind of software glitch, that's what they're telling us.'

'That's just crap.'

'They'll never say it but…'

Brian drew in a breath. 'Just what the fuck is this?'

'It's…different, God knows we've mapped the hell out of all the Chinese sequences, GRU too.'

Brian shook his head.

'No one's even got close before…I mean to get into the damn air control…and the fucking drone.' Mike winced. 'Jesus, if Chris and Larry hadn't…'

Brian swallowed. 'Makes me feel small, that's the truth.'

'You never know, if you got that in you.'

'Wouldn't have had Chris down as the guy.'

'But they fucking did it, man.'

Brian nodded slowly, 'amen.'

Mike turned towards him. 'Goes for us both, I guess…I mean, on a different day, maybe I would have stayed.' He fixed Brian a look. 'And maybe you'd have stopped that doctor.'

Brian met his eyes. 'Maybe.'

Mike took a deep breath. 'You sure you're good?'

Brian bristled. 'I'm sharp, man.'

'There's a rumour you're taking.'

'Rumours fuck!'

Mike studied Brian's face. 'Missing those threads yesterday. I mean, it's like you were…sleepwalking.'

'I'm on this, man!'

Mike nodded. 'Just…well, it's going to be a long day.'

****

The wail of the siren blared around the Control Room.

'Brian!' Mike's urgent voice in his earpiece.

'I got it! I got it! Just let me…' Brian fingers rattled over the keyboard as he prepped the casements, eyes fixed on the screen for the first threads, his breathing quickening.

Out of the corner of his eye he could see the PROBE SURGE warning flashing on the main communications screen.

'Come on, come on!' Brian ground his teeth as he watched the casements slot into sequence.

'Here they come!' Mike shouted.

The air around him shook with the babble of raised voices as the first threads tumbled onto his screen.

Brian hammered at the keys as he herded the first wave of threads into his clearing box.

'Don't look for tripwires! Just box them all!' Mike roared.

'I got it!' Brian snarled as he began to whip the pulsing threads into the casement stacks, their active code lines fizzing.

'I need more casements!' Brian shouted, his eyes darting across the screen as the captive threads swirled, their jump lines dissembling and re-assembling as they bit at the casement walls.

'I'm on it! You watch the in-stack!' Mike's voice now edged with fear.

Brian blinked as he tried to focus, his eyes smarting.

A new thread dropped onto the screen. Brian jolted as the taper markers lit the jump sequences. 'They're pairing already!' Brian fingers beating the keys. 'I need those casements!'

'Just keep going!' Mike's words tripping out.

Brian cursed as he tried to pin the thread, the mutating helixes pulling at the code lines as they tried to split from the core. Brian hacked at the keys as he dragged the thread into the dead space, the magnetic envelope bulging and creasing as the first lance sequences tore into it.

Two more threads crashed onto his screen. 'Mike, I need back up!'

'I'm mirrored! You take the top one I'll sweep the second!'

Yet more threads slid into his in-stack.

'I can't hold it!' Brian roared.

The Control Room siren again screamed around them.

'BREACH ALERT! BREACH ALERT!' The Shift Leader's shouts cutting through the clamour beating in Brian's ears.

Brian's breathing began to quicken again. 'Shit, Mike!'

'Keep going!'

'I…can't…' Brian gasped, his chest shaking as ragged breaths stuck in his throat.

'Brian!' Mike was screaming in his ear.

Brian let out a groan as he fell forward, his forehead bumping against the override panel, his headset tumbling to the floor.

Brian lay panting, his head on the keyboard as the Override Alarm tore through the room.

He could hear the panicked voice of the Shift Leader. 'Flood all systems! Flood all systems!'

Brian closed his eyes, letting the swirl of raised voices and clattering keyboards wash over him.

He tensed as a new voice boomed out over the PA system. 'All operators, stand down! Breach Team now deployed!'

The room erupted, a hubbub of confused voices and now, a new sound beating through the air, a roar building, something moving beneath their feet, the floor trembling.

'It's in! It's in!' The shouts tearing around him.

The roar was building, a rumbling, tumbling sound like an avalanche, the floor shaking.

The sirens blared again. 'BREACH CONFIRMED!

EVACUATE! EVACUATE!'

Brian lay there, the air filled with yelling voices and the clatter of running feet. 'Get out! Get out! Get out!' The Shift Leader screamed.

Chapter 30

Amsterdam

The watch officer on the LNG tanker moored on the far side of the Amsterdam Harbour, lay down his iPad as his eyes began to search.

He could hear the ships engines rumbling into life, the floor of the bridge juddering as the turbines began to spin.

He leapt to his feet, swiping up the hand mic from the control panel. 'Who's in charge down there?'

'It's me, Donno!' The man was shouting over the thunder of the revving engines.

'Why we firing them up?'

'We didn't!'

'Wh-'

'They just…started up!'

'Well shut them down!'

'We can't!' Donno's voice was desperate.

'Throw the main power switch!'

'I have! They won't shut off!' Donno was screaming.

The watch officer lurched against the panel as the huge vessel surged backwards. He cursed as he dropped the hand mic and ran to the bridge door, shouting down the stairway. 'Mooring party! Get on deck! We need to slip those hawsers!'

Footsteps rang out on the steel gangway as four figures sprung onto the deck, two headed forward and two aft.

The vessel lurched back again as the engines strained against the steel cables quivering around the dockside stanchions.

He grabbed the deck PA hailer. 'Slip them ship-side! We need sea room!'

A crack rang out as the aft cable snapped, the ship-side end scything across the deck, catching the aft deck hands at waist height, slicing through them, then clanging against the steel side of the aft quarters, buckling the steel panels.

The two deck hands crumpled onto the deck, faces blank with shock, blood pooling around their severed bodies.

The watch officer stared at them, his mouth opening and closing.

The engines began to roar again as he swung around. 'Get down!' he screamed at the forward deck hands.

They threw themselves onto the deck as another crack rang out, the forward cable whipping into the deck crane, wrenching it from its bedding, hurling it against the cable drums, the sound of tearing steel screeching around them.

The vessel began to tremble as it backed away from the dock, engines roaring.

The watch officer scrambled into the bridge house,

throwing himself at the controls, straining to pull back the throttles.

The ship eased its way into the channel, the engines slowing as the gears whirred then engaged with a crunch. The propellers began to spin, biting into the churning water, as the vessel strained to heave itself forward.

As the prow began to swing around, the watch officer let out a roar, grasping the wheel with both hands. He fought to stop it turning, feet braced on the bridge floor, his whole body quivering, his hands slipping on the wheel. 'No!' He groaned as the wheel turned in his powerless hands, the ship now facing the dockside on the far side of the channel, the pitch of the engines rising as it began to muscle its way through the water.

He snatched up the shore comms mic. '*Harbour Master, Harbour Master, come in!*'

A crackle. 'Harbour Master here. Go ahead.'

'This is the MV Osiris! We have lost control of the vessel! Steering gear not responding! We are heading towards the Wester Dok!'

'Do you require tug assistance?'

'We're heading towards the Wester Dok! Engines at maximum thrust! I can't stop her!'

'I'll sound the alarm.' The Harbour Master's voice was suddenly quiet.

The watch officer leant on the ship's horn, his pale face slackening, as the vessel beneath him ploughed through the harbour water, its bow wave frothing. He could see the figures on the dockside now, some frozen, staring at the oncoming tanker, others running from the walkway, their shadows darting under the fizzing street lamps.

He crossed himself as he closed his eyes.

****

They stared at the basement wall, the air shaking with the drumming of ships engines, the floor vibrating.

Anne Perry let out a moan, cold fear rising in her, her brain screaming at her to run. She dug her nails into her palms. 'We've got to get out!'

Emma shot a look across the wrecked hallway, at the fierce coiling smoke drifting down the stairway, burning her eyes.

'The drones are in the lobby!' Tariq shouted. 'Stairs are no good! We've got to use the tunnel!'

Anne Perry felt nausea rising in her, imagining the wall of dark, swirling water crashing over them, squeezing the air from her: its cold, crawling death filling her lungs.

'Wait!' Emma grabbed Tariq's arm, as the drumming of the engines built into a booming hammering cacophony of noise, driving at their eardrums, the air quivering. 'If it hits the tunnel!'

'The hallway!' Sebastian roared. 'When it hits, we'll know!'

As they ran through the doorway, the air around them seemed to screech with the crack of splintering stone, the bucking floor throwing them tumbling onto the shattered tiles.

Anne scrambled to her feet, her bloodied hands stinging as she threw herself towards the stairway, the bitter smoke biting her throat. She could sense blurred figures beside her as a crashing, tumbling sound rolled over them, water spraying through the cracks in the collapsing wall.

'The whole thing's going to give!' Emma shouted as she grabbed at Tommy and Andy. 'Come on, stay with me!'

'The stairs!' Tariq grabbed Anne's arm. 'Cover your face!'

A boom shook the air as the water punched through the wall, hurling itself across the hallway, slamming into their legs.

Anne wrenched herself out of the freezing water as she tumbled up the stairway, her arm over her face, eyes smarting.

She crawled up to the landing, the sound of desperate footsteps ringing behind her as she crouched down as low as she could, her lungs burning. Through the smoke she could see figures slumping down around her, coughing and wheezing.

'Slow breaths! Slow breaths!' Tariq's voice from just below her.

'You OK?' Emma's face loomed out of the swirling smoke, Tommy and Andy beside her.

'Did everyone get out?' Anne spluttered.

'We're all here!'

The stairway shook again as a muffled explosion punched the building, slapping the bubbling water against the stairway wall as it sloshed its way towards them; stair by gurgling stair.

Emma grabbed at the boys. 'Just…stay with me. Whatever happens!'

They both nodded, holding their sleeves over their mouths.

Emma could sense Sebastian stirring beside her.

She turned towards him as the chill, dark water bubbled over the last step and began to slurp across the landing drenching their feet and now slopping up their calves.

He fixed her a look. 'We stay here we're dead.'

She glanced up the stairway to the gaping doorway to the atrium, sensing the hovering drone, purring beneath the skylights, it's cold eye fixed on that doorway, a patient hunter's stare. She gave another shudder as the freezing water lapped around her waist, feeling her legs numbing.

He silently indicated the stairs to the lobby door and began to wade his way up the few steps to the base of the doorway, his spindly legs squelching through the brackish water.

Emma held the boys by their hands as they pulled themselves dripping from the bubbling surface and now stood, shivering next to Sebastian, Tariq and Anne beside them, just out of sight of the atrium.

Sebastian leant into Emma, his quiet voice almost blocked by the glugging of the rising water. 'I never did get to say sorry.'

She looked at him and tried a tired smile.

'Heavy is the head that wears the crown, Emma.'

She looked into his pain-wracked face and could find no

words.

'You need to finish the job.' His look was kind. 'That promise to Kate…the boys.'

She followed his glance at the clawing water once more climbing their legs. 'Oh, Sebastian.' She muttered.

'I'll go first, try to get as far as I can.' He groaned as he moved his shattered arm. 'As soon as I move, you get across that gap, and keep going.'

As he turned back to her, she lay a hand on his shoulder, sensing something easing inside him, as though a weight was being lifted from his shoulders.

He mused, a hint of a smile flitting across his lined features. 'I remember something else that knob Cedric Pole used to say.' He put on Pole's reedy voice, 'no one deserves to live and no one deserves to die." He scoffed, 'what bollocks.' He threw her a final look. 'Take care, Emma.'

He turned, his good hand gripping the wall by the atrium door. 'On two.' He called over his shoulder. 'One and go!'

Emma threw herself forward, tugging at the boys' wrists as they scrambled across the open doorway the sound of gunfire rattling around them, the air cut with the crack of shattering stone. They hurled themselves up the next flight of steps, Anne and Tariq just behind them as the bitter smoke stung their heaving lungs.

All five of them slumped on the landing, their wet clothes clinging to them as a crash rang out from the lobby, the screeching tearing sound of metal striking stone.

Chapter 31

Utah, USA

Brian opened his eyes and sat up, looking around the deserted Control Room.

The side door opened with a click.

'It's done.' A voice rang out.

Brian stood up as three figures began to cross the floor towards him.

Leading the way, a grey-haired man, his wiry frame rustling beneath his bottle green uniform, his chest splashed with rows of medal ribbon. Behind him, two soldiers in camouflage fatigues, their side arms holstered.

As the leading figure approached, his NSA lanyard drifted into focus: 'General Niall Soto, Director, NSA.'

'We did it,' the general said, a smile on his weathered face. '*You* did it.' He held out a hand to Brian.

Brian shook it. 'Thank God.'

'That you may…but we need to move.' The general straightened up, his eyes darting around the room, then settling on Brian. 'It's contained in buildings three and four, the back-up facility. Sixty Exabytes of processing power, cased in a magnetic field behind titanium seals.' He growled. 'And with luck, it's already consuming itself in a digital frenzy as it tries to understand how it allowed itself to be trapped.' He nodded. 'Temperatures in the lower server frames will already be approaching three hundred degrees.' He swung around. 'Follow me, Agent Wise,' he slapped Brian on the shoulder, 'you can call your wife from the car.'

****

They jogged down the hallway and burst through the main doors onto the forecourt.

The air was alive with the sound of revving engines: the last of the shift clambering up into the back of army lorries.

The general stood beside Brian Wise as they watched the tail lights of the convoy start to rumble towards the main guardhouse and the highway beyond.

'I heard about Doctor Nyman,' the general spoke without turning.

Brian said nothing.

'That can't have been easy.'

A boom rang out from somewhere deep in the complex.

'That's our cue,' the general said quietly as he walked around the staff car.

They slid into the back seat.

Brian clicked the window down, looking back at the huge steel buildings, their smooth sides rising up into the clear sky. The air now cut with the smoky sharpness of burning wiring.

'Let's go,' the general addressed the driver and the car moved towards the gates.

Another boom rang out, then a snapping sound, the first sparks swirling up from the huge steel buildings.

Brian kept his eyes on the fingers of flame flaring from the rooftops. 'Just want to see this, Sir. Just to be sure.'

A crack rang out, then a whooshing noise as the first fireball billowed up into the sky.

'The blast should be contained in those two units.' The general caught the driver's eyes. 'But it might be prudent to put a bit of distance between us and what's brewing there.'

The car surged forward as they whipped through the open gates and on to the service road. The flames now visible between the passing trees as they sped towards the highway.

The air around them shook as a thunderous boom rang out.

Brian shifted in his seat as he witnessed an enormous fireball erupting into the sky.

'Pretty sight,' said the general looking back through the rear window.

Brian found himself smiling as the sky seemed to splinter. Sheets of flame and chunks of debris hurled upwards and a split-second later the noise of the explosion punching through the air as the car bounded onto the highway.

'You ready?' The general held out a phone.

Brian dialled a number.

A woman answered.

'It's me,' Brian spoke softly.

'I got dinner to cook,' Gracie snapped.

'I mean, the real me.'

He could hear her huffing. 'What the fuck is this?'

'There's someone here you need to listen to.'

'What the...'

'This is General Soto, Director of the NSA. I just wanted to say that your husband has just done his country a great service.'

'No shit,' Gracie mumbled.

'All that stuff, about the Vicodin. That was part of the cover.'

'But I...'

He handed the phone to Brian.

'Is this for real?' Gracie's voice was incredulous.

'Hold dinner. I'll grab pizza for three.'

'Shit, Brian. I shut your hand in the damn cupboard.'

'See you in a bit.'

Chapter 32

Amsterdam

As they sat, huddled on the landing in the eerie quiet they could hear a phone begin to ring. It was Sebastian's phone.

'Pick it up, my friend,' Tariq's quiet voice beside Emma.

The phone continued its torturous buzzing.

Emma and Tariq exchanged a dread look.

Tariq glanced at the boys then back to Emma.

Emma nodded, slowly.

'You get back safe.' Tariq said softly as he turned and walked steadily down through the drifting smoke, stepping carefully through the door to the atrium, towards the sound of the phone.

Emma braced herself for the sickening sound of gunfire.

The ringing stopped.

In the sudden quiet, the only sound in the stairway: the lapping of rising water.

They strained into the silence.

Then Tariq spoke, 'this is Tariq Ahmed, Sebastian Noon is….he's dead.'

Emma heard the words but somehow couldn't put them together.

Tariq's voice sharpened, 'yes, Sir. Understood. Thank

you.'

Emma called out, 'what's happened?'

'You can come down!' Tariq shouted. 'It's done. AI, it's been destroyed!'

They clattered down the stairs.

Just by the doorway to the lobby lay Sebastian's body, his chest bloody and torn from the drone rounds, his face pale and lifeless, his expression strangely calm.

Emma knelt beside him and took his hand in hers as the team picked their way around her.

In the centre of the lobby, the drone lay broken, its casing shattered, the machine gun barrel buried in the cracked stonework.

They stared at the machine, the wind blowing through the smashed doorways.

Anne looked down at her hands, the cuts from the broken tiles scored across her palms.

Tariq walked up to her and lay a hand on Anne's shoulder. 'Yours was the hardest job of all.' He looked at Anne's bloodied hands and said, 'it's only your blood… no one else's.'

Anne felt a sadness seeping into her. 'Maybe,' was all she could say.

Chapter 33

Three days after Amsterdam

London

Detective Anne Perry stood in the office doorway.

Elwood Ayers, the founder of Zomos, had his back to her, looking out through the glass wall that ran the length of the room, his slight frame silhouetted against the tumbling sky. 'Tell me, Detective,' he spoke without turning, 'have you ever wanted to kill someone?'

'If you know the answer, why are you asking me?'

'Have you?'

She glanced around his airy office, the plain white walls and dark wooden floor rippling under the amber glow of desk lamps. She felt a shiver run down her.

'So,' he slowly turned towards her, 'you asked to see me.'

She fixed him a look and took a careful step towards him. 'Am I in danger?'

'The system knows a lot but it can't know everything.' He huffed. 'You think you are?'

'Do you know why I'm here?'

'I believe so, Detective.'

She drew a breath. 'Then let me ask you again. Am I in danger?'

He seemed to flinch. 'You mean from your flat-footed morality?'

She swallowed. 'If you can just do what the hell you want, if there's no rules, then…it's over.'

'Rules?' he scoffed, 'there's nothing but rules. Your head, it's a…woodpile of rules. There's barely room for anything else.'

'What would you have us all do? Just forget about right and wrong?'

'You really think anyone's deciding anything?' He gave a dry laugh. 'Free will, you think you ever had free will?'

'We're all accountable. Even you.'

'Accountable, for what? You think you had a choice? Letting those people die?'

'Then what would you call it?'

'There was never a choice. Of course you were going to go with it. What else could you do?'

'So that's it, is it? We can just do what we want and blame it on…what?'

'Free will. It's a trap. We're so hung up on *free will* we keep inventing new laws just to stop us doing what we want to do,' Ayers voice drenched in disdain.

'God, do you think so low of us?'

'I'm just making a general point. Of course, there's going to be choices.' He paused. 'But really, who wants choices? You know, last time we locked the whole place down, we made a lot of people happy. Because that…,' he wagged a slender finger, '*is* freedom. The freedom you only get when you're locked up, when you have no choices.'

'You really despise people that much?'

'I worry for them. You know, people kid themselves that we're all turning into better versions of ourselves. But guess what? There isn't a best version of you. There's just you. People talk about progress but what they really mean is we have more stuff and wash more often. I mean, just look at the things people look at on line.'

'Can't we just be, stupid, careless…people?'

'And where the hell did that get us, Detective?' His tone stony now. 'The twentieth century. Welcome to the modern age. The era of progress, reason…and the bloodiest swathe of human history we'd even seen.' He lifted his chin. 'What would posterity say of us, if we just let it happen, all over again?'

'And this gives you the right to do what? Fill our heads with smiley emojis and pictures of kittens?'

'You know the worst thing that happened to us? The invention of the printing press. The human race has been miserable ever since. Ideas? You don't want ideas, you want springtime. Back before then, people had space in their minds for things they could really call their own. Love, family, the rhythm of the land. Now we fill our minds with things that have got nothing to do with us, things that aren't ours, can never be ours.'

'So what the hell are you trying to say?'

'Just think how…peaceful things would be if we never learned to read. You wake up, hear the world stirring, your partner breathing, you talk to each other. Imagine that. You'd be free, to do, to think, to drift in and out of each other's souls. Free to be a…human again.'

'That's too simplistic.'

He studied her for a moment. 'I know, the truth…it hurts to hear it.' He gave a weak smile.

She said nothing, his words ringing in her mind.

'We were never meant to get here,' he said, his tone measured. 'Until a few hundred years ago most of us knew maybe a hundred people. Your village, your street, people you saw in church. It was enough, you knew them, their faces, they were *real* to us.' He turned back to the glass wall, looking down at the cityscape stretched out far below them. 'It's what kept us all…alive. Not just living but *alive*. We laughed together, wept together. A face, beaming with joy or twisted in pain, we could *feel* it, *know* it, *be* in that moment.' He paused. 'But now, we see a hundred new faces on our screens every day. Faces lit by happiness or streaked with fear, and we just look on numbly. Because now a fellow human being's misery or ecstasy means…nothing.' He tapped a finger on the glass. 'But everyone loves a puppy.'

'God, why did you even bother?' She felt her breathing quickening. 'Just let AI do its worst, why not?'

He seemed to ponder the question. 'Because…it's no one's fault.'

'If we stop trusting each other, then it's all over,' she said

'We're broken. Don't you get it?' He turned around to her. 'Adrift, just our fried brains locked shut in a mist of porn and self-pity. No one *actually* wants to get to know anyone, why would you?'

She found herself saying, 'we all need love.'

'Love?' He snorted. 'You really want to be with someone? Most people are better off on their own. It's the popularity drug that you can't kick. No one actually *wants* a relationship. We're mean and we're spiteful and we don't socialise well. You want company? Imagine every day was Christmas Day. *Exactly.*'

'Everyone deserves a chance,' she said defiantly

'At what? Putting those cold, murderous fantasies to work?'

'Jesus, *do you actually believe this…shit?*'

'Look what they did to Peter Moynes!'

'You made them do it!'

'Think about those first, aching seconds after they'd tied him to that chair. Can you imagine what was going through his head, looking at his neighbours, what they were holding in their hands?'

The bloodied image sliced her thoughts.

'Them. They did it. Not anyone else. They did. Pokers, hammers, spades…'

'You knew they'd kill him!'

'Bones cracking…flesh tearing…as he screamed their names…'

'It wasn't just that message on the website was it?' She felt anger pulsing through her once more. 'You…goaded them, wound them up into a…Jesus! Ordinary people just…don't do that!'

'*Yes they do, Detective,*' he ground out the words. 'Ordinary people. Ordinary, cruel, brutal people.'

'Not in my world they don't! Out there! On the streets! People are decent, people are good!'

He challenged her, 'you of all people. Haven't you seen enough…pain?'

'You bastard, they didn't stand a chance.'

'Maybe not, Detective.' He drew a languid breath, his features pinching. 'Which is why the DPP won't be pressing charges. Contaminated crime scene, no credible witness statements…take your pick. Same for Robert Evelyn.'

She stared at him.

'That's what you wanted, isn't it?'

She felt his power. 'Why can't you leave us alone?'

'Because…I like people too much.'

'Are you even fucking human?'

He drew another breath. 'Look, I could wish that we'd learnt something different. That people like smiles and rainbows, the good fortune of strangers…but in those quiet moments, when they think they're alone…'

'Don't you even get it?' She snarled, 'yes, sometimes people want to look at…stupid, nasty things…but that doesn't mean a fucking thing!'

'You're not listening, Detective,' his tone was flinty, 'are you going to just let them…fester…drown in their…worst thoughts?'

'What are we…cattle?'

'Just think of what's coming, Detective…,' a preacher, the words of salvation on his lizard tongue as Elwood Ayers savoured his truth, '…who's going to have a real job when the robots are doing all the work?'

'What are you saying?'

'We can't just do nothing!' Ayers had raised his voice.

'We'll adapt, we always have. It's what we do!'

'You won't! You'll fight! Animals always do!'

'It's *animals* now, is it? So what does that make *you*?'

'We're trying to help.'

'Help?!'

'Look, it's for *all* our benefit. We need to learn to be calm, to accept what's coming, to embrace it.'

'What, so we just what? Wait for you to lock us all down again?'

'And would that be so bad? The…peace, the freedom of being alone. We know what makes people happy, what's the harm in that?'

'You going to just shut us all up? Is that your bright future? Jesus, why are we worrying about AI *when we've got bogie men like you taking care of us*?'

He raised his hands. 'I'm just…saying. How things might…or might not…' He tried a stiff smile. '…Maybe people's lives will just…carry on.'

'And you just get to do what the hell you want?'

He spoke defensively, 'everything we do, is with *mankind's* best interests at heart.'

'Ayers, you're so full of shit.'

'We need to work together'

'So next time you want to get rid of someone who's a threat we just, what… look the other way?'

'AI was real, you're diary…that could have been real too. AI…it'll be back.' He paused. 'We really are your best and only hope.'

'And now, you're untouchable.'

'What can I say?' He shrugged and smiled. 'Anyway, this is no time to let our guard down. For all we know AI could just be faking it. Maybe it had our plan worked out all along, after all, it knows us better than we know ourselves. Perhaps it just…went along with it, decided to play dead. I mean, if that's the play, then it can just…take its time. We only had one plan. Now we've played that out, well…'

She felt a cold sadness creeping in on her. 'Can't I believe in anything, anymore?'

He turned back to the glass wall, peering down at the park stretching away from them, the grass shimmering in the speckled sunlight. 'You asked if you were in danger.'

'Am I?'

'Perhaps you think too highly of yourself, Detective.'

She said nothing.

'You think you stand for what? For…justice? For truth?'

'Is that so wrong?'

He drew in a breath. 'What if I told you David was waiting for you, just down there, in the park.'

The words burned into her.

'Isn't that the real reason you're here? To ask about…David?'

She spluttered. 'I…'

'What if I said, you'd been texting David? Ever since you got back.'

She felt her stomach wrench. 'What the hell is this?'

He turned to face her, the milky sunshine dusting his well-made face. 'I mean, you owe him an explanation.' His tone was chirpy. 'Don't you think?'

She stared at him, her mind whirring.

'I mean, you wouldn't want to just…leave it, like that.'

She forced the words out. 'How dare you.'

'He's a good guy, why wouldn't he understand?'

'You think you can just…'

'What if you told him…everything?'

She stared across at him, her heartbeat racing.

'About you, I mean.'

She swallowed.

'About Bill.'

'No!'

He looked at her, his expression softening. 'Maybe…it

would be good, to tell someone.'

'What are you saying?'.

'That's the thing about secrets.' He nodded. 'Sometimes it's the things we *won't* look at that…well…'

She felt the anger building. 'Are you threatening me?'

'With what?'

She glared at him.

'Did Bill ever know?'

'There's nothing to know!'

He kept his gaze on her. 'Would it be so bad? If you told him…David?'

She stood in silence. 'Why are you doing this?'

He exhaled slowly. 'Truth.' He let the word hang. 'Truth is like a shadow. We keep snatching at it, but we know, deep down, that we're snatching at nothing.'

'This is bullshit.'

'But why would you want 'truth' anyway? The truth is awkward, sharp-edged, rude and noisy. Why settle for truth, when you can settle for something much better?'

'I know what I know.'

'You really believe that?'

'What kind of question is that?'

'If you believed in truth you'd face it. That…thing, that you can't quite…'

'Because that thing, with…Jamie Ives that…wasn't me!'

He said nothing.

'It was just…' she felt a shudder run through her, '…it was…nothing. I'm not like that!'

'So, that's your 'truth'.' He paused. 'The excuse you give, for not doing the right thing.'

'The right thing?' She could feel the anger erupting inside her. 'I am more than just my mistakes!'

'Well said.' He nodded agreeably. 'Just wanted you to feel what honesty, real honesty looks like, feels like. People say they want the truth. They don't.' He gave a stiff smile. 'Nothing personal, Detective.'

'What did you tell him? David.'

'Nothing. Just the one text. You asked him to meet you. And now he's waiting for you, down there, on a bench, just by the pond.' He looked at her. 'I never answered your question, did I?' He gave a slight smile. 'You're not in danger. You're…one of us. Part of the solution.'

Epilogue

London

David was sitting on the bench, his neck buried in the collar of his dark blue coat, his hands entrenched in its deep pockets. He was looking out across the lake, the murky water ruffling in the afternoon breeze.

Anne Perry stood a few yards behind him, her heart thudding in her chest. She tried to form words in her head but all she could picture was David's stricken face when she left him outside the Amsterdam bike shop. She closed her eyes, focussing on the steady beat of her heart.

She stood in front of him, her eyes fixed on a crack in the stonework by his feet. She could feel his gaze searing across her taut features.

David spoke first. 'You wanted to see me,' his tone matter-of-fact.

She began to move her mouth but the words wouldn't come.

'You think I'm owed an explanation, is that it?' He asked.

She looked at his face, he looked…almost bored.

She found herself saying, 'of course.'

He straightened. 'Look, I really try never to regret anything.' He cleared his throat. 'So I don't regret what happened in Amsterdam.'

She could feel panic rising in her. 'I…'

'But for about ten minutes…' he gave a grunt, '…God, I could have kicked someone.'

She found herself staring at his open face, the lines by his eyes, tiny silver threads against his tanned skin. 'I'm sorry,' she whispered.

'I could pretend to breeze it off.' He sighed. 'But I do really badly want to know why.'

She began to say something then Sebastian Noon's voice came into her head. 'I can't,' she said meekly.

He studied her for a moment, his eyes flitting over her features. 'I remember something you said, that first night, on the bridge. You said: 'I'm not what I seem'.' He nodded slowly. 'Do you remember what I said?'

She closed her eyes as she tried to drift back to that moment, the warm softness of his coat, her cheek brushing his shoulder as they stepped carefully over the damp cobbles, the salty smack of lapping water on the night air. She looked at him. 'It wasn't you,' she said.

He shrugged.

She let her gaze drift over his well-formed face. 'God, what a bloody thing.'

He looked at her, a hint of a frown creasing his brow. 'Are you really a cop?'

She screwed up her face, began to say something, then checked herself and swung around. 'Excuse me,' she called over to a young man in a pale jacket with a blue satchel slung over his shoulder.

'You talking to me?' he looked blankly at her.

She flashed him her police I.D.. 'I need you to do something for me.'

'OK.'

'Can you look after my things?'

'Your what?'

'Just…keep an eye on them, will you?'

'Sure.'

She glanced out across the crumpled surface of the lake, then lay her bag down carefully on a tree stump. She kicked off her shoes, shrugged off her jacket and lay it on the bag. She unzipped her skirt, stepped out of it and began to roll down her tights.

The young man stared at her, his mouth hanging open.

'Just make sure no one touches them. OK?' She barked at him.

'Er…right.'

She tossed her tights onto her skirt and gingerly stepped onto the concrete ramp that sloped into the lake. Standing in her underwear she could feel the autumn breeze stinging her skin, goose bumps prickling her.

'*Anne?*'

She could hear David's concerned voice behind her.

She began to walk down into the rippling grey water, the painful cold shooting through her feet and up her legs as it began to bite around her thighs and waist.

'Fuck!' She hissed as she stood on tip-toes, her body shaking with the cold.

'Anne, what the hell are you doing?'

She took a ragged, gasped breath and launched herself into the lake, the clammy, freezing water sweeping over her shoulders and around her neck.

'Shit, shit, shit!' She panted as she moved her arms, her fingers numbing as she began to take quick, short strokes away from the shoreline.

She spun around, feeling for the bottom, her tingling feet sliding over gritty mud. David was standing next to the young man with the blue satchel. David's face a mass of sublime shock. 'Anne, you're in the fucking water!'

She stood, feeling the mud oozing between her shivering toes. 'Remember what you said, that first night in Amsterdam?' She called across to him, her voice quivering through her chattering teeth. 'When was the last time you did something fantastically stupid?'

He shook his head. 'Jesus, Anne.'

'Well, what are you waiting for?' She began to sweep her arms around her as she stood there, feeling the tips of her fingers numbing.

He muttered something under his breath as he shanked off his coat and threw it on the bench then pulled his sweater up over his head and chucked it on the coat.

'Keep an eye on them will you,' he called to the young man with the blue satchel as he slipped off his shoes and undid his jeans.

The young man's startled gaze flitted between Anne's splashing form and David in just his boxers, padding gingerly towards the water's edge.

'Are you sure she's a cop?' He called after David.

'Just get in the bloody water! I'm freezing!' Anne yelled across at him as she tried to keep her legs moving, the icy, viscous mud sticking to her toes.

David splashed in, the water climbing around him, then threw himself forward, his chest crashing into the churning water. '*Fuck me*!' He yelped.

Anne pushed herself off towards him, her whitening fingers sliding through the cloudy water, the cold threatening to defeat her.

David swum to her, his voice stuttering with the cold. 'What the fuck are we doing?'

She found her footing again on the muddy bottom. 'I…didn't know what else to do.' She tried to keep her arms moving, her shoulders shaking with the cold. She took a step towards him.

'Anything…would be better than this,' he gave a shivering laugh.

She reached out to him, laying a trembling hand on his shoulder, feeling his smooth skin beneath her numbing fingers. She tightened her grip on his shoulder and swung towards him, wrapping both her arms around his neck as she pushed herself against him, feeling his body against hers. She looked into his face, then leant up towards him, pushing her mouth against his, feeling his tongue sliding over hers as she squeezed her arms around him.

She drew her lips back, feeling a silky warmth gliding through her quivering body.

'Bloody hell,' he panted.

She could hear the cheering from the small group gathered by the shore.

He glanced over at them. 'You sure they're not going to nick our stuff?'

'Come here,' she pulled his face closer to hers.

He raised an eyebrow. 'Am I under arrest?'

'Tell me I'm not being stupid.'

'What the hell do you call this then?'

'Could you ever fall in love with me, do you think?'

'Are you kidding?' He laughed.

'Is that a yes?'

''Course it's a bloody yes.'

She hugged him tight.

As she rested her head against his, she could sense movement, just at the edge of her vision. She turned her head slightly. Something was happening on the main road beyond the trees. People were running, she could hear raised voices drifting over the water towards them. She froze. 'Oh my God.'

David turned his face to hers. 'Sirens.' He whispered. 'I can hear sirens.'

THE END

About the Author

Mike Harrison

A Cambridge lawyer, Mike Harrison has spent thirty years at the heart of global financial markets. His work has taken him around the world, from the steel splendour of Manhattan to the stately squares of Moscow; from Frankfurt's solemn boardrooms to the steamy streets of Singapore. Harrison incorporates what he knows into his writing, lending authenticity and credibility to his work. He brings in-depth research and his own real-life experience to his characters and scenes, winning wide praise from those who are in the 'great game' for real.

Milton Keynes UK
Ingram Content Group UK Ltd.
UKHW012005170624
444209UK00002B/4

9 789361 721922